Something Wicked

Also by Carolyn G. Hart
in Large Print:

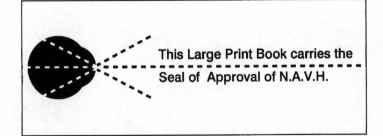

This Large Print Book carries the
Seal of Approval of N.A.V.H.

Something Wicked

Carolyn G. Hart

Thorndike Press • Waterville, Maine

Published in 2004 by arrangement with the Bantam Dell
Publishing Group, a division of Random House, Inc.

Thorndike Press® Large Print Famous Authors.

The tree indicium is a trademark of Thorndike Press.

The text of this Large Print edition is unabridged.
Other aspects of the book may vary from the original edition.

Set in 16 pt. Plantin by Minnie B. Raven.

Printed in the United States on permanent paper.

Library of Congress Cataloging-in-Publication Data

Hart, Carolyn G.
      Something wicked / Carolyn G. Hart.
          p. cm. — (A death on demand mystery)
      ISBN 0-7862-6743-7 (lg. print : hc : alk. paper)
      1. Darling, Annie Laurance (Fictitious character) —
Fiction.   2. Darling, Max (Fictitious character) — Fiction.
3. Women detectives — South Carolina — Fiction.
4. Booksellers and bookselling — Fiction.   5. Actors —
Crimes against — Fiction.   6. South Carolina — Fiction.
7. Summer theater — Fiction.   8. Large type books.
I. Title.
PS3558.A676S66 2004
   813'.54—dc22   2004055348

To my mother, Doris Akin Gimpel,
who gave me lots of Nancy Drews,
raspberry parfait chocolates,
and love.

National Association for Visually Handicapped
------------------------ serving the partially seeing

As the Founder/CEO of NAVH, the only national health agency solely devoted to those who, although not totally blind, have an eye disease which could lead to serious visual impairment, I am pleased to recognize Thorndike Press* as one of the leading publishers in the large print field.

Founded in 1954 in San Francisco to prepare large print textbooks for partially seeing children, NAVH became the pioneer and standard setting agency in the preparation of large type.

Today, those publishers who meet our standards carry the prestigious "Seal of Approval" indicating high quality large print. We are delighted that Thorndike Press is one of the publishers whose titles meet these standards. We are also pleased to recognize the significant contribution Thorndike Press is making in this important and growing field.

Lorraine H. Marchi, L.H.D.
Founder/CEO
NAVH

* Thorndike Press encompasses the following imprints: Thorndike, Wheeler, Walker and Large Print Press.

As Will and Agatha often warned,
Something wicked this way comes.

1

The bicycle tires left a single track across the rippled tideflat. The rider pedaled slowly, obviously enjoying a sunset outing, admiring the silvery glow of the chalky gray strand, the creamy gold of the gently waving sea oats on their wind-sculpted dunes. Every so often a weathered gray boardwalk provided access from the beach to the homes hidden behind the dunes. But the rider was oblivious to the tangy salt scent and silken caress of the breeze now flowing back to sea as the sun set. Instead, it was the emptiness of the scene that pleased, for no one moved on this stretch of Broward's Rock beach so far as the eye could see.

So, the first objective had been met, an unobserved approach.

At the next boardwalk, the rider dismounted and dropped the bicycle on its side. The scuff of sneakers against the sand-filmed wooden slats couldn't be heard over the rustle of the breeze through the sea oats. It took not quite thirty seconds to reach the patio behind the

Buckners' rambling beachfront house. A pink-and-yellow plastic sea horse rocked in the shamrock-shaped pool. Blue terrycloth beach towels hung from webbed chairs. A *Fortune* magazine fluttered on a cane table, held in place by carelessly dropped, salt-rimmed goggles.

"Sandy? Dick?"

The call hung unanswered in the hush of twilight.

The bicyclist stepped over a furled beach umbrella, called out again, and knocked sharply on the French doors, but, just as expected, no answer came. The Buckners were not at home. There was always noise, motion, confusion, and disarray when Dick and Sandy were there.

A warm flush of anticipation suffused the bicyclist. And when the door, unlocked, swung in, there was a sharp, heady sense of triumph. Of course, Dick and Sandy left their doors unlocked. They were careless, messy, and heedless.

The den smelled of pipe smoke and an odd combination of dried newsprint and paints from Sandy's collages. The Sunday papers littered the floor. Across the room the last shafts from the setting sun glittered on the glass panes of the gun case.

Now, crumpled gardening gloves were

pulled from a jacket pocket and donned. A gloved hand twisted the handle.

An ugly twist of sheer fury flamed for an instant.

The hand rattled the handle. Locked. Locked!

But they were so careless, so idiotically undisciplined. . . . The haze of anger cleared, cold analytical thought returned, the gloved hand swept above the case, and a key clattered to the floor.

Less than a minute later, the bicyclist rode off into the dusk. Two target pistols in a capacious carryall thudded against the right leg as the rider pumped, a solitary figure against the dusky sky, enjoying the solitude of an evening outing on the beach.

2

Shane shifted the tiller, and the wind kicked into the sails. *Sweet Lady* surged ahead. He savored the heavy heat of the noon sun, the beading of water against his bronzed skin. He glanced down at the matted golden hair on his chest. By God, he still had the body women lusted for. He ignored the puffy softness of his belly and admired his trunk-thick legs. He recalled the quick glance of interest from that dark-haired girl on the *Dancing Cat*. Maybe he'd ask her over for a drink when he got back. He liked the look of her legs, long and slim, and a soft little butt. The familiar heat coursed in his crotch. Then he remembered. Shit. Another rehearsal. But only a few more days and all that would be over. He would be free. Free of this stuffy, boring island. Free of Sheridan. His shoulders hunched. Sheridan kept badgering him to learn his lines. Said it would look better. Hell, what difference did it make? God, he'd be glad to see the last of Sheridan, go his own way.

Only a few more days.

3

Carla knew the room was a perfect backdrop for her: the muted bone of the linen-sheathed sofa and chairs, austere yet luxurious; the woven cotton rug with alternating diamonds of rust and brown, cobalt and moss green; the crystal clarity of the glass coffee table with its gleaming beveled edges. She moved through the open doors and stepped out onto the balcony overlooking the sound. Moonlight swept over her. She glanced down at her soft satin trousers. Turning, she slowly looked back into the living room and the mirrored wall opposite. Her reflection shimmered in the moonlight — jade green silk jacket, ivory trousers. She saw an apparition from long ago, cheeks faintly flushed, long ebony hair hanging straight and still. God, she hadn't looked like this since . . . Her mind veered away, but the pain that slumbered in her marrow flared, and she felt a moment's panic. She'd sworn that it would never happen again. Never. It hurt too much.

She glanced at the crystal goblets waiting on the jewel-like table for the finest, lightest white wine, the best she could offer. And after wine, after conversation, words with long pauses and longer glances, she knew what would happen. A touch, a caress, and the explosion of passion that hurt and destroyed but transformed.

And yet, she knew — in her heart — she knew how it would end. But she was so tired of loneliness and the shell she had built to keep out the world. So tired. So hungry to be touched.

The front doorbell rang.

Carla glanced once more at her own loveliness, then — her face uncertain, her eyes clouded with yearning — she moved toward the door.

4

Agatha crouched atop the coffee bar, her amber eyes glittering with pleasure, her plump black paw poised.

Annie deftly avoided the swatting paw as she bent down to open the box. "Why don't you go outside and find a mouse, sweetie?"

Agatha's tail switched a millimeter, her shoulders hunched, and she launched herself with fluid grace into the just-opened box.

"Agatha, no!" Dropping to her knees, Annie swiftly retrieved the silky cat, who immediately began to writhe, indicating *extreme* displeasure.

"I know. It's Sunday. You're bored. You want to play the string game, at the very least, but I have to hurry. I have to hang these watercolors, and I don't have time to play with you."

The cat emitted a choking hiss.

"You don't scare me, kid." Annie turned, bearing her squirming bundle, toward the back door of Death on Demand.

But Agatha, who could exhibit the liquidity of an eel, undulated free, and, with a final, outraged, over-the-shoulder hiss, disappeared into the darkness of the rattan-chair area of the bookstore, seeking sanctuary beneath her favorite fern.

Annie grinned. If there's one thing Agatha had, it was spirit, just like her namesake. Agatha would return, more determined than ever to investigate that tempting box. Annie wished that she, too, could hiss. As she lifted out the top painting, she had a wonderful vision of a world where people hissed and flipped bouffant tails to indicate displeasure. Boy, would she ever switch a tail at the next rehearsal, right in Shane's meaty face. And she would waggle a tail, even if at long distance, at her well-meaning but *maddening* mother-in-law-to-be.

Still grinning, she focused her attention on the first painting and gave a whistle of admiration. This was the first time Nan Allgood had painted for Death on Demand, and Nan had outdone herself. Spreading the five mounted watercolors on the floor, Annie nodded in satisfaction. They were wonderful! And so perfect for the romantic month of June. Her customers would have a fabulous time meet-

16

ing the challenge of naming the books and authors they represented. Although she knew it was immodest, she congratulated herself anew on her cleverness in running a monthly contest to draw whodunit fans to her mystery bookstore, which was, of course, the finest this side of Atlanta.

In the first painting, a young woman stared at gray stone house with mullioned windows, rising above a terrace and lawns that sloped to the sea. A lovely house. But closer inspection revealed that decay flourished. The drive was choked by weeds, pressed upon by unbridled trees, overborne by gigantic hedges, and in the garden, rhododendrons loomed against the moonlit sky. Yet the young woman's face seemed to hold a memory of the house as it once was, the windows warmly lit, the curtains moving in the gentle night breeze. But the reality, forevermore, was desolate ruin.

In the second painting, a dark-haired young woman in a knee-length black dress and fur-collared coat stared in horror at the contents of a devastated linen closet. Fire had blistered the white paint of the door, and flames had singed the body that lay crumpled on the floor. But the flames hadn't destroyed completely the victim's silver fox jacket or the red silk negligee she wore.

A golden-bronze statue of Apollo dominated the third painting. A woman in a torn and dirty dress, her neck bruised and swollen, reached out to cup her hands in the water of a spring. Her companion, his face and hands still streaked with blood, his clothes showing evidence of a fierce battle, held out a gold sovereign to drop on the plinth in front of the statue.

The fourth watercolor brought to mind the glorious days when archeologists were first recovering the treasures of Egypt from the Valley of the Dead. A darkly beautiful woman raised a lantern high within the dusty confines of a burial chamber. The flickering light sculpted the terror on her face. Above her, rows of vultures painted on the stone wall watched implacably.

The fifth painting had, as did the first, an unmistakably dreamlike quality. The interior of the greenhouse was just blurred enough to hint at nightmare rather than reality. A striking young woman with short black hair and deep blue eyes held a shattered glass flask in her hands. She studied it in sickened fascination while the hundreds of orchids which surrounded her seemed to move and rustle and talk, willing her to die. The orchids ranged in color from white to mauve to deepest purple, and one monstrous bloom, a golden-tawny Great Empress, looked as though it were streaked with blood.

As she hung the painting of the gray stone house, Annie remembered the first time she'd ever read the book, and that haunting opening line. The words shimmered in her mind, as luminous as moonlight on dark water. What a *wonderful* writer. And how much pleasure she'd given millions of readers over the years.

It didn't take long to hang all five. As Annie folded the stepladder, she quickly scanned the paintings again. Each brought back memories of exquisitely pleasurable, long ago Sunday afternoons, plates of chocolate chip cookies, and Uncle Ambrose handing her a stack of books and saying gruffly, "Pretty good, these. Think you'll like them."

The sharp peal of the telephone shattered her reverie.

Annie eyed the telephone with all the enthusiasm of a Roderick Alleyn fan stuck on a desert island with a crate of Mike Hammer books.

But, at Ingrid's stern nod, she sighed and said grumpily, "I'll get it."

"Yo," her clerk replied from the cash deck. Ingrid, too, had a strong suspicion as to the caller's identity and had no intention of running interference. "Bunter I am not," she had explained firmly, defending her cowardice.

"Death on Demand," Annie answered and knew she still took pleasure in so announcing the finest mystery bookstore on the Atlantic coast, even though her tone at the moment was clearly defensive.

Laurel Darling Roethke's voice flowed over the line like gin at a Pam and Jerry North cocktail hour, smooth and mellow. The undercurrent of laughter, wonderment, and other worldliness was as unforgettable as Shirley MacLaine's performance in *The Trouble with Harry*.

Annie could feel her face softening in a smile, despite her near certainty that the call heralded yet another outrageous suggestion for the coming wedding.

"My sweet," Max's mother caroled, "I actually feel as though I've had a vision of feathered-serpent rainbow wheels. It's quite mystic, actually, and it all springs, of course, from the approach of the Harmonic Convergence."

As Laurel rhapsodized over the glories to be experienced later in the summer when the earth entered a new phase of evolution, which would climax in 2012, Annie's hand tightened spasmodically on the receiver. She'd considered Harmonic Convergence, a hodgepodge of New Age philosophies, Mayan lore, sixties-style radicalism, and Buddhism, to be quite amusing until her future mother-in-law had telegraphed in April from Egypt:

ATOP PYRAMID. EXPERIENCING LOVE, HOPE, EAGERNESS FOR ARRIVAL OF HARMONIC CONVER-GENCE — AND VISION OF WEDDING!! OPPORTUNITY TO CREATE MULTI-CULTURAL EXTRAVAGANZA!! WILL SERVE AS COSMIC REVELATION TO YOUNG LOVERS AND TO WORLD!!!

"So, of course," Laurel now cooed in Annie's ear, "I know you and Max will come round to my view of the wedding. Annie," and now the husky voice was solemn with a catch in it, "this is truly a *historic* opportunity."

Annie tried not to wail, but her voice rose wildly. "Laurel, I just want a *simple* wedding. Nothing extravagant. Nothing grand. And I'm certainly not going to turn it into a three-ring circus by trying to make

21

some kind of cosmic statement."

For an instant, she felt a swell of pride. She'd laid it on the line, been pleasant but firm. Her relief was short-lived, however.

Laurel gave a tiny golden laugh. "Oh, my sweet, don't worry, you will receive enlightenment, I'm sure of it."

It was like trying to seize motes in a sunbeam.

The graceful notes of laughter sounded again. "I want you to relax, Annie. Breathe deeply. Think of blue. That's a lovely color, isn't it? And then I know you'll become a part of an ever-growing swell, a life-loving Force, and you will see just how marvelous it will be to create with this wedding, with the exchange of vows between you and Maxwell, a perfectly lovely representation of wedding customs from around the globe. Now," and she was suddenly brisk and efficient, if a bit chiding, "you know that you needn't concern yourself with the spadework at all! I'm taking care of everything. I will discover the finest, the most unusual, the most meaningful customs that have represented love's true glory in every nation, and I shall bear them to you like Cupid hoisting garlands upon a silver salver." She paused to draw breath, then added triumphantly, "I know you will be enchanted, my dear, to discover what the groom does in Korea."

Annie waited in stony silence.

Undaunted, her mother-in-law-to-be trilled, "It's so *dear!* The groom rides a white donkey to the bride's house, and he's carrying a goose and a gander as symbols of fidelity. Did you know those glorious creatures mate for life? Isn't that quaint!" (Since Rudolf Roethke was Laurel's fifth husband, Annie thought the description interesting.) "Anyway," the husky voice flowed on cheerfully, "I've thought about it." Her voice dropped a little. "Of course, it's hard, since it's here at home. Without a pyramid, you know. But I climbed the apple tree in the north meadow and I have an interpretation. Max can come to your house in a white Lincoln Continental and he can present to you on a white satin pillow a most lovely charm bracelet with a goose and a gander — and you can wear it at the wedding!"

"In addition to the gold whale's tooth?" Annie asked acidly. "Won't I start to clang? (In Fiji, custom demanded that the groom give to the bride's father a whale's tooth, representing riches and status.)

"Oh. Oh, dear. I'd forgotten the whale's tooth! Mmmh. Of course, we can't have you clanging. Don't worry, Annie, I'll re-solve it."

And she rang off.

Annie looked toward the cash desk.

Ingrid raised an inquiring eyebrow.

"Korea. Groom on white donkey carrying goose and gander."

Ingrid turned back to an order list, but not in time to hide her grin.

"Just wait," Annie warned. "Let Laurel get her teeth into what you'll wear as matron of honor — then we'll see how funny you think it is."

The phone rang.

Annie jumped and stared at it as warily as she would regard a hungry boa constrictor.

It rang again. Annie took a deep breath and lifted the receiver.

The sibilant hiss over the line hit her eardrum with stiletto sharpness. "Annie, it's time we got to the bottom of the problem."

Although this somewhat enigmatic pronouncement might be expected to puzzle her, Annie had no difficulty identifying the whisperer and her preoccupation. Leaning back against the coffee bar, she relaxed. "Hi, Henny." She carefully kept amusement from her voice. Annie still felt a little awkward addressing her long-time and perhaps most avid customer, Mrs. Henrietta Brawley, in such familiar terms, but since they'd both joined the cast of the summer production of *Arsenic and Old Lace*, Mrs. Brawley had insisted on being on a first-name basis.

"Shh!"

Annie jerked the receiver away from her ear.

"No names, please!" The S's rustled richly. "It's time for action. We've got to *save summer theater!*"

The corners of Annie's mouth edged upward. "Oh, it's not *that* bad." (In comparison to geese and ganders, Annie felt Henny's concerns were mild.) "And maybe," she added cheerfully, "whoever's doing it will get bored."

"Evil ignored flourishes like the green bay tree," Mrs. Brawley intoned, forgetting to whisper.

Annie wasn't sure whether this was an adjustment of a Biblical quotation, an observation based on the reading of more crime novels than any other resident of Broward's Rock, or merely a social comment, so she ignored it and asked pragmatically, "What do you want to do?"

The whisper returned. "You and I can

25

take turns camping out overnight at the theater."

So far as Annie was concerned, camping — indoors or out — was a wonderful pursuit for pilgrims, pioneers, or extremely hearty party-goers, but she, personally, preferred to be pampered at a Hilton Inn, and even a Ramada would do in a pinch.

"Absolutely not." Pleasantly, but oh, so firmly.

Once again the whisper fled, this time replaced by indignation. "Annie Laurance, I'm surprised at you! What do you think Hildegarde Withers would do?" A disgusted sniff. "Well, if I have to do it all on my own, I will!" A brisk click broke the connection.

Annie stared at the receiver for a moment, then slowly replaced it. Her sense of quiet amusement seeped away, and not because of the undisguised disappointment in Henny Brawley's voice. The unease over the play that lurked just below the level of conscious thought burgeoned like a spark fanned by a willful wind. Actually, Henny had every right to —

"Penny for your thoughts."

She looked up and flashed a brief smile. "Hi, Max. I didn't hear you."

"A phone call?" he asked tentatively.

26

His tone was just ingenuous enough to excite her suspicion. She looked at him sharply. "Has your mother called you, too?"

Max smiled airily. "The Japanese have a wonderfully liquid approach to such a solemn occasion. The bride and groom exchange sips of sake and become husband and wife after the first sip. *We* could substitute scotch."

Damn, he would think Laurel's plans hilarious, but Henny's call made light conversation impossible. Annie frowned.

He leaned comfortably against the coffee bar and looked at her curiously. "Are they building a nuclear generating plant next door?"

That jolted her. "For Pete's sake, I hope not. Where did you hear that?"

Max managed not to look toothpaste-ad handsome because his regular features — nice strong nose, firm jaw, and lake-blue eyes — had a slightly rakish air, not quite Mephistophelian, but assuredly not Eagle Scoutish. Those eyes now gleamed with quite as much pleasure as Agatha was exhibiting as she poked her head out of the painting box to watch them.

"Had I not been taught to be forthright and honorable at all times, I would claim to have heard about it over beer at Ben Parotti's Bait Shop and Bar, and soon a whirlwind of rumor would sweep our tiny island. There would be torchlight parades. Mystery novelist Emma Clyde would chain herself to the Post Office flagpole in protest. An absolute explosion of excitement." He smiled regretfully at a luscious prospect denied. "To tell the truth, however, I made it up just now."

Annie sighed gustily in relief, then glared at him. "Why?"

"You looked so worried," he replied earnestly, as if that explained everything.

Slowly, reluctantly, she began to laugh. "So okay," she agreed, "nothing's *that* bad." Then her brows drew down again. "But, Max, I am worried about the play."

"The play? Oh, well, sure. But what else is new?" He walked around the coffee bar and lifted down two mugs from her collection. Each mug carried in bright red script the name of a famous mystery.

Annie automatically noted the titles, *The Innocence of Father Brown* and *The Rasp.* "Do you think we have time?" She glanced at her watch.

"There is always time for coffee," he said reverently.

As he poured, Annie sniffed the richness

of the dark Colombian brew. Oh, well, she and Max usually arrived promptly for rehearsals, and almost everyone else ran late. She accepted the mug.

"So, why are you upset about the play?" He paused, and rephrased the question. "Or, more upset than usual? Has anything else happened?"

"Mrs. Brawley called." She cleared her throat. "Er — Henny."

He sipped and waited.

Annie struggled to explain. "Now, look, you know I don't let things bother me."

A thick golden brow arched sardonically over one quizzical blue eye.

"I mean," she amended quickly, "I know I stew around and get mad, but we've agreed to go with the flow over the play."

An encouraging nod.

"I can be relaxed, too," she insisted.

He patted her shoulder, his expression unaltered.

"Dammit, Max," she spewed, now pushed to the limit, "I am not uptight!"

"I didn't say a word," he said virtuously.

"It's just that all those things that have happened, well, you have to admit they are worrisome."

"The play is being presented by the Broward's Rock Players. The director is

Sam Haznine, the famous Broadway director. The stage manager is Burt Conroy, president of the players and a moving force in the Broward's Rock Merchants Association." He recited it as a litany. "In short," and now his tone was brisk, "this production is not, as we've discussed before, any responsibility of the charming proprietor of Death on Demand."

"Yes." It was an unwilling agreement. "Darn it, I wish we'd never agreed to be in it. After all, we didn't have to."

"We had a gilt-edged invitation."

"Yeah," she said ruefully. "Us and Shane." She grinned. "Maybe we all deserve each other. Just because you produced a couple of plays off-Broadway and I tried to be an actress, we're classified as big New Yorkers with experience in The Theater. That's just about as phony as Sam Haznine being a big-deal director."

"Actually, Sam *was* a fairly big deal, until he had three flops in a row," Max said mildly. "That's why the players were able to hire him to direct the first play of the summer. He has to have some success somewhere, even if it's a little island like Broward's Rock. And you have to admit Shane has more experience than we do. He really was in all those surfer movies in the sixties."

"Where he learned nothing," she said darkly.

"How to surf?" As always, Max's tone was gently amused and reasonable.

She shook her head impatiently. "Shane isn't the point. He may," she admitted, "be part of the problem, but he isn't the point. I'm worried about Henny."

Max looked surprised. "Is she going to quit or something?" For the first time, he sounded concerned. "Actually, she's a great Abby."

"Quit? You've got to be kidding. She's enjoying this more than anything since she bought a full run of Nero Wolfe first editions in jacket from an estate dirt cheap. No, it's all the mess. She wants to *investigate!* Find out who's behind all the trouble." Annie's brows drew together once again in a tight, worried frown. "Max, maybe we ought to help her."

He finished his mug of coffee, put it down with a decisive bang, reached over, and gently smoothed away the line above her nose. Then, with elaborate gestures, he curved his hands as if lifting an extremely heavy round object from her shoulders.

"I do not like mimes," she said stiffly.

31

He shook his head and repeated the movements.

"What are you doing?" she demanded suspiciously.

"Lifting the weight of the world from your bowed shoulders."

The corners of her mouth twitched. "So okay. Point taken. I'll lighten up. And you're right, I guess. I'm not the director. I'm not president of the players. So —"

"That's my girl. Come on, let's go to rehearsal and wow 'em. And who knows? Maybe everything will go great today."

The Porsche swept into the lot behind the high school. Designed and built in the fifties, the dingy, orange-brick building had the ramshackle look of a once avant-garde structure whose glory days have passed. The endless facade of slanted windows, with a later addition of a blue tint to shade the subtropical sun, looked cheerless and tacky. Even the palmettos had a ragged air, and the untended yard was hummocky.

It wasn't Broadway. It wasn't the Helen Hayes. It wasn't even a real theater, but the high school auditorium had it all over a storefront or the local Moose Lodge, so the players needed to be duly appreciative of the loan of the premises from the

Broward's Rock School Board (for a set percentage of the gross, of course). Without the auditorium, the players would have no stage at all. Ever since a January fire left the Broward's Rock Playhouse a blackened shell, it had been touch and go whether the summer season could be mounted. And this summer season had to succeed, or the campaign to rebuild the playhouse, the ruins of which Annie could see from the front windows of Death on Demand, would founder and fail. The insurance coverage wasn't nearly enough to meet present-day construction costs.

The players faced enormous obstacles, from overt and legal maneuvers to underhanded and deceitful sabotage.

Max suspected Harley Edward Jenkins III of engineering the setbacks which had dogged the company since rehearsals began.

Of course, Annie knew Max was prejudiced, to say the least. He'd despised Harley ever since the businessman had attempted to hire Max and his problem-solving agency, Confidential Commissions, to take some compromising photos of a competitor. (South Carolina statutes made it tough to establish a detective agency; Max insisted no law prohibited an energetic entrepreneur from solving assorted problems.) As for the photos, Harley wanted to use them for leverage in a business deal. Max had made it very clear that Confidential Commissions didn't stoop to that kind of snoop.

So it was no surprise to Max when civic appeal left Harley unmoved, and that Harley, as CEO of Halcyon Development, creator of the resort community on the island, was vigorously opposed to rebuilding the theater on the choice location overlooking the sound. Instead, Jenkins wanted to open another retail shop there. The playhouse had never brought in as much as a business would at the site, but the original bylaws, offered by Halcyon Development and agreed to by property owners, provided for the continued support of a theater there "so long as the theater company meets its own expenses." No one foresaw the burning of the theater and the subsequent cost of rebuilding. The Broward's Rock Players insisted the clause mandated that the theater be rebuilt by Halcyon Development. The corporation disagreed, and claimed, moreover, that if the players didn't have a successful (i.e., debt-free) summer season Halcyon Development would be free of any further responsibility for the theater, and could build and lease the site to any business of its choice.

At this point, Sunday, May 31, the players were determined to mount a successful summer season to maintain their claim to the harbor-front site and, hopefully, to force Halcyon Development to rebuild in the fall.

As the Porsche jolted to a stop, gray dust rose in dispirited swirls in the unpaved lot.

Max surveyed the skipping dust-devils. "We'd better remind Burt to have somebody wet down the lot before opening night."

Annie was hopping out. "Let's hurry. It looks like almost everyone's here." She noted the half dozen cars, and the two bikes, Henny Brawley's bright red ten-speed and director Haznine's cheaply rented bent and battered old-fashioned no-speed.

She moved eagerly toward the school. Despite the problems with the production — and God knows there were many, ranging from the miscasting as Teddy of a California surfer running to fat to the series of odd tricks that had plagued the play since rehearsals began — she still looked forward to rehearsals. She loved *Arsenic and Old Lace*. She loved the dear old sisters so busily dispatching lonely old men to, they were certain, a finer world. She loved nervous, alcoholic Dr. Einstein with his plaintive "No, Chonny, no!" And she adored Max as Mortimer. There was something about Max in a double-breasted suit and a snap-brim felt hat that melted her bones. She picked up speed. She heard a soft chuckle behind her as she pulled open the faded red door.

Then she pulled up short, stopped by a frazzled voice climbing until it neared falsetto.

Sam Haznine, his pudgy shoulders tightly hunched, stood with his back to them, clutching the receiver of the pay phone in the lobby. "I *know* it's hot. Goddamn, I've been hot ever since we hit this godforsaken outpost, but, sweetie, it's gonna get better. Stick with me, honey lamb. We're going to bust out of this swamp right back to Broadway. *Please,* sweetie, don't go. It's just one more week and we open and then it will all be gravy, I swear to God." He paused, pulled a wilted handkerchief from a hip pocket, and mopped the back of his neck. The director's seersucker pants hung limply on his pear-shaped frame.

Annie held a finger to her lips and began

to tiptoe across the scuffed tile to the double doors at the center aisle. One door sagged from its hinges. Once she and Max were safely out of the foyer, she said softly, "Poor Sam." Then, a little wearily, "Poor us. What'll you bet it will be some rehearsal today?"

But Max was looking toward the stage. "Not all the fireworks are going to come from Sam."

She looked down the aisle and saw Hugo Wolf rising from his seat as Burt Conroy darted out on stage.

Even in the somewhat dingy auditorium, Hugo commanded attention. As he stalked with measured tread toward the stage, every eye turned toward him.

What was it that distinguished Hugo? Not his size, although he was over six feet and solidly built. Not even his looks, although he had a dark, twisted countenance that made her think of a Borgia contemplating a dinner partner. Hugo had presence, that mysterious quality that makes men stand out from their fellows. You *knew* when you looked at him that he was a heavy hitter, and, if the set of his shoulders meant anything, and she was quite certain it did, he was ready to unload this afternoon.

It was easy to understand, when Hugo reached the stage, why he was cast as Jonathan, the menacing, saturnine older brother who has returned to terrorize his screwball family. Hugo's thick, silvery eyebrows tufted in a grim frown as he glared down at Burt Conroy.

"Dump Shane." His hard-featured, broken-nosed face was implacable.

To Annie's surprise, Burt Conroy didn't crumple on the spot.

Feeling a little as though she was intruding in a death scene, Annie slipped into the third row. She cringed as her chair squeaked. Max quietly joined her.

But every eye was focused on Hugo and Burt.

Standing in the center of the stage, the president of the Broward's Rock Players and stage manager of *Arsenic and Old Lace* pleated his hands nervously against the trousers of his pale blue leisure suit, but his reedy voice was firm. "I am surprised at you, Hugo," he chided. "You are experienced enough to know that the director makes all casting decisions and —"

"I'm experienced enough to know this play's a disaster." Hugo's gravelly baritone carried from the first seat to the last.

Everyone watched, mesmerized, because

there was no mistaking the icy fury in his voice.

Serving as president of the players, despite the customary internecine squabbles among its members, hadn't prepared Burt Conroy for this confrontation. Nor had his years as a successful owner and manager of Stuff 'N Such, a knickknack shop on the waterfront that carried everything from memorabilia to quite old and valuable wooden duck decoys. Burt's normally grayish face flushed a dull saffron and he took a deep breath, but Hugo plowed right ahead, his deep voice and superb diction flooding the auditorium.

He had an audience, all right. Of course, not all the cast members were there. Only Act II was on this afternoon's schedule and several of the characters didn't appear in it. But those present hung on every word.

Carla Fontaine, the set designer and chief carpenter, rocked back on her heels and looked up tensely. Her shining long black hair shadowed her patrician face, but her hands gripped a hammer so tightly that her knuckles blanched. Normally, she was remote and aloof, immersed in her work on the set, not even accepting graciously the compliments that had been showered over her superb creation: the Victorian stairs that dominated upstage right and were so essential to a successful production of *Arsenic and Old Lace*. Now her worried eyes showed just how much the production meant to her.

Arthur Killeen, the local druggist who played Dr. Einstein with raffish charm, stood at stage left, waggling his hands in helpless dismay. Brushing back a strand of thin black hair, he tried to break in, "Now, Hugo, it's too late to make changes." Hugo ignored him, increasing his volume just a little.

Henny Brawley bounced on her sneakered feet at the top of the downstage left steps. Her bright black eyes darted from face to face and her fox-sharp nose quivered with interest. In her brilliant crimson warm-up and with a calico headband holding down her salt-and-pepper hair, Henny looked like a bony geriatric jock, but she could pick up and discard personalities faster than Sherlock Holmes could fashion a disguise. She was a superb Abby. At this moment, she looked torn between being a theater stalwart and jumping ship to join Hugo's insurrection.

The Horton family stood in a clump at downstage right. Although they were near each other physically, their familial bonds, were, as usual, stretched to the breaking point. Cindy, the nubile teenage daughter who fancied herself the eighties' answer to Marilyn Monroe, so far forgot her lacquered persona as to permit a scowl to crease her normally unsullied brow and twist a mouth generously fashioned by the wettest-looking lipstick the local drugstore could provide. As a stagehand, she hovered backstage at all hours, but her thoughts were seldom on the play. She was wildly infatuated with Shane Petree, which everyone except her mother recognized.

Her mother, Janet, was no prize in the brains department. At the moment, she was registering ladylike disapproval, with several sad little headshakes at Hugo's ungentlemanly behavior. A somewhat limp but moderately attractive midforties, Janet played Martha surprisingly well indeed and was an accomplished enough actress to recognize the truth in Hugo's furious bellows. But women are notoriously blind to flaws in their beloveds, and the whispers around the island made the odds ten to one that Janet was another of Shane's foolish conquests.

T. K. Horton looked to be odd man out on every front, with his daughter pursuing Shane with the tenacity of an overripe hound in heat, and his wife reverting to giggly, preteen behavior whenever the great lover appeared. T.K. was such an unlikely center for domestic tragedy. As he watched Hugo, his jowly face began to look years younger. Hope flickered in his spaniel eyes. If Shane were kicked out of the play — God, T.K. obviously could taste it!

Another face watched with burgeoning hope, and the sight really made Annie sad. Eugene Ferramond was *born* to play Teddy Roosevelt. He had the same bluff good looks, the same orange brush mustache, even the rimless eyeglasses that hung from a cord. He was burly as a bear, moved with a bouncy swagger, and was as nutty as his hero about history. Until this year, he could always count on playing Teddy whenever the players revived *Arsenic and Old Lace*.

But not this summer. Instead, when the cast was announced, Eugene was picked to play Officer O'Hara. Now, to be sure, that was a wonderful role, the cop who desperately wants to be a playwright and is consequently sublimely oblivious to the presence of a wanted murderer. He concentrates instead on selling his plot outline to the theater critic Mortimer Brewster,

42

who is frantically trying to save his old aunts from incarceration as murderesses and simultaneously foil the deadly plans of his dangerous brother Jonathan and Jonathan's sidekick, Dr. Einstein. Even as Hugo raised his volume another notch, Annie thought in passing what a *wonderful* Mortimer Max was.

Eugene was a very good Officer O'Hara. But he didn't want to be Officer O'Hara. He *wanted* to be Teddy.

It was Henny Brawley who had gotten the real scoop and shared it with Annie when she dropped by Death on Demand to pick up her latest batch of books (two by Liza Cody, two by Jim Stinson, and three by Anne Morice). According to Henny, Burt Conroy had forced the director to pick Shane for Teddy because Sheridan Petree, Shane's wife, had agreed to underwrite all the expenses for the play. And that was too tempting a plum for Burt to refuse. After all, if the play didn't cost a penny, every cent of ticket sales could go for profits and make it that much more likely that the summer season would turn a profit — and Burt Conroy loved his community theater with a passion that most men reserve for their wives, mistress, or cars.

Hugo reached his dramatic finale. "God knows why Sam picked Shane! It would take a deity to understand that incredible decision. I consider it one of the world's inexplicable mysteries."

(*But not to Henny,* Annie thought.)

Hugo hit full vocal stride. "Shane's an unmitigated disaster as Teddy. He's a disaster as an actor. Although, God knows, it would help just a little bit if he would learn his lines. Is it too much to ask," and now his voice dripped venom, "that the sorry bastard know his lines five days before we open?"

An ebullient call erupted as Sam pushed through the center aisle doors. "Kids, kids, let's get ready! Time's a-wasting." Sam bounded toward the stage, clapping his hands. "Act Two, that's the ticket. Everybody ready?"

Even Sam noticed something curious in the quality of silence that greeted him, but he shook his head, and the blondish fringe of hair that stuck out in tufts like a friar's headpiece quivered with energy. "Come on now, lots to do, kids. Jonathan, stretch out in that armchair, look like the lord of the manor. You're back home, king of the hill. Come on —"

Hugo didn't make a move.

Sam squinted up in concern. "Sorry to be late." His watery blue eyes flickered away. "Having trouble locating the programs."

But Annie saw the pain in those eyes and in the sudden droop of the director's mouth. So "sweetie" was still hellbent to leave the island.

Hugo looked down at Sam, in the manner of an executioner measuring rope. "Take your pick. Shane or me."

The stuffy, airless heat in the foyer had leeched the last vestige of freshness from Sam's seersucker trousers. Sweat ringed the armpits of his faded Grateful Dead T-shirt. His pink-rimmed eyes fluttered nervously as he looked up against the overhead lights at Hugo's determined face.

"Now, Hugo . . ." he began placatingly.

But Hugo wasn't having any. "Less than a week to go." His voice clanged like a closing cell door. "And this show is hopeless. If that fat moron louses up again today, I'm walking."

If it were possible for cherry red cheeks to blanch, Sam's did. "Oh, Jesus! You can't do it! Without you, we're sunk. Dead. Rigor mortised."

"With Shane, we are an abominable embarrassment to the world, and I'm not going to put up with it any longer. I'm telling you right now, Sam, if that sweaty stallion doesn't know his goddamned lines today, I'm going to break his goddamned neck — and then I'm going to walk out of here a happy man."

Sam jiggled unhappily on his tiny feet. "Hugo, Hugo, you don't mean it, man. Why, you're marvelous as Jonathan. The critics will go nuts. You want to go to Broadway, don't you? Well, listen, I got news. I got great news. Listen, everybody. Hey, everybody, gather round, I got news."

And that, of course, was when Shane made his entrance, slouching down the center aisle like Elvis Presley on a bad, late day.

"Coming, everybody. Coming." Twenty minutes late at least, but there was no hint of apology in his voice. He was so full of himself it was miraculous that he didn't explode like an overinflated balloon. Shane had starred in a series of low-budget surfer movies in the late sixties, and he still had the body of a Huntington Beach golden boy, except for the softness of his belly. Well over six feet tall, at a distance he looked like a casting director's delight. Close up, he carried puffy pouches under his eyes from too much scotch and too many late nights.

Oblivious to the varying shades of disgust and dislike aimed at him, he sauntered up the stage right steps with a quick wink at Janet and a hot little glance at Cindy.

Hugo glared.

Sam swiped nervously at his perspiring face.

Cindy's well-endowed bosom quivered.

Janet's pale blue eyes widened rapturously.

T.K. stared glumly down at the boards.

Carla turned away and began to pound a nail into a loose tread of the stairs.

Eugene sighed, tugged on his orange brush mustache, and dropped heavily into a seat beside Annie.

Burt's color turned muddy, offering an unpleasant contrast to the sky blue of his leisure suit.

Arthur batted nervously at that lank piece of hair dangling near his eyes.

Henny's mouth formed a perfect O.

Max poked an elbow in Annie's ribs, but she didn't need a warning. Anyone could decipher these storm signals.

"So," Hugo sneered. (And Annie put the tone right on a Richard Widmark level. Damn, Hugo was *good*.) "God's gift to summer theater has deigned to join us — finally."

Shane gave him an indifferent glance, then thrust out a middle finger in the immemorial gesture of disdain.

Hugo's dark visage twisted with fury, and he lowered his head to charge.

Sam sprang forward, grabbed Hugo's arm, and hung on like a limpet.

"Sweetheart, sweetheart, toss it off, 'cause I got news," and he dug in his heels. He wasn't big or strong enough to stop Hugo and was being pulled over the boards, but his voice kept rising with banshee desperation. "Producer!" he shrieked. "Broadway producer! Listen to me, Hugo, I got a Broadway *producer* coming for open ing night!"

Hugo stopped. His clenched hands and flexed biceps slowly loosened. Slowly his head turned, and his glazed eyes focused on Sam.

"A Broadway producer?"

Sam knew he had his fish; all he had to do was play in the line. Sweat coursed down his face in rivulets. Panting, he poured it out. "God's truth. Cross my heart. Solomon Purdy. You know who he is." Sam looked around at his captivated audience. "Everybody knows him. Right? Three Tonys. Successful revivals of *The Crucible* and *Who's Afraid of Virginia Woolf?*

And he's casting *Cat on a Hot Tin Roof.*"

On the rare occasions when Hugo directed his attention to anything other than himself, he was fond of discussing Tennessee Williams's plays. He considered Williams the quintessential American playwright. And, since his retirement as a trial lawyer at the peak of his career, Hugo considered himself the greatest undiscovered actor in America.

"Opening night?" Hugo repeated.

Sam's shoulders heaved in relief. The fish was hooked. "Yeah, sweetheart. So, let's go after it, baby. Give the brass ring a big try. Come on, Hugo, show these folks how they do it in the big time. You're Jonathan and you're so goddamned pleased with yourself —"

And, easy as that, they slid into the rehearsal of the first scene in Act II.

Annie never could decide which act she enjoyed the most. As Jonathan lit his cigar and leaned back comfortably in the armchair to the left of the table, Abby and Martha perched uneasily atop the window seat, while Dr. Einstein relaxed in his chair. Did she like best that wonderful moment in Act I when Mortimer finds the body in the window seat? Or his incredulity when he discovers that his aunts are merrily providing destitute elderly men with poisoned elderberry wine? Or the scene when Mortimer proposes to Elaine (her own fun role)? But Act II certainly had its moments, not least of which was Teddy's enthusiastic agreement to dig another lock in the Panama Canal (the nice deep holes in the basement which the old dears utilized for gravesites).

As Teddy stomped out onto the balcony, wearing a solar topee and carrying a book, Eugene moved restively beside Annie.

She shot him a quick sideways glance. Eugene's underlip drooped, and he suppressed a weary sigh. For once, in a life filled with conversational gambits, Annie couldn't think of a thing to say.

Unfortunately, Eugene saved her the trouble. She knew, before he spoke, that he was going to share with her yet another flash of information about the life of his idol and look-alike, the redoubtable Teddy. Eugene was a walking authority on the interests, achievements, passions, and pursuits of the twenty-sixth president.

"The head of the African Cape buffalo that hangs over the mantelpiece in the entrance hall at Sagamore Hill was shot by TR on a safari to Africa in 1909." Eugene nodded happily. "Oh, the colonel was a great hunter. And you know, it was a cartoonist's rendering of a bear hunt in Mississippi in 1902 that got the rage started for teddy bears."

Annie made a noncommittal noise. As the act progressed and Teddy came onstage again, she learned that Roosevelt was very partial to natty and stylish gray trousers.

It was with a feeling of relief that she made her escape. It was almost time for her to come onstage as Elaine. She didn't know which bothered her the most, Eugene's devotion to his idol or Shane's wooden performance in the role. Each made the other worse.

As she waited backstage to enter through the front door of the set, she watched Abby and Martha resisting Jonathan's orders to go upstairs and go to bed. (Jonathan is eager to clear the lower floors of the old ladies because he and Dr. Einstein have their own corpse which they wish to smuggle into the house.) Jonathan bellowed at Martha, and she started reluctantly up the stairs.

Annie heard a rustling behind the backdrop not too far from where she stood. A rustling, a high giggle, then a squeal. "Oh, you better not! I'll tell my daddy on you — if you don't do it more."

Martha stopped midway up the stairs, and her head swung toward the backdrop. The image of Martha dissolved, and as it did, Annie saw Janet clutch her throat in shock, her usually placid, somewhat obstinate face crumpled in pain.

Another suggestive giggle, and a murmured, "Come on! You can do —"

"Cindy!" The name exploded from Janet's contorted lips. Taut silence behind the backdrop.

"Hey, what's the matter, Janny?" Her husband's voice came from the auditorium.

A rustle of movement behind the backdrop, a quiver as someone moved against the curtain.

Janet clung to the banister. She was breathing in jerky gasps, her face an unhealthy pinkish red.

"Janet?" T.K. lumbered solicitously toward the down stage left steps.

At that moment, Janet proved to Annie that she could indeed act. She lifted her head, took a deep breath, then turned to face the auditorium. "It's all right. I just felt faint for a moment. That lunch. I *know* I can't eat chili." She managed a light laugh. "I'll rest for just a moment offstage, and I'll be all right."

T.K. peered up at the stage. Concern warred with suspicion on his face. Obviously, he hadn't heard the exchange behind the backdrop. Just as obviously, he had an inkling that there was more to this moment than indigestion.

Sam clapped his hands. Clearly, he knew damn well what was going on behind the curtain, and he was determined to keep the Horton menage tamped down. "Let's pick up at the top of the act with Einstein coming back up from the cellar." But he gave a worried glance offstage, hoping, no doubt, that Janet would keep her mouth shut until she came back onstage.

Damn Shane's proclivities. Annie's entrance was now delayed until they ran through the first half of the act again. She tossed a glower over her shoulder but didn't see anyone in the dimness. Then she turned back to watch, keeping an ear cocked for a first-class row, but a pastoral quiet reigned behind her. It figured. Janet was much too ladylike to mount a virago attack on her daughter in public, even though she had just had a traumatic shock. Annie shook her head. However could Janet have missed the byplay between Cindy and Shane?

The scene with Jonathan and Einstein went superbly and even Janet did well when she returned as Martha. Annie began to have a cheerful conviction that, by golly, the show was going to be a success, as by all rights it should be. Her good cheer remained until Shane entered as Teddy. Then the mood shattered. For his entrance was even more off-key than usual.

Shane looked excited, horny, and overpoweringly masculine. It was that rampant sexuality that made him so wrong for the role. Teddy is one of life's innocents and Shane's dissipation seemed almost obscene as he swaggered downstage. And, as usual, before he spoke, his eyes darted at the nearest prop, which held a prompt card. He was the only cast member who had yet to master his lines. In desperation, Carla had taped cards at various spots on stage so Shane could read Teddy's dialogue. Shane's cavalier attitude toward his lines enraged Hugo more than anything else. If Shane would learn his lines, Hugo groused, he could be a passable Teddy. Not a great Teddy, like Eugene, but passable, because beneath that layer of self-adulation and self-indulgence, lurked a minor talent. But the flicker of talent wasn't enough to offset the wooden delivery of badly read lines.

Shane leaned closer to the table. "General Goethals," he boomed, "says out damned spot —"

Sam's high explosive scream sounded like a toreador gored by a bull.

Everyone swung to look at him.

Sam jumped up and down, absolutely out of control, his fringe of blondish hair flapping like mast flags in a hurricane. "Oh, Jesus X. Christ, I give up! So friggin' hot it's like rehearsing in the Black Hole of Calcutta, a stage that even a corn-pone outfit would sneer at, and now this hot-panted excuse for Teddy queers everything! Jesus, now there's no hope at all!"

Cindy began to giggle.

5

Shane stared at him, open-mouthed.

Quivering with frustration, Sam slapped his hands against his temples. "What kind of friggin' idiot are you?"

"Hey, wait a minute, buster! What the hell's wrong with you?"

"Wrong?" The director's reedy voice wobbled, then cracked, as he glared at his star. "Oh, God, what *isn't* wrong? A Teddy who has about as much class as a Hollywood bimbo and who won't learn his lines. Or maybe you're so damn dumb you *can't* learn them! That's what comes of casting a hunk out of a surfer movie. And now, this!"

Shane lunged forward, grabbed the front of Sam's T-shirt, and hauled the little man up on his toes. "Listen, creep, I don't have to take this shit."

Sam wriggled like a gigged fish.

Max moved to rescue Sam, but Hugo was nearer. The big actor clamped a vise-like hand on Shane's arm. "Let go."

There was an instant's stillness, but the

outcome was never in doubt. It would take a brave man, and Annie felt sure Shane didn't qualify, to ignore the steel in Hugo's voice.

Shane's grip loosened. Sam bounced on his heels and rubbed at his throat. His chest heaving, the director's face contorted. Weeks of cajoling Shane and placating the other cast members boiled over into flaming rage. "Shit?" he exploded. "Who're you to talk about shit? You trying to ruin the play? Put us out of commission? We might as well close the doors now. You know what happens when somebody quotes from *that play!*"

"Quotes what?" Shane asked blankly.

There was another instant of silence, this one freighted with disbelief. Then, joining Annie in the wing, Carla began to laugh derisively. Brushing back a strand of long, dark hair, she stared at Shane disdainfully. "You don't even know what you just said." It wasn't a question. It was an observation, a damning pronouncement that here, ladies and gentlemen, was the dumbest son of a bitch in captivity.

Shane's blue eyes narrowed, indicating heavy thought.

Burt hurried onstage, his glance jerking from Sam to Shane, his grayish face creased in a scowl. "What's wrong, Sam? Somebody sick?"

"I'm sick," Sam growled. "This idiot" — he stabbed his forefinger at Shane — "he quoted from *that play*."

Burt's face registered instant comprehension, but Shane clearly remained bewildered. The watching faces now included those of T.K. and Eugene, who had surged onstage from the auditorium.

Everyone gathered in a circle, except for Henny Brawley, who edged around the group to study the white index card taped to the top of the table. Just a moment ago, as Abby, her movements had reflected gentility and, bony as she was, she had exuded an aura of pleasing, elderly plumpness. Now, as she arched forward, her dark eyes avid, she was a bloodhound on the scent.

Janet pressed a hand against her lips. But, of course, she would take the incident to her breast and hug it lifeless, Annie thought. She adored drama, real or manufactured. Her beefy husband shook his head in disgust, whether at Shane's stupidity or at the breaking of the theater taboo, Annie couldn't tell. Hugo's dark eyes glittered with irritation. Arthur, who was such a charming Dr. Einstein, suddenly looked enormously weary, as if he longed to be back at his drugstore. Eugene leaned forward, his orange brush mustache quivering with eagerness, hoping, of course, that this would be the final straw. Cindy, craning past Annie's shoulder, obviously didn't care what had happened or why. Her eyes were too busy fondling Shane.

"You have to know what you said," Burt said flatly. He usually affected an uneasy geniality, a product of his years as a merchant, but he shed it now like a bill collector dunning for a bad debt. His lips thinned into a tight, angry line.

Shane shrugged, a gesture not even bothering to hide his disgust. "What the hell's wrong with everybody?"

At that moment, as Annie feared violence might actually erupt, Henny stepped forward to fill the crackling silence. She spoke so precisely that Annie suddenly pictured her in another milieu, wearing a crisp navy blue dress with a white ruffled collar and standing before a class. "It's a quote from a famous Shakespeare play, Shane. Those extra words in your line. And it's considered bad luck, the very *worst* kind of bad luck, ever to quote from this particular play in any theater."

Sam's bleary eyes focused on Shane with

sheer hatred. "Bad luck! You'd better believe it's bad luck. The time I was in Chicago and we were producing it, God, the
leading man got mugged in an alley back of
the house, the lead actress got malaria. You
ever heard of anybody getting malaria in
Chicago? Oh, Jesus, it was a disaster — and
that's just what this play is, a damn —"

"Sam!" Burt spit out the name like an
expletive.

The director swung to face him, his eyes
wide. "Burt, I tell you, we got trouble,
baby. This is just the tip of the iceberg.
What's happened so far will make the *Ti-
tanic* look like a Sunday afternoon row on
the river!" He jerked around to glare again
at Shane. "And you can't tell me this Hollywood yo-yo didn't do it on purpose."

Ignoring Sam, Shane elbowed through
the watchers to the table and stared down
at the prompt card. Then he grinned. "You
people are a bunch of dingdongs. Three
little words and all hell breaks loose." He
surveyed the grim-faced assemblage, his
mocking eyes moving from Janet, hand still
pressed against her mouth, to Sam, livid
with anger. "What a bunch of crazies." He
snickered. "Out damned —"

Sam bellowed and lurched forward.

Max dodged between them, and over the

rising tide of imprecations, Burt's reedy voice announced, "Rehearsal's over!"

Annie measured the expresso-grind chocolate Viennese coffee to the two-cup level, plugged in the mini espresso-cappuccino machine, and switched it on. As she poured half-and-half (fat content be damned, glory be to calcium) into a pitcher, she glanced through the kitchen doorway. Max was stretched out happily on her rattan couch, the most comfortable pillows bunched behind his shoulders.

"Max," and she knew her tone was half plea, half demand, "we have to *do* something!"

The first drops of luscious brew spattered into the carafe, so Annie tilted the cream pitcher beneath the steam nozzle and turned it on. With a rushing, hissing sound, steam roiled into the half-and-half and foam began to rise like a spume on a breaker. The steam nozzle emitted more vapor with a piercing squeal that reminded her uncomfortably of poor, tormented Sam's final shriek. She yelled over the rising whistle, "Don't you think we should?"

The bubble and hiss of the steam nozzle drowned his reply. She tipped the pitcher as the half-and-half frothed, and smiled in anticipation. It took only a moment more to pour the rich dark coffee and the foamy half-and-half into yellow pottery mugs, sprinkle a dash of cinnamon, and load the tray. She paused thoughtfully, contemplating a package of Oreo cookies. Max was much too rigid in his approach to food. Still, she *was* using half-and-half. Feeling virtuous, she added a plate of lemon tea cookies and carried the tray into the living room. (She could always munch an Oreo later.) (If he wanted home-baked cookies, he could marry the kind of girl who bought a food processor with Green Stamps.)

The late afternoon sunlight flooded through the eleven-foot windows in her hexagonal living room. Max still laughed at her tree house, but Annie knew she would miss it after the wedding, when they moved into the home they were building near the twelfth green of the Island Hills Golf Course.

She paused, glancing around the tiny, cheerful living room at her bookcases filled with paperback mysteries, with most of her very favorites, the Mary Roberts Rinehart and Leslie Ford books, plus some by the new mistresses of mystery, Charlotte

MacLeod, Dorothy Simpson, and Linda Barnes. Her most recent photographs, including a marvelous shot of a rare Canada goose, strikingly beautiful with its black neck and head and white cheeks, were pinned to the corkboard. She had a funny feeling for just an instant, a moment of breathlessness, the scary kind of feeling that precedes any new adventure, any step into the unknown. But, for heaven's sake, Max wasn't an unknown. Marriage with Max would be . . . She grinned, recalling the day's events. Lively, that was for sure.

The subject of her thoughts was looking up at her quizzically. "When you withdrew to the kitchen, you were consumed with angst about the future of the play. Did the joy of cooking," here she decided to ignore the irony in his voice, "drive away your dark thoughts?"

She pushed aside the latest copy of *The Armchair Detective* and put the tray on the rattan coffee table in front of the couch.

"I was just thinking about this fall. After we get married."

"Good thinking. Lots more fun to speculate about than the identity and/or motives of the prankster who's making life miserable for Sam." He sat up, grabbed her hand, and tugged her around the coffee table to sit beside him. "You know, I was afraid you'd forgotten there was a world that existed after June twenty-eighth. Let's focus on what really matters. We're getting married in September, and it's going to be a *blast*."

"It would be difficult to forget our upcoming nuptials, since I am in almost daily consultation with your mother," she pointed out.

"Mother is excited, isn't she?" he exclaimed cheerfully. "You know, she's really throwing herself into it." Whistling "Get Me to the Church on Time," he slipped his arm around her and managed a sip of the cappuccino in one smooth move.

"Dexterous, you are," she commented.

"Oh, you bet. I can kiss a girl and drive a car at the same time. Chew gum and think. Star in a play and —"

The phone rang.

They looked at each other. Two minds with but a single thought: Laurel.

It rang again.

After four rings, the answering machine would play her recorded message.

But, after all, if she married Max — and she was going to marry Max — Laurel would be her mother-in-law. It behooved her to remain on good terms with her prospective family member. Especially since the dutiful son was regarding her with mild but prompting inquiry.

She poked off the answering machine, managing to smile as she did so. The smile might possibly be a trifle strained.

"Hello?"

"Annie, my sweet." There was a moment's pause, then the golden voice asked gently, "My dear, did I catch you at a bad moment? I do feel that I detect stress." The words became muffled. "When I press my hands to my temples, I can sense emotions. Annie, I sense confusion!"

Annie pictured the receiver cradled between chin and shoulder and almost said she sensed contortion. But, looking at Max, whose lips were curved in a fond smile, she thought better of it.

"Actually, Laurel, I'm so glad you called now. Max and I are having coffee and discussing the wedding. Here, you can talk to him." She thrust the receiver determinedly at her beloved.

After an exchange of delighted greetings, Max began to nod and say, "Mmmm. Mmmm." He took occasional sips of his cappuccino and once said, "Not really!" And finally, "Oh, that's a *grand* idea."

Annie regarded him like Pierre Chambrun sizing up a flashy gent in the bar at the Beaumont.

When the fond farewell was complete and the receiver once again rested innocently in its cradle, he cleared his throat and said, a little tentatively, "Now, Annie, I'm not going to try and sell you on any idea you'd regret. . . ."

It was her turn to say, "Mmmm."

Max slid his arm again behind her shoulders.

Annie sat up very straight.

"But Laurel does have interesting ideas. . . ." he ventured.

She could have changed the subject, discussed her latest issue of *Mystery Readers of America Journal*, shared her excitement over a new divine mystery, *The Unorthodox Murder of Rabbi Wahl*, or wondered aloud what Ngaio Marsh would advise in regard to the *Macbeth* quote, but the Gordons' *Undercover Cat* had nothing on Annie when it came to curiosity.

"What is it this time?" she demanded.

"Laurel is an enthusiastic traveler."

Annie considered this observation in silence.

Max cleared his throat. "She had a wonderful trip to China last year."

Annie's eyes narrowed.

"Lovely wedding customs there. Visually quite striking."

Annie tensed.

Max raised his dark blue eyes to study the ceiling, remarking conversationally, "Red's a jolly color, isn't it?" His eyes moved to her face, then quickly away. "Of course, in China red signifies joy and love, and the bridal dress and candles and gift boxes —"

"No."

"No?"

There was a moment's silence, before Annie asked, strangled voice, "Where else did Laurel travel last year?"

"Mmmm. Here and there."

She looked at him steadily.

"Let me see. Thailand. East Pakistan. The Congo Republic. Cameroon. Algeria. Nicaragua."

At the mention of the last country, Annie stared at him in surprise.

"Just a fact-finding tour. For her local world peace group."

"Maybe she'd like to go back. In September."

Max's dark blue eyes were reproachful.

"Just kidding," she said grimly. But she felt enmeshed in a gossamer web, and she had a dreadful fear — one she hesitated even to put into words — that Laurel would prevail. Even the thought triggered a shudder, and she knew she must not permit her mind to envision the awesome possibilities of a wedding successfully engineered by Laurel.

She would not think about it. She would not. What had they been doing before Laurel called? Oh, of course. The play. The quote from *Macbeth*.

"Max, we've got to figure out who's sabotaging the play." She handed him the plate of cookies.

He scooped up three. "Why?" he asked mildly. "Let good old Burt take care of it."

"And what if he doesn't? Does Burt have our expertise? Max, I love that play, and I don't want to see it ruined. Come on, let's think. Surely we can figure out who's causing this trouble."

He popped a cookie in his mouth and crunched. "Hmm. Pretty good. You make 'em?"

She merely stared at him.

"Oh, sorry. Didn't mean to say the wrong thing." He grinned.

She would have admired the way his eyes crinkled when he was amused, but he got too much attention as it was. Instead, she sucked the froth from the top of her cup.

Max drank more of his cappuccino, then asked suspiciously, "Did you put cream in this?"

"Absolutely not," she said indignantly. Half-and-half wasn't *cream.*

She took a big sip, then popped up and crossed the room to root in the telephone desk for paper. The more active she was, the harder she thought about the play, the more Laurel's latest *outré* proposal receded in her mind. She found book order forms, copies of programs from last summer's plays, muttered "Damn," when she pricked her finger on an errant needle (What was a needle doing in there?), and was burrowing beneath a mound of bank statements when the front doorbell was prodded sharply three times.

Sucking on her finger and still scanning the living room for something to write on, she reached out and opened the door.

A high-pitched voice burbled as Henny Brawley swept inside. She wore a large gray flannel skirt with a droopy hem, a full blouse with a lacy panel down the front, a shapeless rust-colored cardigan, lisle stockings, and extremely sensible brown shoes. She looked twice as big as she actually was. Her salt-and-pepper hair blossomed in springy sausage-roll curls.

"Annie, Max, there's no time to be lost. It's imperative that we investigate at once. I know that if we fasten our teeth into this problem, we shall shake out the truth, like pigs hunting truffles."

Annie was, for once, at a loss for words. She gaped.

"Henny, how are you?" Max asked cheerfully as he got to his feet.

"Dear boy, I am in full cry." She marched across the room. As she hurried, an apple tipped out of her skirt pocket and bounced on the floor.

Annie reached down automatically to retrieve it.

Henny paused, pulled another apple from the pocket, polished it on her skirt, and took a generous bite.

Annie began to grin.

Managing somehow to chew and talk simultaneously, Henny gestured with the partially eaten apple. "I *know* who's behind the sabotage!"

"Really!" Annie exclaimed.

"Good going," Max applauded. "Who is it?"

"It's obvious, clear as the nose on your face. No two ways about it." An English accent became pronounced at this point.

They waited.

Henny Brawley nodded emphatically and the complex hairdo began to wobble. "Our troublemaker is Shane Petree."

She said it so confidently that they both leaned forward, entranced.

"How do you know?" Annie asked eagerly. "Did you see him with the prompt card? Did you find some cards in his car? How did you figure it out?"

Their visitor ignored the questions. Instead, she gnawed ferociously on her apple, chewed, swallowed, then demanded, "Who *obviously* doesn't want to be in the play? Who was cast *only* because his wife made it a condition of her financial support of the players? Who has *refused* to learn his lines, been consistently late to rehearsal? In short," and she spaced the words out dramatically, *"who — is — the — only — person — not — trying — to — make — the — play — a — success?"*

"Shane!" they chorused.

Henny beamed her approval at their sagacity, then finished the apple, tossed the core toward a wastebasket, which it missed, and wiped her hands on her cardigan. Another apple bounced onto the floor. Annie picked it up.

"Proof?" Max inquired mildly.

"Proof? Why, a woman's intuition, my

dear. You can count on it every time."

Swinging around, Henny darted back to the front door, and another apple went careening across the room. "So, just wanted you both to know. Just in case."

"Just in case what?" Annie cried, as the door opened.

"I'm off to keep an eye on Mr. Shane Petree. He won't do any more dark deeds, I can assure you," and she was through the door and gone.

Annie looked down at the two apples in her hand. "Ariadne Oliver," she announced.

Max was stretching out again on the couch. "Spare me. I don't think I want to know any more than you've already told me."

Annie crossed to the bookcase, slipped her hand along the C's, withdrew *Hallowe'en Party*, and tossed it to Max. Then she threw an apple.

Absently, she began to eat the one she held. "Darn it," her voice was indistinct, "she really had me going. I thought maybe she was on to something."

Max firmly put his apple and the Christie novel on the table and picked up his coffee mug.

Annie gave a muffled whoop of pleasure

as she found the notebook she'd been seeking underneath a stack of *Ellery Queen Mystery* magazines.

Max watched indulgently as she listed the malicious tricks that had been played on the cast and crew of *Arsenic and Old Lace.*

SABOTAGE

1. May 6. Blocking rehearsal. Someone erased the chalk marks denoting furniture placement from the previous blocking rehearsal. A minor inconvenience, time-consuming. Assumed at the time to be accidental.
2. May 8. Stink bomb explodes in basement dressing room. Cast driven out of auditorium by smoke and fumes.
3. May 13. Notices removed from the callboard, so cast members missed next rehearsal.
4. May 19. House curtain collapses. Rope, $3/4$ inch jute, partially sawn through. Curtain's weight ultimately tore through the remaining strands. Could have caused injury had anyone been under the curtain when it fell.

As for number five, was that an unforgettable night! Janet had dropped the glass of elderberry wine she was offering Mr. Witherspoon and screamed, pointing up. Everyone looked toward the ceiling of the auditorium. Up, up, up, at the beams in their gridwork. A hand dangled from an opening. A limp hand and arm. Max, followed closely by Annie, tore down the center aisle and up the front-of-house steps to the balcony and the door to the light booth. It was open. Into the booth and up the narrow steps to the attic opening, then Max, waving Annie back, inched carefully across the narrow planks that crossed the dangerous ceiling with its square openings for the lights. And finally, as they waited breathlessly, his voice floated eerily through the dusty space. "A dummy. For God's sake, a dummy!"

5. May 22. *Annie wrote.* Dangling dummy.

The laconic notation did not adequately represent the dreadful moments when they believed a body was lodged precariously in the far reaches of the attic.

Max grabbed up a pen from the coffee table and began to write.

74

6. May 31. Quote from *Macbeth* inserted in Shane's prompt card. Sam goes bananas.

"Hey, do you have a copy of the rehearsal schedule?" Annie looked around for her purse, but Max was already pulling the mimeographed sheet from his pocket.

He spread it open and she peered at it. "Look, that's what I thought," she said triumphantly. "When somebody let off the stink bomb, it was a rehearsal for Act Two. So that lets out the people who appear only in Acts One and Three. And the stink bomb is the only piece of sabotage that had to have been done by someone in the auditorium at the time."

Quickly, Max made a list of the cast for Act II: Henny Brawley as Abby, Janet Horton as Martha, Hugo Wolf as Jonathan, Arthur Killeen as Dr. Einstein, Shane Petree as Teddy, Annie as Elaine, himself as Mortimer, and Eugene Ferramond as Officer O'Hara.

Annie took another bite of apple. "We have to count T.K. He doesn't come on as Lieutenant Rooney until Act Three, but he hasn't missed a rehearsal yet. And, of course, Sam and Burt are always there."

"And Cindy and Carla," Max added. "So we're back to the same people who were present today. Is that any help?"

"Well, we can at least drop Father Donaldson, Ben Tippet, and Vince Ellis from consideration." They played, respectively, Dr. Harper (Act I), Mr. Gibbs (Act I), and Officer Brophy (Acts I and III).

Max wrinkled his nose. "Sorry to be discouraging, old top, but I don't think we are making much progress."

Annie wasn't ready to quit detecting. "Look," she said hurriedly, forestalling suggestions of other pastimes (Max had a certain gleam in his eye), "we've got to look at the people involved. That's the way to go about it. Like Poirot says, running about to and fro like a dog with a bone won't get you anywhere. We've got to look at the psychology of it all."

"Okay," Max said equably. "Who fits the profile?"

She nodded approvingly. He was getting into the spirit of it.

She printed PROFILE, then frowned. After all, it was impossible to have any idea of the perpetrator's personality unless they knew his (or her) objective. She scratched out PROFILE and substituted OBJECTIVE, then wrote busily,

1. Ruin the season.
2. Get Shane canned.
3. Drive Sam berserk.
4. Raise a little hell.

Max took her pen and circled the last line.

She looked at him inquiringly.

"As a general proposition —" he began.

Annie shushed him. "Don't distract me. I think we really getting somewhere. Let's see who might fit each category."

They didn't agree in all cases, but they did come up with some possibilities.

1. Ruin the season. Harley Edward Jenkins III got top billing. As everyone in town knew, Jenkins vociferously opposed rebuilding the theater on the harbor front. Certainly a lousily produced first play of the season would lessen the chances of a profit-making summer.

As far as Annie and Max knew, and they chewed this over thoroughly, it would not be to anyone else's advantage to prevent the theater from rebuilding on the harbor front. Certainly Burt Conroy was determined to see the theater rebuilt at its original site, both because he was president of the players and the community theater was his guiding passion in life, and, more prosaically but perhaps as importantly, because it was to his economic advantage as a shopkeeper to prevent Jenkins from building and leasing to a competing business.

"However," Max objected, "Harley was not in the theater when the stink bomb went off. So, if he's involved, one of the other cast or crew members is doing his dirty work."

Annie put *conspirator* in parentheses with a question mark by Harley's name.

Then she shook her head. "Why would anybody do that?"

"Money."

"You think Harley would bribe someone?"

"Honey, I think Harley's capable of any number of deceitful and disgusting acts. Besides," Max said triumphantly, "none of the cast or crew members has any reason to ruin the season."

"Except Eugene," Annie said reluctantly.

"Still smarting because Burt forced Sam to cast Shane as Teddy?"

"Obviously, it still smarts. Have you seen Eugene's eyes when Shane comes on the set as Teddy?" Annie sighed.

Under *Ruin the season*, Max wrote *Eugene Ferramond* in small script. Under *Get*

Shane canned, he printed the name in big block letters.

"That's more likely," Annie agreed. "But Eugene sure doesn't stand alone." She printed *T. K. Horton* in similarly large block letters, took another bite of apple, and added *Hugo Wolf* and *Sam Haznine.*

Max quirked an eyebrow over the last entry. "That's pretty subtle."

"If Henny's gossip is right, Burt forced Sam to cast Shane. Don't you think Sam would do anything he could to make Burt change his mind?"

"I've never thought Sam could be that Byzantine."

"Speaking of Byzantine, do you think there's anything to Henny's idea that Shane's behind the sabotage? You know damn well that if his wife is determined for him to be in the play, he wouldn't have the guts to go against her wishes. But if he could cause enough trouble, fluff his lines, make Sam mad enough, and get himself fired, well, Sheridan could hardly blame *him,* could she?" Annie had a swift vision of Sheridan Petree's feline face. She suspected that Shane had developed a lot of Byzantine qualities in the years he'd been married to her. The woman was awesome in the force of her personality. She reduced most people, including her surfer-handsome but aging husband, to rubber-stamp marionettes.

Under *Drive Sam berserk*, Annie listed Shane and Eugene again, with one caveat.

"I really don't think Eugene has that small a personality. I know he aches to be Teddy, but he's doing an excellent job as Officer O'Hara, and he's always cheerful."

"Cheerful — and full of facts and figures about TR. It's almost an obsession." Max drew a line under Eugene's name. Under *Raise a little hell*, he wrote *Cindy Horton*.

Annie looked at him curiously. "On the theory that she's an oversexed snot and is capable of anything?"

"That young lady is quite hostile to her mother," Max observed. "Maybe she doesn't want to see Janet succeed as Martha. Maybe she thinks she could make more time with Shane if he weren't tied up in a play."

They studied their list of suspects.

1. *Ruin the season.*
   Harley Edward Jenkins III
      (conspirator?)
   Eugene Ferramond
2. *Get Shane canned.*
   Eugene Ferramond

Sam Haznine
Hugo Wolf
T.K. Horton
Shane himself

3. *Drive Sam berserk.*
   Shane
   Eugene

4. *Raise a little hell.*
   Cindy

Then Max added a final category, *Unknown*. "And that's my best suggestion yet."

At the bottom of the sheet, Annie penned: *Possible suspects but without known motives: Annie Laurance, Max Darling, Carla Fontaine, Henny Brawley, Janet Horton, Arthur Killeen.* She finished her mug of cappuccino, then lifted Max's from the coffee table, and saw, with regret, that it was empty, too.

Max flipped the notebook shut with a purposeful snap and moved closer. "Now that that's taken care of, let's consider some more pleasurable pursuits," and his arm slipped around her shoulders.

But Annie looked down at her watch. "We're due at the Petrees'. Remember?"

"Oh, hell." Then he suggested brightly, "Let's skip it."

Annie was tempted. She almost slipped

comfortably into his embrace.

Max said silkily, "After all, do you really want to go to an enormous bash put on by Sheridan Petree ostensibly to celebrate the beginning of the theater season, but actually to showcase that god-awful house and herself?"

It was his mention of the house that was his undoing. The house *fascinated* Annie.

Clapping her hands together, she said, "Oh, come on, Max. Let's go. I mean, you never know what's going to happen at the Petrees'."

Which was, she agreed later, the understatement of the year.

Max drove slowly, obviously in no hurry to reach the Petrees'. But he smiled at her, and his eyes did that nice crinkle. She smiled back. Max was born to wear a dinner jacket. The crisp white emphasized his even tan, the flash of his dark blue eyes, and his blond hair, tousled now by the warm air sweeping through the open sunroof. And was there a more perfect place in this world than Broward's Rock on the eve of summer? The sweet scent of blooming magnolia mingled with the sharper tang of the salt marsh. The offshore breeze rattled the palmetto fronds and the glossy magnolia leaves, but the loudest evening sounds came from frogs singing their mating melodies. Then the Porsche headlights swept over a salt marsh, and Annie glimpsed a four-foot-tall Great Blue Heron, with a long yellow bill and distinctive black plumes trailing from his white head. Startled, the majestic bird squawked and rose into the night sky, his three-foot wings flapping majestically. The road swung inland, and great spreading branches of live oak trees, festooned with Spanish moss, met overhead.

Annie slid forward eagerly in her seat when they reached the enormous circular drive that served the Petree mansion. The drive was jammed with cars parked along both sides. Two stewards from the country club served as valet parking attendants. Light spilled from every window of the two-story, Mediterranean-style home, and the blare of Dixieland jazz reached the foot of the drive. As they began the long walk up to the front door, Annie began to feel festive. She loved Dixieland, Sheridan always had fabulous food, and the interior of the Petree house was unsurpassed for grandiosity.

Max considered the house, which had the stark grace of a villa perched on a

Greek headland, to be an abused possession, lovely on the outside, rotten on the inside. In sunlight, its white stucco exterior glistened, as hard as Portland cement. Now, at night, it had the rich gleam of a moonlit Parthenon. Spotlights in the garden illuminated the brilliantly purple bougainvillea clinging to the facade. But the exterior of the house didn't hint at the opulence of the interior, the sheer, overwhelming, sense-assaulting ostentation. Ribbed brass ceilings glittered like gold bullion, satin-covered furniture glistened like luxurious pincushions, bronze-and-crystal chandeliers gleamed like shiny ribbons of neon. Here was a material glorification of the sensual, the visual equivalent to a romp in a California hot tub or its historical precursor, a Roman bath. Annie wondered if the other guests shared her faintly decadent feeling. If so, they hid it beneath social faces as they eddied across the pink marbled foyer into the enormous living room with its lush polar-white carpet, mirrored back wall, and, centerpiece of the room, a six-foot-tall oil derrick of gleaming Steuben glass.

Sheridan Petree stood beside the shimmering statue, her scarlet lips curved in a faint smile. Her hair swung long and loose and was the dusty gold of the Serengeti Plain. Her backless lamé dress, molded to her generous figure, repeated the gold motif of the ceiling. She looked past a circle of admirers at Annie and Max and lifted a heavy crystal goblet in salute.

"All she lacks is a twenty-one-gun salute," Annie murmured.

Max took her elbow and maneuvered her past a group of grazers clustered near the buffet. "Do I sense hostility, love?"

"There's something about Sheridan that rouses even my most dormant hostilities," she admitted. Was it because to her Sheridan and Shane epitomized the idle rich? But Max was, most of the time, idly rich. She couldn't pretend his forays for Confidential Commissions amounted to more than an interesting hobby. But Max was *attractively* rich. And the Petrees, to her mind, were most unattractively odious, self-absorbed, snobbish, lazy — and very, very rich. Sheridan's father had been quite famous in west Texas. Hunter Prentiss was a roistering, self-made oil man who had made and lost a half dozen fortunes, but, fortunately for Sheridan, was on a high roll when he was killed nine years before in a barroom brawl. Sheridan made reference to Hunter Prentiss on every possible occasion. A larger-than-lifesize portrait hung against the far mirrored wall, mounted between an elephant head and a tiger pelt, animals the oil man had killed with his very own .458 Winchester Magnum, displayed on a mahogany rack nearby. There was no corresponding portrait of Shane. Annie wondered if sometimes Sheridan's husband didn't weary of hearing incessantly about Daddy's exploits. Of course, in Annie's view, if Sheridan was not a delight, Shane was certainly no prize. If it wasn't a marriage made in heaven, it seemed a nice combination of people who probably deserved each other.

As Max and Annie came even with the elephant head, Eugene Ferramond, dignified in his tuxedo, waved a genial hand.

They paused and said hello.

"Pretty nice, this," Eugene observed.

Annie looked at him sharply. She would have thought Eugene would find this room distasteful in the extreme, but he was nodding serenely at the elephant head. And, my God, if he wasn't Teddy to the life tonight!

"Big-game hunting is quite a test of a man."

"Actually, quite a test of the prey, don't you think?" Max asked.

Annie could have hugged him. It might not be murder to gun down magnificent creatures, but it ranked high on Annie's sin list.

Eugene was oblivious. He looked admiringly at the mounted gun. "You know, TR was partial to the Winchester. He always used forty-five-caliber bullets of three hundred grains, backed by ninety grains of powder, when he hunted elk. Of course, he made it a rule never to shoot at anything but bucks — unless it was the rutting season."

"Good," Annie said dubiously.

"The bucks' flesh is poor then."

They edged away, leaving him absorbed by the elephant's head.

When they reached the crystal oil derrick, their hostess held out her hand and took Annie's in it. "So glad you both could come," Sheridan murmured insincerely.

They exchanged smiles, which had all the warmth of a west Texas winter sunrise.

Sheridan's voice was cool, too, uninflected, with only the faintest hint of her southwest origin. Her accent owed more to her Boston finishing school and her ricochet around the jet-set ports of call — Malibu, Monte Carlo, St. Thomas, Rio, and, now, Broward's Rock.

The smile scarcely caused a ripple across Sheridan's face. Her skin was smooth and unblemished, thanks, Annie felt sure, to the very finest of plastic surgeons. Not a single wrinkle splayed out from her amber eyes, even though she must be in her early forties. Was she older than her husband?

Feeling vaguely guilty, Annie increased the wattage of her smile. "Oh, we wouldn't have missed it for the *world*," she cried heartily and felt embarrassed when she saw Carla's quick, sardonic glance as she joined them.

Sheridan looked past Annie at Carla. "Everyone's raving about the sets, my dear."

Carla flushed with pleasure and ducked her head.

The contrast between the two women was striking. Carla stood at an awkward angle, her dark hair falling across her face, while Sheridan posed beside the crystal derrick, her body as clearly on display as a Rubens nude. Most women wouldn't have dared to stand beside the glittering oil derrick, fearing they would be overshadowed, diminished. Sheridan was not. She dominated the room, and she knew she did so. It was clear in the arrogant lift of her head, the satisfied curve of her scarlet mouth, the blatant play of her dress against the glistening brass ceiling. And tonight, she was clearly in high good humor. She squeezed Carla's arm, then waved an imperious, diamond-heavy hand, beckoning Sam Haznine nearer.

Sam swerved immediately toward Sheridan. The pudgy director clutched the hand of a girl who couldn't be a day past nineteen and who sported the spikiest purple-and-pink hair Annie had ever seen. This must be sweetie, she thought, carefully avoiding Max's twinkling eyes.

Sheridan's disdainful glance moved from the top of that neon-bright hairdo to the white, out-of-style sandals, just slightly scuffed. Then she looked away, dismissing the girl. She spoke to Sam as if he were alone. "Come tell us what happened today, Sam."

The girl's face flushed, and she grabbed at Sam's elbow. "Let's go get something to eat," she said loudly.

Sam gave her a hunted look, but he scuttled directly to Sheridan, the girl trying to hang back.

Sheridan's lips curved.

Annie had a sudden sharp desire to puncture that envelope of self-satisfaction. What would Sheridan do if Annie loudly announced how Shane had performed behind the backdrop with a randy refugee from the sandbox set? Annie profoundly wished she had been endowed with what Miss Marple so lovingly described as "a wicked tongue."

Sheridan proceeded to underline her lack of regard for social niceties. Turning her unreadable amber eyes toward Sam, she drawled, a ripple of amusement in her voice, "Here I am with the director and two stars of the opening play. Now's my chance to find out what happened this afternoon. Shane came home from rehearsal as puffed up as a tomcat in a backyard brawl, and I can't get a word out of him."

Sam looked seedy in a dinner jacket that had seen better years. The collar had frayed and the cummerbund wrinkled against his paunchy abdomen. He had approached his hostess with a smile. Now it stuck to his face like garnish on yesterday's tea sandwich.

"Nothing much," he said sourly. "Somebody's screwy idea of a joke." But his watery blue eyes were full of dread. He stuttered in his eagerness to deflect Sheridan. "Want you to — to — to meet Tonelda. This is Tonelda Divine — and she's going to be a great actress."

The flush was receding from the girl's face. She puffed her spiky hair and simpered.

Sheridan nodded curtly. "Come on, Sam. What's it all about?" she persisted. "Shane muttered something about a Shakespeare play."

Carla moved restively, and almost spoke.

"A superstition. Theater people are chock-full of them," a robust voice announced at Annie's elbow. She looked up at Vince Ellis, who had an Irish face and a mop of brilliant red hair. He played Officer Brophy in the play and was also owner and publisher of the *Island Hills Gazette*, the weekly newspaper that served Broward's Rock. "Has something else happened at the theater?"

Sam made a valiant stab at looking unruffled. "Naw. No big deal. Listen, I meant to tell you what a great Brophy you are, kid." It wouldn't have played even in Paducah, and Vince was nobody's fool. With mounting curiosity he looked at Annie and Max.

Brusque as always, Carla broke the short silence. "Oh, come on, Sam. You can't keep it quiet." She turned toward Vince. "Somebody included a quote from

Macbeth on one of Shane's prompt cards."

Vince whistled.

Boredom replaced the avid interest in Sheridan's eyes. "Is that all?" she drawled. "What's so bad about that?"

Carla clenched her big hands. "It's supposed to cause lousy luck if anyone even mentions that play in a theater," she said gruffly.

Sheridan's full lips curved in an amused smile. "Oh, that's really funny."

"Funny!" Sam's voice rose sharply, and he hunched his shoulders as if cowering against a blow.

Tonelda yanked at his arm. "Flip her off, Sam. Tell her to go get screwed."

"Sweetie —" His tone was strangled.

Max hastily intervened. "It's a deep-seated taboo," he informed Sheridan, moving between her and Tonelda. "Some people think it started in Shakespeare's time and had to do with the supernatural elements of the play, that when you invoked the witches it summoned evil spirits who would then injure the players. But some experts believe it was simply because a lot of people took sick playing in *Macbeth* during the Restoration period, and the feeling got out that if you quoted from the play, you could be struck down, that it was very, very bad luck."

Vince moved closer to Sam. "You know, maybe it's time to do a story on all this in the *Gazette*."

Galvanized by this new threat, Sam reached out and grabbed Vince's arm. "Oh, no, buddy, you don't want to do that. You're an island booster, right? You want everything to go swell — and that kind of story could scare people away. You want us to have a good season, don't you?"

"That's what everybody wants," a deep voice boomed. "Right, Sheridan?"

Harley Jenkins III, all 295 pounds of him, resplendent in red dinner jacket and green-and-red-checked trousers, clapped a meaty hand on Sheridan's bare back. The head of Halcyon Development's thick lips spread in a loose imitation of a smile that wasn't reflected in his eyes. "Sounds like a bunch of nuts to me. I don't believe in bad luck. A man makes his own luck." He pulled Sheridan's sinuous body close to his, gave her a hug. "Now, here's the kind of luck any man can enjoy — and I don't mind telling you it would take a woman like Sheridan to bring me out for this bash."

Sheridan gave him an enigmatic smile,

then gracefully slipped free of his embrace. "It always helps for opposing camps to talk." She looked earnestly at Sam, who was watching Harley like a rat who's just spotted a cobra. Annie thought the mantle of civic helpfulness rode uneasily on Sheridan's smooth, naked shoulders. "I asked everyone to come tonight, hoping we could all work together for the artistic community. It seems such a shame for creative people to be at cross-purposes."

"Cross-purposes?" Carla's violet eyes raked Jenkins's broad figure. "It's the same old story, a bully wanting his way."

Jenkins's bonhomie evaporated faster than a stack of quarters in Las Vegas. The veins in his mottled face bulged. "And I always get my way, you better remember that." He turned his back on Carla, once again reaching out to clasp Sheridan's arm.

Carla started forward and stumbled. Her hand went up and a cup full of purple punch splashed on Jenkins's back. "Oh, Lord, so sorry. Turned my ankle."

Annie gasped, Tonelda clapped her hands in pleasure, Max gestured for a waiter to come, and Jenkins whirled toward Carla, his face apoplectic.

6

They made their escape during the mop-up and took refuge near the terrace windows on the lee side of an alabaster statue of Pan that should have been in the Getty Museum. As they looked out on the swirling currents of the party, Max tried to restrain his glee, but found it hard going. "Not that I would wish our friend Jenkins ill," he said virtuously, "but his spirits did seem dampened."

"That punch is damn sticky," Annie observed, wiggling her silver pump, which matched the smoky shade of her silk dress. "I stepped in it." Across the room, a waiter offered a second wet towel to Jenkins, who shrugged it away, his empurpled face twisted in a furious scowl. Carla was swinging around, head down, evidently on her way out, when Sheridan caught her arm. The hostess patted her guest on the shoulder, nodding warmly. They spoke for a moment more, then Sheridan turned back toward Jenkins.

"That was thoughtful of Sheridan," Annie forced herself to say. "I suppose

Carla's terribly embarrassed about the whole episode."

"Embarrassed, hell. Carla did it on purpose," Max chortled. "She's a well-coordinated woman, even if she does stride around like an Amazon." He frowned thoughtfully. "You know, she must think Harley's behind all the trouble, too." Then he grinned. "Sure glad we came. You were right. You never know what will happen at the Petree house." He shaded his eyes, as if peering into desert distances. "I think I see a bar over there somewhere. Since it's still a sexist world, I'll go for our drinks," and he plunged into the crowd.

She hissed at that, but absently, because she was scanning the sea of faces. People were jammed elbow to elbow despite the sixty-foot length of the Petrees' baronial living area. All the movers and shakers of Broward's Rock were present. For the first time, Annie noticed the ten-foot banners strung across the center of the room, blazoning the titles of the five plays scheduled for the summer: *Arsenic and Old Lace*, *The Mousetrap*, *Blithe Spirit*, *My Sister Eileen*, and *The Moon Is Blue*.

Annie's eyes narrowed. Wait a minute. Wait a minute! *The Mousetrap* was already in rehearsals, because, in common with most summer theater groups, the players produced one play while simultaneously rehearsing the next. While the number two play ran, rehearsals would be underway for *Blithe Spirit*.

But Annie hadn't heard of any problems with *The Mousetrap*. Was the sabotage limited to *Arsenic and Old Lace*?

She stopped gazing at the milling throng with mild interest and began to hunt. She saw the mayor listening attentively to a banker, Police Chief Saulter shaking hands with the Island Hills golf pro, a damp Harley Jenkins sullenly sampling some of the buffet extravaganza, and there, near the mirrored back wall, the very person she sought.

When Annie reached the edge of the admiring circle, mystery author Emma Clyde smiled a greeting. Annie waited until she'd finished signing several autographs, then wormed her way closer.

Emma welcomed her genially. "How's crime, Annie?"

As always, Emma's frosty blue eyes seemed to delve into the untidiest corners of Annie's mind and Annie had to fight the impulse to flee. Tonight Emma wore a startling print dress, magenta begonias against an emerald background, instead of her customary caftan. She still looked like a housewife playing jet set . . . until you looked into those piercing eyes.

"Crime pays you better than it does me," Annie responded.

The best-selling author chuckled. "It pays when I concoct, but I'm finding that a little hard these days. I don't know why I ever agreed to direct *The Mousetrap*."

"Oh, I know why. It's the fascination of seeing a Christie plot come to life."

Emma nodded appreciatively. "Perceptive of you, dear."

"How are rehearsals coming? Have you had any difficulties?"

Not only had the crew and cast of *The Mousetrap* not suffered any hitches, the entire experience had gone exceptionally smoothly: cast members who liked one another, word-perfect rehearsals, props all gathered in two weeks ahead of time, a perfect attendance record by all the players.

"How nice that it's all going so well," Annie said cheerfully, as she thought how fascinating it was that *The Mousetrap* appeared exempt from the sabotage which had so crippled *Arsenic and Old Lace*.

As they parted, Emma said briskly, "I've been meaning to get over to the store. Will you order those TR books for me?"

Annie looked at her blankly. Had Eugene somehow instilled his mania for Teddy Roosevelt in Emma? She seemed a most unlikely recruit.

With a shade of impatience, the writer said, "You know, the books with Roosevelt as the detective: *The Big Stick* and *Speak Softly* by Lawrence Alexander."

In her relief, Annie nodded excitedly. "Oh, sure. Certainly. Yes. *Those* books. Yes, I will. As soon as possible."

She was aware, as she backed away, smiling and waving, that Emma was studying her with renewed interest. She wondered if she would appear in Emma's next book as a young entrepreneur suffering a nervous breakdown.

She struggled back toward the French windows. Max, if he ever returned with libations, would surely seek her in that area. She found the statue of Pan and leaned against it, lost in thought.

If the objective was to ruin the season, why was play number two apparently immune?

Were she and Max off on the wrong foot entirely? Was disruption of the summer season not the point of the sabotage? Was the animus directed simply and solely toward the cast and crew, or perhaps the director, of *Arsenic*? But the sabotage hadn't stopped rehearsals. The major result had been a lack of cohesion, a sense of unease among the cast and crew members, like corralled horses who have heard the unmistakable *thu-rumm* of a rattler and know he's out there somewhere. Could that generally nervous atmosphere be the point of all the petty tricks? It scarcely seemed worth the effort. Of course, the most recent irritant, the inclusion of the *Macbeth* quote, had certainly affected Sam. But why would anyone want to devil the high-strung, emotional director? Maybe the same kind of person who liked to pull the wings off butterflies.

Then a passing figure caught her eye. She strained to see better. What the hell was Henny Brawley up to now?

No one else appeared to be paying the slightest attention to Henny, and that demonstrated just how much everybody, except Annie, had had to drink, because Henny was strikingly noticeable. She now appeared to have a quantity of mousey brown hair tinged with gray that was drawn back in a bun, the whole, including an Alexandra fringe of bangs, quite firmly controlled by a net. She wore a substantial hat with a mass of ribbons at the back and a clump of forget-me-nots and pansies on the left side. A pale complexion. Only the fox-sharp nose couldn't be tamed. But there was no mistaking, Annie felt sure, the smooth, controlled passage of Miss Maud Silver.

And she might as well have stalked across the floor with a magnifying glass held high, she was so obviously in pursuit of someone.

Annie stood on tiptoe. Across the room, Max stood in a four-deep line at the bar. She whirled just in time to see Henny slip through the French windows and out onto the terrace.

Of course, she wouldn't be drawn. It was just Henny playing sleuth.

But why had she gone out on the terrace?

Annie took a few steps toward the French windows. After all, it wouldn't hurt a thing just to take a peek. And the blare of the trumpets and the thick haze of tobacco smoke were wearing. Really, it was awfully hot. She slipped out onto the terrace, welcoming the cool, fresh air tinged with unmistakable dampness from the nearby lagoon. Lights in the southern red cedars danced on the dark water. Where had Henny gone? Annie started down wooden steps The cattails along the lagoon wavered in the night breeze, and the willows rustled. She had almost reached the base of the steps when she realized there was an embracing couple in the gazebo at the foot of the slope. Tactfully, she turned and began to climb. Midway, a dark shape brushed past her. Was that Henny? She stopped. No, there was a darker shade near a tall planter's vase at the edge of the terrace, and she saw a flicker of moonlight on straw. Henny's hat. So who was she watching? Then the figure that had passed Annie reached the wash of light from the windows. Janet Horton stopped on the terrace and pressed her hands against her eyes. Even in the diffused light, Annie could see the trembling of her mouth, the tears glistening on her cheeks. She took several deep shuddering breaths. As she blundered back into the house, her mouth was twisted into a smile that was painful to see.

Annie paused and glanced back down the steps. She didn't have to go and see who embraced in the gazebo. Janet's face told her that. Abruptly, footsteps grated on the stone terrace above her. T. K. Horton's burly shoulders were slumped, and his face a study in misery. He hesitated, staring after his wife, then, face hardening, swung around and rushed down the wooden steps, moving so heavily that the boards shook beneath him.

"T.K. —"

He brushed past Annie as if she weren't there, and she knew nothing existed for him but the reality of his daughter in Shane's arms, and the haunting figure of his wife, running away from the discovery.

Oh, God. Annie took two steps up toward the house, changed her mind, turned and started back down, stopped again and flapped her hands indecisively. What should she do? Well, it wasn't her business to do anything. But somebody could get killed. At least, somebody would, if this were a Leslie Ford novel of love and lovers gone wrong.

Over the bleat of the Dixieland five and the chorus of amorous frogs, she listened, waiting for screams, shouts, blows —

It was almost anticlimactic when T.K. emerged from the gazebo, his hand clamped to his daughter's arm, hauling her up the steps, a hostile, protesting bundle of teenage animosity. "Daddy, let go of me! I can kiss whoever I want to — and I don't care what you and Mama say. You're jealous. Both of you."

T.K. didn't say a word. His face looked like leather that had been out in the sun too long.

Annie squeezed back against the railing to let them pass. Neither seemed to notice her. The Hortons were too involved in their own emotions to spare a thought for onlookers. It was a funny feeling to be invisible. But T.K. and Cindy were surely visible on the light-flooded terrace as he yanked the shrilly protesting teenager toward the side of the house. And who was standing, framed in the window and looking down the steps, but Sheridan. The light etched her glamorous silhouette for a long moment, then she turned back into the room.

Annie would have given a good deal to have seen Sheridan's face.

The wooden steps quivered beneath her.

"Hey, Annie baby, how's about a little kiss?"

Shane reached out for her, and Annie adroitly dodged his seeking hands and ran lightly up the steps, carrying with her the cloying smell of bourbon and the picture of a flushed face streaked with lipstick.

She paused at the top of the stairs. "Better wipe your face off, honey lover —

or your wife may be curious about your taste in cosmetics."

"Oooh. Sounds like the lady's jealous." Shane swayed and grabbed the railing to steady himself.

"God, you do flatter yourself."

As she stepped through the window, she saw Henny's hat-laden head poke out from behind the urn. So she was still tracking Shane. Even Miss Silver might find some of his activities daunting.

Annie welcomed the tobacco-thick haze of the house. It and the battering pound of the music were preferable to the emotional dangers lurking outdoors. Searching for Max, she jumped when a heavy arm slid around her shoulder. "Aw, come on, Annie, you can give the host a little kiss, can't you?"

She saw Max approaching, with drinks in both hands. "Go find another play-mate," she snapped, sidestepping Shane and starting toward Max.

Shane lumbered at her heels.

They came even with Hugo. Glowering down at Burt Conroy, the big actor looked even more dangerous than when he was portraying Jonathan. Edging past, she heard Hugo snarl, as he gestured violently with his cigar, "Get rid of him, Burt!"

Burt's narrow face set in stubborn lines. "Look, Hugo, I know he's a pain, but you've got to look at the money —"

But Hugo wasn't listening. He'd spotted Shane, and his malevolent glare was now directed at the drunken host.

Tra-la, tra-la. What happiness and joy Shane was bringing into the lives of his fellow players.

Annie put on a burst of speed. Reaching Max, she held out her hand for her drink. She'd never looked forward with quite the same eagerness to a gin and tonic, but this was one of the driest evenings she'd ever —

Shane bumped against her shoulder, and her drink sloshed, spattering her new evening slippers.

She looked at him in exasperation. "Shane, will you please —"

"Annie, I've just had all I can take." His words were slurred, but he spoke loudly enough that people standing near turned to look.

He was drunk, but not so drunk he didn't know exactly what he was doing. His eyes glittered with malice.

"Yeah. I mean, why don't you leave a man alone? Callin' me, comin' after me all the time. I keep tellin' you, honey, I'm a married man, so, cool it, will you?" The words might be slightly slurred, but he delivered them with more force than he had ever exhibited on stage.

Annie's mouth hung open. The louse. The creep. The almighty jerk!

Shane looked past her. "Jesus, honey, I just took it as long as I could."

Sheridan's smooth face turned toward Annie without a flicker of emotion.

Annie took a deep breath. "You may be drunk, Shane, but that's the sorriest excuse for a joke I ever heard."

Some onlookers tactfully turned away, but there was no escaping the curious sidelong glances. Someone snickered. Annie's face flamed.

Sheridan ignored her, nodding at her husband. "Shane, come over here. I want you to meet the Fishers' guests from Key Biscayne," and they were gone, leaving Annie and Max in a little circle of cautious avoidance.

"I could kill him!" Her voice was a frustrated screech, and she was the object of renewed appraisal, which made her even angrier. She stamped her foot furiously and longed for something to throw. "Have you ever in your life seen anything sleazier? The sorry bastard. He made a pass at me outside, and *I* told *him* to get lost." She glared at Max. "What are you laughing at?"

"Annie, love," he said sweetly, "if you could just control your appetites."

"Max!" She took a deep breath, preparatory to launching a vitriolic attack on his misplaced sense of humor, when most un-partylike sounds and movements erupted near the punchbowl.

"Oh, my God —"

Spinning around, Annie saw a woman in emerald green silk clutch at her mouth, then begin to vomit.

She was the first of many. Soon, the spectacularly appointed dining area with its twin ice sculptures of the tragedy and comedy masks, its sumptuously loaded buffet table, its tall silver vases filled with sweet-scented iris, was as gruesome as a scene from a teenage horror flick.

The bell sang as the front door of Death on Demand closed after Ingrid. Annie had urged her assistant to take her time over her late lunch. June, of course, was the beginning of high season for tourists, but the rush always slacked off between one-thirty and two-thirty. Annie often wondered why. Late lunches? Afternoon siestas? Erotic frolics? Speaking of — She glanced down at her watch. Max should be here soon. But that reminded her of last night and Shane's little joke. All right, she'd given Max an earful on the way home. He'd been properly penitent, but there was still a glint of laughter in his blue eyes. Moreover, he had soothed, nobody with a working mind would believe a word of it. Sheridan might — wives had been known to swallow incredible tales from husbands — but everybody else on the island knew Shane's habits. Still, it was *insulting!* But she was able this morning to dredge up a tiny smile. Grudgingly. After all, she didn't want Max to think she lacked an appreciation for the absurd. And, of course, the finale to the Petree party had certainly proved a distraction. Probably nobody would even remember that short exchange between Shane and Annie. Thank God she'd *never* liked passion-fruit champagne punch. At least, Chief Saulter believed the onslaught of illness could be traced to the punch.

Of course, she couldn't help wondering whether there was a connection between the sabotage at the theater and the illness at the Petrees' party. She'd persuaded Max to see what he could find out, not because she gave a damn about the Petrees, but she still cared about *Arsenic and Old Lace.* She really couldn't take the time to nose around too much because these were the very best bookselling days, and it was unfair to expect Ingrid to handle the flood of tourists alone. Moreover, there were so many unsettled issues in the planning of the wedding. She flicked a hunted look at the telephone. Still, she itched to be involved.

But she had work to do, and fun work it was, choosing the books to be displayed in the north window. She'd already prepared the background poster: *Died Laughing, or Fifty Years of Funny Mysteries.* The window space lent itself beautifully to a semicircle of five novels. More than that seemed cluttered. Of course, she must include *A Blunt Instrument* by Georgette Heyer. Her mouth curved as she remembered P. C. Glass and his Biblical injunctions. Then she realized she was smiling at the unresponsive form of Edgar, the stuffed raven perched by the front door. Edgar was a wonderful symbol to mystery lovers since his namesake, Edgar Allan Poe, is credited with creating the mystery, but she suspected the somber bird's personal taste in crime fiction might run more to the terrifying, such as Stanley Ellin's *The Dark Fantastic* or Jim Thompson's *The Killer Inside Me*. She gave Edgar's sleek feathers a swift pat. "I'll do your kind of book next month." Eager to fill her display, she hurried down the central aisle and paused to study the caper/comedy shelves. *A Blunt Instrument*. Oh, and of course she would pick *Murder's Little Sister* by Pamela Branch. Or should she select Branch's *The Wooden Overcoat*, with its many moveable corpses? But *Murder's Little Sister* was so wry, so sardonic, so absolutely marvelous. Annie slipped both titles off the shelf and tucked them under her arm. She spent several long minutes surveying the Constance and Gwenyth Little books. Which one? *The Black Shrouds*? Or maybe *Black Corridors*? Oh, well, she'd come back in a minute. She reached the T's and nodded decisively. A Leonidas Witherall mystery was a must. Annie adored the erudite sleuth, who could compare the final rousting of a murderer to Cannae, a famous battle in 216 B.C. in which Hannibal defeated a superior Roman force. Witherall looked like Shakespeare and was the delightful creation of Phoebe Atwood Taylor writing as Alice Tilton. After considerable thought, she settled on *File for Record*. Her eyes moved up. Oh, yes. A Craig Rice. She retrieved

Home Sweet Homicide, or the kiddie brigade to the rescue. Her hand darted out unerringly for *God Save the Mark*, Donald E. Westlake's hilarious recounting of the saga of Fred Fitch, the quintessential sucker. Or should she choose *Dancing Aztecs*? Maybe she could cheat, put one behind the other and count it as a single entry. Oh, dear, she knew this would happen. She couldn't leave out Joyce Porter and her gluttonous Chief Inspector Wilfred Dover. And how about those fresh funny voices belonging to Joan Hess, Bill Crider, and Frank McConnell? She picked out more titles and carried her treasures to the front desk. She had the best of intentions to winnow, but, before she knew it, in between ringing up purchases, she was deep in the adventures of Leonidas Witherall, aka Bill Shakespeare, as he struggled to compose a letter about a lost-and-found department, French bread, and laundry hampers to his friend, Ross Haymaker.

The phone rang, and she reached out absently to answer.

"Death on Demand."

"Oooh," the golden voice cried. "Such a *grim* name, when the world needs Love on Demand. Oh, no, no, that doesn't have quite the right ring. Perhaps" — a pause for thought, then a triumphant pronouncement — "Oh, yes, I have it. Love Forevermore."

Annie strove for patience and forbearance, those saintly qualities. "This is a mystery store, Laurel."

"But love *is* a mystery, my dear."

Annie knew just how Doc Cummings often felt in the Asey Mayo books: speechless.

Laurel burbled ahead. "Max tells me you are adamant about the red wedding gown." There was the tiniest upward inflection to wedding gown.

"Yes. Yes. Definitely yes." Then Annie wondered wildly if she should have been shouting *No.*

"Your dressmaker — did I tell you I've been talking to her? Dear Mrs. Crabtree. *She* thinks red might be an enchanting theme color. We could special-order those glorious tulips from Holland. Of course, there's always the difficulty of season, but in hothouses —"

"Not red."

"How succinct you are darling. It must come from all your reading. Oh, well" — Laurel was never one to beat a dead horse — "there are so many ways we can proclaim our love for mankind while we prepare for the ceremony. There is so much *unity* to be achieved. And I want you to take very good care of yourself."

Was it a non sequitur?

"Yes, we definitely want to pamper you as much as we can."

Annie waited with growing apprehension.

"Every society has its customs."

Here it comes. Annie's knuckles whitened on the receiver.

"In Morocco, the bride enjoys a ceremonial bath five days before the ceremony. Her friends adorn her with makeup and jewels" — a pause, then in a hopeful flood — "and help her paint henna swirls on her hands and feet."

"Laurel, I know you mean well." The words almost stuck in her throat, but Annie forced them out. "I mean, I really know you do. But I'm not going to —"

"They wouldn't show," Laurel said plaintively.

The front doorbell jangled. Annie would have welcomed Count Dracula. However, her eyes widened as she saw her visitor.

"A customer, Laurel. Sorry. Have to go. A customer." She banged the receiver down.

A remarkable vision stood before her:

114

flyaway white hair, a shapeless quilted brown raincoat (she must be sweltering), and a quite astounding bird's-nest hat. Yes, that hat could easily hold eight forged passports.

"It's definitely an inside job." Henny Brawley's version of a New Jersey accent was interesting. "I've interviewed the caterer and three of his assistants. No one could have tampered with the champagne. Now, the ginger ale is another matter entirely."

Annie couldn't resist teasing just a little bit. "What's an inside job?" she asked blankly.

"Annie." Patient forbearance. "I *assumed* you kept abreast of events. It was *ipecac* in the punch, of course."

This startled Annie into an exclamation. "No kidding!"

Henny ignored this sleuthing gaucherie. "It was *obvious* to me right from the moment. Of course, I confirmed it with Chief Saulter this morning. Now," and her voice dropped, "here's the important point. The only persons who could have tampered with the champagne, fruit juices, and lime sherbet were the caterer and his two assistants. *They* have no motive. However, the ginger ale was taken from a store in the pantry. Therefore, the ipecac was in the ginger ale. Now, the Petree house is well-equipped with burglar alarms, there is a live-in butler, and there is no indication that anyone other than a member of the household had access to the pantry. You see," she said chirpily, "where *that* inescapably leads." A brisk throat-clearing. "There's no doubt about it — that punch was poisoned by either Sheridan or Shane. And," Henny concluded inelegantly, "I'll put *my* money on Shane."

She might be masquerading as Emily Pollifax today, but she was still Henny Brawley with a bee in her bonnet.

"Well," Annie temporized, "there must have been more than three hundred people there last night."

"The facts, Annie. The facts." A touch of *Dragnet* here?

"Oh, sure, Henny. The facts, by all means."

Henny nodded briskly in approval, and the massive hat wobbled precariously. "I'll keep in touch. And don't worry about me. Brown belt, you know." The doorbell sang as she departed.

Definitely Mrs. Pollifax, taking some time off from her new geranium greenhouse.

Seven customers later (Elmore Leonard's latest was hot, hot, hot), she waved a welcome to Max and Ingrid, who sauntered in together.

Relinquishing the cash desk to Ingrid, Annie led Max to the back and poured steaming coffee into two mugs. (*The Crooked Hinge* and *Love Lies Bleeding*.) She handed the latter to him.

He studied the red script for a moment, then murmured, "Sulking doesn't become you."

"Just kidding."

He didn't pursue it. Grinning, he straddled a wooden stool. "I come bearing news."

"Ipecac," she replied.

She took pity on his amazement.

"Not witchcraft, Max. Henny Brawley."

"Oh. Well, if you already know everything, I could have had a jollier morning drinking beer at Parotti's Bait Shop and Bar, or continuing my scientific study of the reduction in area covered by this year's swimsuits. Purely from the standpoint of style. More as a divination of manners and mores than —"

"Sulking doesn't become you," she interrupted.

"So okay, tell *me* what happened."

"According to Henny, it's an inside job, and she's convinced it was Shane."

"Chief Saulter will be intrigued by that suggestion. The last I heard, Sheridan was breathing fire and threatening to call every senator she knows if Saulter didn't fingerprint all the bottles, then send them for chemical analysis. He keeps trying to explain that it doesn't matter a damn what bottle they do or don't find the stuff in, there were three hundred and seventy-two people at that party last night and any one of them could have dumped ipecac in the punch."

Could they?

"Sure, it was a mob scene," Annie agreed doubtfully, "but wouldn't it have taken a lot of guts for a guest to pour anything into the punch? Nobody would notice a waiter, but the other seems definitely chancy. Beside, Henny says the ipecac was in the ginger ale and only the Petrees or one of the help had access to it." She put her coffee down untasted. "Max! Maybe Henny's on to something. Neither Sheridan nor Shane got sick!"

He shrugged that away. "So neither one of them drinks purple passion punch. Does that surprise you?"

"Oh. I guess not."

"And if that's your criteria, Janet Horton can be crossed off the suspect list. She was 'sick as a dawg,' as T.K. described it."

"Have you talked to everybody this morning?"

"If by 'everybody' you mean our friends and compatriots in the theater, yes. And Janet was the only one who got sick."

"Hmm." Annie relished her coffee. Its taste was absolutely unambiguous. As for Janet, she couldn't be cleared merely because she'd drunk the punch. It could be like *Crooked House.*

Feeling like a hound distracted by false scents, she returned to the central point. "But, look, if Henny's right about the ginger ale —"

Max shook his head irritably. "Creative deduction on her part. Saulter doesn't have any idea where the ipecac came from."

Annie thought back to Henny's revelations. Maybe it was inductive reasoning on the order of: Shane did it, he couldn't have monkeyed with the ingredients supplied by the caterer, ergo, the ipecac was in the ginger ale.

"Here are the known facts." Max ticked them off. "Sheridan added champagne to the punch at nine-thirty, tasted it herself —

and didn't get sick. Ipecac works within minutes of ingestion. The first party-goer bit the dust shortly before ten. Therefore, the ipecac went in the punch a few minutes before ten."

"I wonder if any of our people were near the punch bow during that period," Annie said thoughtfully.

"Sure," he said cheerfully.

"Did you tell the chief about the problems with the play?"

"Yeah. He's not terribly impressed. Says it could be. But he says it also could be a nut, somebody who doesn't like the Petrees, maybe a disgruntled caterer. Maybe the butler. Who knows?"

Annie refilled his coffee mug. "Max, had I told you? Everything's dandy with *The Mousetrap*. I talked to Emma Clyde, and she said they haven't had any problems at all. So it looks like the animus is directed at *Arsenic*."

"I'd say the animus was spread pretty wide last night," he objected.

"Maybe the circle of sabotage is widening," Annie suggested.

"If the ipecac is connected to the other stuff."

"How many creepy-crawlies do you think the island holds?"

"I don't know. Why don't we ask Henny?"

"She's busy tailing Shane at this very moment, no doubt."

"I think we can safely leave the search for clues to her and the chief." Max settled against the coffee bar.

"Sometimes, I fear that I detect a tinge of laziness in your manner. You promised that we'd keep looking for the saboteur." She cradled the mug in her hands and looked at him meaningfully. "After all, the owner of Confidential Commissions, an investigative organization that claims the ability to sniff out the answers to any and all troubling, difficult, or nefarious situations, surely can be counted upon to do his civic duty."

Max studied her with concern. "Have you been talking to Laurel this morning?" When she took an extremely deep breath, he held up both hands. "That's all right. That's fine. You needn't answer. I'll do anything you wish — almost." He gave a good-humored shrug "Off to sleuth I go. And I do have an idea."

He waited for an appropriate response. He got it.

"Oh, good. What?"

"I'm going to see if I can find any kind of connection, beyond the obvious, between Harley and our cast and crew."

So Max still believed Harley was behind all the problems. Well, that could be. As he left for Confidential Commissions and an afternoon on the telephone, Annie waved him a thoughtful good-bye. She drank her coffee and brooded.

She was convinced that the unpleasant incidents were aimed at torpedoing the players' season and preventing the rebuilding of the theater at the harbor, but there were some puzzling questions. She found a pad, this one with the logo (a bright green toad mouthing TODAL PROTECTION) of the T. K. Horton Insurance Agency, and made a list of questions:

Why no problems for The Mousetrap?

Was the ipecac in the punch a venomous attack on the Petrees?

Or was the object of spite the players or perhaps Burt or Sam individually?

She chewed thoughtfully on the end of her pencil (BUY AMERICAN), and added a final question:

What's going to happen next?

Max waggled the computer printout at her. "Instant bios. Everything you ever wanted to know — and more — about your fellow thespians."

"Terrific." She took the sheets and gave a whoop when she saw *HENRIETTA HOLLIDAY BRAWLEY* was the first name.

"I'm not playing any favorites," he remonstrated.

"Not Henny," she objected. "I'll bet her life's an open book."

"Actually, her life's damned interesting. Did you know that she —"

"I know she's a chameleon. But right now, I'm more interested in whether you traced a connection between our people and Harley."

The Porsche gave a throaty purr and sprang forward. The sun was slipping behind the live oaks, and a pleasant mellow glow touched the marsh with enchantment, gilding the cord grass and the silvery sea myrtle. Annie welcomed the sweep of air through the open sunroof, but the breeze ruffled the sheets, so she slipped the printout into her woven wicker carryall.

"Give me the scoop," she asked eagerly.

As Max turned the car onto the blacktop and they picked up speed, he asked, "Aren't you going to read it?"

"Nope. You can play Archie to my Nero Wolfe."

He hooted. "Thank God, I don't see any real resemblance."

"Mentally, dear, mentally. I am trenchant —"

"Trencher, did you say?"

The Porsche veered sharply toward the bank as she pulled his ear for that one.

But, as he summed up his afternoon's work, Annie was just as pleased she hadn't plowed through the pages.

"So you didn't come up with any tie to Jenkins?"

"Nothing I can put my finger on. Oh, Burt leases his shop from him, of course, or from Halcyon Development, to be superaccurate. But I can't discover that Jenkins is pressuring him in any way." He frowned darkly. "Of course, they'd keep it pretty quiet, if he's doing Harley's dirty work."

"But he's president of the players!"

"What could be a better cover?" Max slowed to wave to the guard manning the checkpoint at the solitary entrance to the resort homes and condominiums. They drove two blocks and turned left into the parking lot of Broward's Rock High School. Carla's sporty yellow MG, the classic with the jaunty running boards, was slewed carelessly into a parking space just past the entrance to the auditorium, and, as they walked toward the doors, gray dirt

124

spewed as Shane's glistening black Mercedes wheeled in.

"The heartthrob of America," Max observed slyly.

Annie would have snarled, but she was too fascinated by the appearance of Henny Brawley, a red blur on her tenspeed, coming up the road in hot pursuit of the Mercedes. Instead, she satisfied herself with giving Shane a cold glare as they climbed the steps.

In the foyer, Carla was perched on a stepladder by the entrance doors to the center aisle, struggling with a loose hinge. She looked up briefly to smile at Annie and Max. When she saw Shane, her mouth drew into a thin line. She bent back to her work.

Shane glared at her. "Hey, Carla, my car's got a knock. You want to take a look at it?"

Carla reached jerkily for the screwdriver on the ladder tray, and it clattered to the floor.

For once, Max's amiability deserted him. He grabbed Shane's arm and hustled him down the aisle.

Shane's irritated voice rose. "But she asks for it, doesn't she? And I'm sick of her looking at me like I'm some kind of maggot."

Annie bent to pick up the tool. She handed it to Carla, appalled by the burning hatred in the set designer's eyes.

"He's a creep," Annie offered briskly. "Don't let him bug you. He's just jealous he can't do anything well. Your sets are fabulous."

Carla swallowed painfully and tried to smile. "It's all right. I've heard worse. But, God, he's sickening." The hand that accepted the screwdriver trembled, and the thin shoulders beneath the faded denim work shirt shook.

The auditorium door opened, and Henny charged in. "Hi, Carla. Hi, Annie. Hope I'm not late." She paused beside the ladder. "Oh, Carla, how nice of you to fix that door. Really, you go above and beyond duty. Good work, my dear." Henny took Annie's arm. "Time for us to get to it."

Annie surged down the aisle with Henny. Obviously, this was Henny, actress, not Henny, investigator.

Although Annie had expected a lousy rehearsal because of yesterday's dramatics, including the *Macbeth* quote and Sam's frenzy, everyone had it pretty well together this Monday evening. Janet was pale, which came as no surprise since she'd been unlucky enough — or careful enough? —

to imbibe the doctored punch. Henny was marvelous, as always, her sense of timing superb. Only Shane was his usual wooden, ineffective self. If she were Shane, it would make her highly nervous to be on the receiving end of the glares from Hugo. But the magic of the play absorbed her, as it always did, and she stopped thinking about the various cast members and their rivalries.

They were nearing the marvelous scene when Mortimer lifts the window seat and finds the body, one of the most delicious moments in theater. Onstage, Max strode around the living room. Janet picked up her pail from the sideboard and her cape, hat, and gloves from the table and left for the kitchen. Alone, Max continued his search for his lost manuscript. Annie's lips parted in an anticipatory smile.

Max lifted the lid of the window seat. The business called for him then to drop it, walk away, do a double take, and dash back. Instead, he remained in a half crouch, staring down.

Henny and Janet were just offstage, of course, ready to come on.

Max turned, his face grim.

Henny and Janet stepped onstage, puzzled, then hurried to him.

He reached out to bar them from the window seat. Janet craned to look past him, her hands flew to her throat, and her high, agonized scream rose in the musty air of the auditorium, then splintered into choking sobs.

7

"Freddy," Janet wailed. Fat tears coursed down her face; her makeup was streaked and blurred. "Somebody killed my Freddy!" And she rocked back and forth, clutching the stiff, bloodstained carcass of a huge orange cat.

Her cries brought everyone running. Max reached out gingerly, offering to take the animal. Annie joined him and thrust some wilted tissues at the hysterical actress.

Hugo and Arthur rushed up from the subterranean dressing rooms. Backstage steps led down to the greenroom, the men's and women's dressing rooms, even two small cubicles with tarnished stars pasted on the doors, restrooms, and a labyrinth of partitioned-off areas, including the prop shop, wardrobe, storage, and a dimly lit boiler room. Hugo glared dourly at the dead animal, as if it were a personal affront, while Arthur wrung his hands, mute and miserable.

Vince Ellis jammed a hand through his

flaming red hair. It wasn't often that anything caught the *Gazette* owner off balance. Annie would bet at that moment he regretted trying out for the role of Officer Brophy.

Father Donaldson, present for his role as Dr. Harper in Act I, hurried from a wing. "Here, Janet," he intoned in his deep, soothing voice, "let me have Freddy." Somehow, he succeeded in lifting the cat from her arms. Max looked relieved. The Episcopal priest, who good-naturedly played clergy for the summer theater in everything from *The Importance of Being Earnest* to *Murder at the Vicarage*, continued to quietly reassure, his ruddy face grave. T.K. jerkily patted his wife's heaving shoulders.

It was the Hortons' cat. The information came out in choked fragments from a shocked Cindy, for once subdued. Her father stood red-faced and silent. Freddy hadn't come home this morning. They had worried a little, but he was a tom and occasionally roamed, although he usually stayed in their backyard. He liked to sun on the patio. Cindy last saw the cat before they left for the Sunday afternoon rehearsal. "He was asleep on the retaining wall."

"Freddy was almost fifteen years old. We

got him when Cindy was just a baby. Oh, how could anyone do it?" Janet moaned. Father Donaldson, with another reassuring word, carried the body offstage.

T.K. cleared his throat several times. "Come on, now, honey. It won't help to cry. Freddy wouldn't want you to cry. He's not hurt now."

If she were Freddy, Annie thought, that would hardly be her attitude, but T.K. was desperately trying to console a desolated Janet and might be forgiven a little latitude with the truth.

In the downstage right wing, Sam backed away from Father Donaldson. At the moment, he looked decidedly green and his eyes were scrupulously averted from the carcass. Ben Tippet, who ran Tippet's Garage and was onstage for a few minutes in Act I as the prospective boarder who is saved from poisoned elderberry wine only by Mortimer's frantic intervention, looked from the cat to Sam to Janet, then muttered, "I gotta go. A transmission to put in," and scuttled offstage.

"This is beyond the pale," Burt announced shrilly. "I want to make it clear that if I ever discover who perpetrated this outrage, that person will never in my lifetime take part in any production mounted by the players."

To Burt, of course, that fate was far worse than being cast out into the wilderness.

Even Shane looked sickened. "This is shitty."

Henny Brawley, lean as a whippet in bright crimson warmups, was staring at Shane, her face creased in a puzzled frown.

Eugene's broad face puckered. "Who would do such a thing?"

And that was the question in every mind, Annie knew. How could anyone stalk a pet, murder it, then plant the bloodied corpse, and wait for its discovery?

She looked at the watching faces and wondered.

The freckles stood out starkly on Vince Ellis's ruddy face.

Carla stood with her hands jammed into the pockets of her dungarees, her arms tight to her body, as if she were cold. Long, dark hair framed a sensitive face, frozen now into immobility. Her violet eyes kept glancing at Janet and then away. Once, she shook her head, as if irritated at her own inability to help. Annie admired her compassion, because she felt certain that Janet was the kind of dithery, male-dependent female Carla most abhorred.

Hugo's silvery black eyebrows were bunched in a furious line. Annie wondered if he were angry at the disruption of the play, or if he liked cats. One thing she was sure of . . . he didn't especially like Janet. Funny. She didn't have an idea in the world what Hugo was thinking behind that brooding, saturnine face.

Sam held a hand to quivering lips. "I think I'm going to be sick."

Burt shot him a look of unconcealed contempt. "For God's sake, it's not even your cat."

"Blood," Sam said faintly. "Can't stand blood."

"Don't look."

Janet's face was beginning to puff from her weeping, and her hiccoughing sobs shook her plump shoulders. T.K. grabbed her elbow and glared at all of them impartially. "We're leaving," he said harshly and began to steer Janet toward the steps. He moved with lowered shoulders, ready to bull his way ahead, an ex-jock in uncharted seas.

Henny held up a hand. "Do wait a moment."

"What for?" T.K. demanded gruffly.

"Someone brought Freddy here," she

said firmly. "Don't you think we should try to find out who?" She scanned the waiting faces. "One of us, don't you think?"

There was a moment of stiff, shocked silence, then voices erupted.

"That's absurd!"

"Just a minute, Henny —"

"Not me!" Shane objected loudly. "I'm no nut case. But somebody damn sure is."

Arthur tossed his head, flipping the dark hank of hair out of his eyes. "I would hate to think it of one of us."

Sam seized on Shane's response. "Jesus, the hunk put his finger on it. We've got us a nut. Oh, God, that's all I need now. A nut!" He clapped his hands to his head, moaning.

Eugene twirled his eyeglasses on their long black ribbon and looked like TR learning that his Bull Moose party had gone down in defeat.

"Cool it, everybody." Max's voice and demeanor were as pleasant as always, but the voices stilled. "Henny's right, you know. Somebody brought Freddy in here and put him in the window seat. We have to find out who did it."

T.K.'s bristly blond brows knitted in concentration, and his heavy head began to nod. "Yeah. Goddammit, yeah. One of us.

Who the hell else?" He peered suspiciously from face to face.

"I don't think so." Carla's voice was cool. She stared a Max thoughtfully. "I was the first to arrive tonight, and I didn't see anyone carrying anything large enough to contain the cat."

"Of course not," Henny observed.

Burt shot her an irritated glance. "If nobody carried the cat in, how the hell did the cat get in the window seat?"

"The operative question is when, not how," Henny retorted, "and the answer's quite obvious. The deed occurred some time between rehearsal yesterday afternoon and Carla's arrival tonight." Henny's bright dark eyes gleamed.

"I got here the same time as Annie and Darling." Shane was, as usual, supremely self-centered. "I wasn't clutching no bloody cat."

"The thing to do is look around and see if the building's been broken into," Cindy offered. It was her first suggestion. Annie shot her a look of surprise and grudging respect. She'd always assumed Cindy was stupid as well as horny, but now the teenager's sea green eyes were calculating and intelligent.

Max's voice sliced through the chorus of

assent. "All right — but we'll look in pairs."

"Do you figure it's dangerous?" Eugene demanded.

Hugo smiled sourly. "I rather think Max would prefer no one do a solo survey and produce a conveniently broken window."

They divided into pairs, with Annie and Eugene left to guard Freddy, who had been placed in an empty cardboard box by Carla. The box sat by the prop table. "I don't want it to disappear," Max said briskly. "We can at least see whether the bullet that killed Freddy can be traced."

Annie's mind whirled with fragments of thought about bullet and cartridge case comparisons, rifled bores, and powder pattern distribution. But a ballistics department needed the gun to make a match. Was Max trying to frighten one of his listeners?

The search was fairly simple, since an iron grille, locked with a padlock, separated the auditorium and its front foyer from the main corridor leading to the schoolrooms. That left the auditorium itself, the front foyer, the attic area, and, of course, the bewildering labyrinth of nooks, crannies, and hallways branching dark and twisted beneath the stage like the gnarled offshoots from a cypress.

Annie waited, listening to the faint eddies of the voices of the searchers. She looked occasionally toward the box just offstage. Freddy was missing after rehearsal on Sunday. Most of the cast arrived for to-night's rehearsal around seven p.m. A space of little more than twenty-four hours. The three Hortons had been absent from their house for the two hours of rehearsal Sunday — and again for the period of the Petrees' party Sunday night. Freddy was last seen shortly before two p.m. Sunday.

Had anyone been late to rehearsal Sunday?

Shane.

The name popped up like a red cherry on a slot machine.

But, for God's sake, why would Shane kill the Hortons' cat?

But then, why would any of them kill Freddy?

What could possibly be the point of this macabre and distinctly nasty exercise?

But what was the point of erasing the chalk marks from the stage, setting off a stink bomb, removing rehearsal notices from the callboard, sawing through the rope to the house curtain, artistically draping a dummy from the gridwork, and inserting the lines from *Macbeth* in Shane's prompt card?

What had been accomplished?

A harassed director. A furious president of the players. A skittish cast. And, today, a thoroughly demoralized — and perhaps even terrified — group.

Annie stared at the box. The pranks had gone from sophomoric to vicious — which certainly removed three possible suspects: the Hortons — T.K., Janet, and Cindy.

She turned and paced downstage and stared sightlessly out at the empty auditorium.

Eugene cleared his throat once, but said nothing.

But *were* the Hortons above suspicion?

Was it her own advancing age that said, "Oh, yeah? Wait a minute!" Or did it spring from years of consorting, in a literary way, with writers who could invest with horror such commonplaces as an eight-year-old's playhouse or a cheery mound of bright yarn and shiny knitting needles: Ruth Rendell, P. D. James, Margaret Millar, Helen McCloy, Charlotte Armstrong.

What the human mind can conceive, Richard Lockridge once remarked. . . .

T.K. adored his wife. But he must know that Janet was emotionally tied in some way to Shane — and it didn't take a Basil

Willing to figure out just how. Just how angry might T.K. be?

As for Cindy — To what lengths would the sixteen-year-old go to strike out at her rival for Shane's attentions, even though the other woman was her own mother? Could anyone so cold-bloodedly kill a pet that had grown up with him? Briefly, with a shudder, Annie thought of *The Bad Seed.*

Could Janet be distraught enough over Shane to kill her own pet to inflict unhappiness on Cindy?

Footsteps sounded behind her. She swung around to face Eugene as he joined her in looking out over the auditorium.

"TR was an outstanding success as police commissioner in New York. He would go out late at night to see if the beat patrolmen were on duty. The tabloids nicknamed him Haroun-el-Roosevelt."

Annie stared at him blankly.

Eugene smiled genially. "That was after the famous caliph who enjoyed slipping around Baghdad unrecognized after dark."

A nut. Sam was looking for a nut.

She felt a quiver of relief when the steps leading up from the dressing rooms creaked. Hugo emerged brushing a dribble of cobweb from his immaculate pinpoint oxford shirt. It matched perfectly the sky blue of his faded denim slacks. But Hugo didn't look pretty in his outfit. His face was too rugged, his dark eyes too daunting, and his manner too assured. "Anybody who wanted to get in this godforsaken hole could have gotten in."

Carla moved out from the shadows behind him. "There's a loose window in the wardrobe area. And just some cardboard in place of window panes in the east corner of the prop department."

Shane and Henny followed close behind them. "The door leading outside from the boiler room is secure," the latter announced.

Father Donaldson and Vince, murmuring earnestly to each other, stood in the balcony. Then Vince shouted, "Nothing open or broken up here." The Hortons came down the center aisle from the front foyer, and Sam and Burt returned through the left wing.

"Tighter than a drum," T.K. reported.

Burt was frowning. "We didn't find anything open." Sam nodded morosely.

Max poked his head out of the right wing. "Carla, did you come in through the stage door today?"

"No. The front entrance."

"Arthur and I found the stage door open."

The sudden relaxation of tension was as palpable as the emergence of the sun from a cloud bank. It was abruptly much cheerier in the dusty auditorium; the world was now suspect, not just this select group.

Burt turned to Carla. "Did you check the stage door before you left Sunday?"

"No, no, I didn't." Was Carla's answer a shade too eager?

"So anybody could have done it," T.K. said ponderously.

"Anybody? Any citizen presently residing on our golden isle?" Hugo asked, his gravelly voice rising ever so faintly in inquiry.

Everyone looked at him.

"I do hate to cast a pall on the resurgence of cheer. But there is a minor matter."

"My God, Hugo, spit it out. How much foreplay do you want?" Sam was impatient.

"Think of the circumstances. The cat in the window seat."

The director drew his breath in sharply, but Hugo held up an imperious hand to forestall an outburst. "Think, my friends. I know, of course, that *Arsenic and Old Lace* is one of the most popular — and familiar — plays in the world. However, how many people know or would remember that the window seat is opened in Act One?"

They waited uneasily.

"A goodly number, I admit. However, I don't believe this can be considered common knowledge on the island. I believe, in fact, that we must limit our suspicions to those who have been involved in theater productions now or in the past." Hugo's probing dark eyes touched each face briefly. "No, my friends, I think the fox is in the chicken coop — and the fox is *one of us.*"

The sun slid behind the cloud bank again.

"Hugo's point is well taken," Burt said grimly. "In any event, I want to make an announcement. I'm taking Freddy to Chief Saulter." (Annie suspected Max's prepping here.) "If there's any way to trace the bullet that killed him, I'm going to do it."

"Good for you," Henny said warmly.

"Further," he continued, "I want to make one thing perfectly clear."

It was so quiet they could hear a mouse skittering backstage.

"If one more piece of sabotage occurs, this play is canceled."

Sam began to pace, his hands flapping wildly. "Now wait a minute, wait a minute. I got a contract. I got a producer coming. I got to stage this play. Dead or alive, I got to stage it! No way am I going to let some loony ruin my chance." He halted in front of Burt, his fringe of yellowish hair quivering, and poked Burt's chest with a pudgy finger. "You can't do this to me! No way can you do this to me!"

Burt ignored him. "The sabotage has to stop. It's going to stop. If it doesn't, this play's canceled."

Sam moaned. "Done in by a crank. Oh, God, what am I going to do?"

"Now, if anyone has any idea who's behind all of this, come and talk to me." Burt paused, and the silence crackled with uneasiness and quick, sideways glances. Burt finally cleared his throat. "All right. Everybody knows the score now. I'll see you here tomorrow night for a run-through of all three acts." His upper teeth gnawed on his lower lip for an instant, then he concluded gruffly, "That's all."

There was a moment of uncertain quiet, then a general movement toward the exit.

Hugo's clear, carrying voice rolled across the stage. "An addendum, my friends."

Everyone stopped. His voice commanded obedience.

Hugo waited just long enough to give the pause an edge. "As long as we are making pronouncements, I wish to make one of my own." His craggy face was grim. "I have no intention of participating in this play unless it is presented in a professional manner — and that means that not only must there be no more unpleasant interruptions. It also means that every actor must know his lines."

His black eyes challenged Shane.

8

Max stared over Annie's head into the refrigerator. "My God, don't you have anything *edible?*"

"Sure. There's leftover pepperoni, leftover barbecued ribs, and —" She poked a lump of foil. "Oh, yeah, leftover shrimp toast."

He moaned. "I don't want to ask anything too personal," he said mildly, "but have you ever made any meals from scratch?"

"You mean, like bought the ingredients at the grocery store?"

"Exactly."

"Of course. How about bacon and scrambled eggs."

Max sighed. "I can see that come September, I may have to prepare little grocery lists."

"For whom?" she inquired politely, her face attentive.

"For the chef. And I guess we both know who that will be."

"That will be lovely," Annie said serenely. "You know how much I enjoy your cooking."

He bent down, slid out the pizza box, and turned toward the microwave.

Annie set the table. She had real plates, but she reached past them to the stack of nice pink paper ones. It wouldn't do for Max to get set in his ways. She did whip together a tasty salad, just to throw him off balance: Bibb lettuce, cherry tomatoes, diced avocado, green onions, mushrooms, celery, and green pepper. Luscious thick Roquefort dressing for her, oil and vinegar for Max. (Did he want to live forever?)

The timer on the microwave beeped and the telephone rang at the same instant. She gestured for him to answer, while she lifted out the pizza.

"Oh, hi, Laurel." An indulgent smile crossed his face, and he leaned comfortably against the wall, obviously propped up for a lengthy conversation.

Annie sighed. After a moment's thought, she transferred the pizza to a pie tin and stuck it in the conventional oven to keep warm, then poured beer into frosty mugs and wandered into the living room. Handing a mug to Max, she plopped on the couch. But her ears weren't stoppered. An occasional phrase reached her.

"No kidding, Laurel!" "Oh, say, that sounds great." "Thrones? I'd like that." "Would the roots go into the wedding cake?"

Annie studied him dispassionately. Long. Lean. Good-looking. A perfect ass.

He glanced her way and grinned.

She resisted an almost overpowering impulse to retrieve the pizza and drape it over his head.

"A *coupe de mariage?*" He whooped with laughter. "Sounds more like the winner's cup at a horse race." He stifled his laughter. "Sorry, sweetheart. Of course I'm serious about it. It *is* a glorious opportunity to —" He paused. "How did you put it? Oh, yeah, a glorious opportunity to create unity. Yeah. You bet. And I've been thinking, Ma, how about a casino night? We can —" He listened. "Well, no, it's not a custom anywhere so far as I know, but we can create some *new* customs. Like a treasure hunt. First prize — a round trip to Peking. Now, that's international, isn't it?"

Annie turned her head away and stared determinedly at her bookcase. Her eyes focused on *Marriage Is Murder* by Nancy Pickard. Wasn't it just?

Then she stiffened.

"Annie? Oh, sure, she's right here, but

147

maybe you'd better talk to her another time, Ma. She's up to her elbows in the kitchen." He slapped his leg in appreciation of his own wit.

Annie scarcely dared to breathe.

"Sure. I love you, too. And it's going to be a blast, Ma." A pause. "Of course I'm taking it seriously. You can count on me. Night, now."

His eyes brimmed with laughter as he hung up.

Annie didn't say a word.

Max tipped his head to study her. "Did anybody ever tell you how cute you are when you're mad?"

"Max!"

He bounded across the room and pulled her up and into his arms. "Oh, come on, Annie. Grin a little. Laurel means well — and who knows, it may turn out to be the wedding of the century."

"I don't want the wedding of the century. I just want a —"

"— simple, dignified, unpretentious ceremony. Annie, relax. Go with the flow."

She only hoped she wouldn't be swept away. Laurel was capable of generating a *torrent*. Annie kept trying to make this point, but Max's lips kept getting in the way. Finally, she recalled herself enough to remember the pizza.

"Dry," she murmured. "Leathery." And she pulled away and steered him back to the kitchen.

The pizza was hard, but the beer helped. However, Annie found it difficult to concentrate on food. And she was determined not to inquire about thrones or roots. Roots in the wedding cake?

It might not be pleasant to dwell on the recent rehearsal, but it did distract her — at least a little — from Laurel. "I wonder what will happen at the run-through tomorrow night?"

"Don't borrow trouble, as my grandmother used to say."

If it was a saying by his maternal grandmother, she must have used it to survive life as Laurel's parent. That, however, started the same old cycle of concern. (Where was Laurel *now?* What was Laurel *doing?* What was Laurel *planning?*)

Max refused a second serving. Even Annie had only managed one. It was pizza that could walk unaided. It only took seconds to clear the table, and the dishes (paper plates) were no problem, so Annie made cappuccino and they settled on the couch.

Max sighed happily and slipped his arm

behind her shoulders, but she jumped up and darted across the room to paw through her wicker carryall.

She returned, waving the printout he'd given her earlier, and plopped down beside him.

Max groaned. "I thought maybe you'd forgotten."

"Forgotten? After Freddy?" Then she squinted in concentration. "Max, why Freddy?"

"Why concentrate on Freddy? Why *any* of it? Why the cut curtain-rope, why the —"

"No. Freddy's important," she insisted. "That was vicious. Don't you think it shows a particular malice directed at Janet? Why else would such a hideous notion even occur to anyone?"

"Maybe it's as simple as the fact that our creepy friend wanted to put something nasty in the window seat. And what could be nastier than someone's pet? You're probably lucky they picked on Freddy."

She stared at him, appalled. Her voice stricken, she said, "You don't think somebody would shoot Agatha. Do you?" She leaped to her feet.

Max reached out and grabbed her hand, pulling her down. "Annie, I'm sorry. Of course nobody would shoot Agatha. That would be really crazy."

"Maybe somebody is crazy," she whispered.

"No, no," Max insisted.

"So, okay," she demanded, "if nobody's crazy, then what's the point of the sabotage?"

"If I knew, I'd tell Saulter, and get the nut —" He stopped and waved his hands. "No, no, I don't mean nut — get the *prankster* arrested. You can bet there's a rational reason. Somebody's gone to a hell of a lot of trouble. There has to be a reason."

"Maybe we ought to go over to the store. Check on Agatha."

"Annie, she's all right. Relax."

But she wasn't satisfied until they'd driven at a furious pace to Death on Demand, and she held a sleepy and surprised Agatha in her arms. Then the cat, thoroughly irritated at being disturbed, wriggled free, jumped to the top of the coffee bar, and glared.

Annie got out fresh food, crooned endearments to an unimpressed feline, and put on a fresh pot of coffee, decaffeinated chocolate.

Max settled comfortably at the wooden table nearest the coffee bar and watched with amused eyes. "Satisfied?"

"I guess. But I'd almost board her for a while."

"Nobody's going to catch Agatha with her paws down. You know how she disappears when strangers come in. She'll be all right."

Annie pulled the printout from her purse and spread it on the table. "We *have* to get to the bottom of this." She tapped the sheets. "We know these people. I mean, you can't rehearse for a month without learning more than you ever wanted to know about everybody's basic personality. We should be able to figure out who's causing the trouble." She riffled through the pages, then asked, "Do you think we should include Vince Ellis, Father Donaldson, and Ben Tippet?"

"Because they were on hand for Freddy's discovery? Nope." Max was emphatic. "Not unless you think we have two saboteurs at work."

"Two?"

"The saboteur had to be among us when the stink bomb went off. That was an Act Two rehearsal. Father Donaldson, Vince, and Ben weren't there."

That limited their list, at least a little. Max ticked the others off on his fingers. "Henny. Janet. Hugo. Arthur. Shane. Me.

You. Sam. Burt. T.K. Cindy. Carla. Eugene."

Max picked up the printout and began to read aloud. (He did enjoy the sound of his own voice. Attractive as it was, she wondered if this foretold lengthy excerpts from newspapers and magazines after they were married. She preferred reading her morning newspaper in absolute silence.)

"HENRIETTA HOLLIDAY BRAWLEY. Born July four, 1923, in Baton Rouge, Louisiana, only daughter of prosperous cotton broker. Convent educated. Attended Sophie Newcomb, left college in 1943 to train in the Women's Airforce Service Pilots. Trained at Avenger Field, Sweetwater, Texas, receiving her silver wings, September 1943. Served as a test pilot and is credited with developing an innovative landing technique for the P-thirty-nine fighter. Married Robert Brawley, Captain U.S.A.A.F., December 1943. (Major Brawley killed in bombing raid over Berlin 1945.) At Wright Field, Dayton, Ohio, became one of the first jet pilots, testing the YP-fifty-nine, twin-turbine jet fighter. Honorable discharge, 1946. B.A., University of Texas, 1948. Taught English lit in

San Antonio, Texas, at a girls' school, retiring 1975. Received a gold watch and a commendation for never having missed a day of school in twenty-seven years. Joined Peace Corps, spent two years in Zaire building fish ponds and teaching English. Proficient in Tshiluba. Commended for supervising construction of more fish ponds (thirty-seven) than any volunteer in the history of the Peace Corps. Spent next two years backpacking around the world, including jaunts to Tibet and Antarctica. Returned to U.S. in 1979, having inherited property on Broward's Rock from a cousin. Member Altar Society, St. Francis of Assisi; moderator, Broward's Rock Public Library; champion bowler, Cha-Cha League; member, League of Women Voters —"

Annie held up a hand. "More?"

"Another half page."

"I get the picture."

They grinned at each other.

"Maybe we should leave it to Henny," Max suggested.

"She was so sure Shane was the culprit, but I saw her staring at him and shaking her head tonight. Who knows? I'm sure she'll keep us informed." Annie reached for the printout.

The phone rang. Annie jumped and stared like a deer at bay.

"Tsk tsk." Max evinced grave concern. "I'm worried about you, Annie. What's happened to your nerves?"

She glared at him. He knew damn well what had happened to her nerves.

The phone rang again.

Annie didn't want to answer. She was only too afraid she knew who was calling. But she had never been able to resist the imperious summons of Ma Bell. With a strangled groan, she yanked up the receiver.

"Death on Demand."

"Annie, I'm so glad I caught you." A pause. "You don't sound quite yourself. Is everything all right?"

"Of course I'm all right," she replied sharply. "Henny, how in the world did you know I was here?"

"Your place, Max's, or the shop. Where else?"

For an instant, Annie felt nonplussed. Was she really that predictable? After all, she certainly had many interests unknown to Henny Brawley. But Henny was plowing right ahead.

"I'm starting over, my dear. One point is

clear. Shane, whatever else he may have done, certainly didn't hide that cat in the window seat. I followed him home after rehearsal Sunday. He didn't leave the house all afternoon. When the first guests arrived, I ducked into the pool cabana and changed for the party. Then, right after the party, I pedaled back to the school, already had my bedroll on my bike, and spent the night. Right onstage. Then I popped up, brewed some tea in the parking lot on my Primus stove, and pedaled back to the Petrees' — and I followed him all day yesterday." She sniffed.

Annie didn't feel like inquiring into the activities that prompted that disgusted sniff. She grappled instead with the barrage of information.

"So Shane could've killed Freddy, since he was late rehearsal Sunday, but he never had a chance to put him in the window seat 'cause you were either on Shane's tail or at the school from Sunday afternoon on."

"Right." A discouraged sigh. "So, obviously," and a Virginia accent became noticeable, "I've misinterpreted my data. Well, I'll just have to look a little harder. And it seems to me the only thing to do is not to leave the stage unguarded for an *in-*

stant. And I won't." The Southern accent was heavy now. "Never fear. *Nil desperandum!*" And the connection was broken.

Annie stared at the receiver for a bemused instant, then shook her head slightly. "Miss Julia Tyler. I'm pretty sure."

He looked at her inquiringly.

"Southern accent and quoting Latin. Probably wearing a charming blue chambray dress. Miss Tyler is Louisa Revell's retired schoolmistress-sleuth."

He was impatient. "Does she really clear Shane?"

Annie repeated Henny's report, then sketched the times on the bottom of the printout.

1:45 Sunday (approx.) — Freddy sunning on retaining wall.

2:00 — Rehearsal begins.

"Remember, we finished our coffee so we were a few minutes late. I guess we got there about ten after," Annie recalled.

2:30 — Shane arrives.

4:10 (approx.) — Burt ends rehearsal. Which was a simple way of saying he called it off after all hell broke loose.

4:15 — Henny follows Shane home.

10:45 — Henny camps out onstage.

Monday — Henny tails Shane all day, up to arrival at rehearsal.

There was a moment's quiet while they studied the timetable.

"I'm confused," Annie admitted.

"It's pretty straightforward. Shane could have shot Freddy before he arrived at rehearsal around two-thirty on Sunday *but* he didn't bring the body then and he was under surveillance from that point on."

"Under surveillance," Annie repeated. "That has a nice ring to it. Henny would be thrilled."

"So, it looks like Shane's out of it," Max concluded. He rubbed his jaw. "The tricky part is, when was Freddy shot? The Hortons didn't see him after they got home from the rehearsal. Of course, they probably weren't thinking about the cat at that point. But, in all likelihood, since he didn't show up for dinner, he was already dead. Let's say he was killed some time between one forty-five and six p.m. That means someone hid him, then trucked him over to the school after rehearsal let out and before the Petrees' party started."

"There wasn't time for anyone to have shot him before rehearsal," Annie objected.

"Except us," he pointed out.

She ignored that and threw up her hands. "Everybody else was at the rehearsal when we arrived, which means they all must have gotten there about two p.m. So nobody in the cast and crew could have shot him!"

Max nodded thoughtfully. "Okay, if none of us could have killed Freddy, then that means someone who *wasn't* at the rehearsal shot him." His eyes glowed. "Harley Jenkins!"

"Harley wasn't in the theater when the stink bomb went off," Annie argued.

"Obviously, Harley has a confederate." He sighed. "But I didn't find any link to Harley among the cast and crew, except the obvious ones. Burt and Carla lease store space from Halcyon Development. T.K.'s been in some business deals with him." He snorted. "Harley uses Eugene's cleaners. Dammit." He glared at the printout. "Somewhere in there, there has to be a clue. Let's stop worrying about Freddy and concentrate on the people who we *know* were in the theater when the bomb went off. Surely we ought to be able to figure out if one of them is slimy enough to have planned the sabotage."

Annie glanced absently at her bookcase with its glorious collection of paperbacks, augmented by some hardcovers. Ira Levin's *A Kiss Before Dying* caught her eye.

She shivered. Who could really be sure of what might be found in anyone's mind? Dreadful images rose.

"It's the psychology we have to understand. Just like Poirot," she insisted, scanning the top shelf of her collection. Psychology was everything in *The Hollow* and *Crooked House*. "If we understood *why*, we'd know *who*," she explained.

Max gave her an absent nod. It was more polite than Poirot's disdain for Hastings's intellectual processes, but not much. So she continued to study her titles, searching for inspiration, while Max pursued the fruits of his afternoon's research.

The labyrinth of the human mind was explored so well in Celia Fremlin's *The Hours Before Dawn*. And frighteningly so in Patricia Highsmith's *Strangers on a Train*.

Annie sat up straight, feeling as if she were on the verge of a great discovery. A sick and cunning mind but capable, oh, so capable —

"Don't you think so?" Max demanded.

"Huh?"

"Annie, haven't you been listening? I laid it all out."

The faint glimmer in her mind faded. "Sorry. Tell me again."

He managed not to look long-suffering,

but just barely. If he were a cat, his ears would have slanted sharply backward. She almost told him so, then brought her mind to heel and listened respectfully.

"— Burt is actually the most likely person."

Intense, hardworking Burt with his passionate devotion to community theater, his long hours of effort to keep the players going, good years and bad?

"Max that's absurd!"

He held up a printout. "Just listen.

BURTON HOWELL CONROY. Born March three, 1927, in Savannah, Georgia. High school chemistry teacher. Retired five years ago. Widower. Used savings to set up gift shop on harborfront. Two years ago borrowed heavily from local bank against the store. Used money to meet medical expenses of spinster sister in Pine Bluff, Arkansas. Still deeply in debt, even though shop is prospering."

He looked meaningfully at her. "So, Burt needs money."

"Of course." Annie's head bobbed in agreement. "That's why he's working so hard to get the theater back on the waterfront. Performances will draw people in the evening, but it won't compete with his gift store. So your argument's a boomerang. Burt would be the last person to torpedo the play."

"Isn't he perfect for that bloated rat Jenkins to corrupt?" he demanded. "What if Jenkins offered Burt ten thousand dollars to blow the season?"

Annie stared at him. "Oh, that's creative. Do you have any proof that Jenkins might have done that?"

Max had the grace to look uncomfortable. "Well, no. It's inductive reasoning."

She raised an eyebrow. "A little careless of Burt's reputation, isn't it?"

"I'm not telling anybody but you. But he's the only one who really doesn't have an extra dime, except Sam, of course."

"Actually, I can see Sam taking a payoff long before I can see Burt with his hand out."

"Oh, no," Max objected. "Sam's desperate for good reviews. And those, money can't buy. Look at his bio."

Obediently, Annie read:

SAMUEL BRATTON HAZNINE. B. 1953, Brooklyn, N.Y. B.A. in Dramatic Arts, New York University, 1973.

First directing experience off-off-Broadway. Received notice for work on TV soaps. Made it to off Broadway in 1979, then meteoric rise, hottest young director in town, with raunchy comedy, *Kiss 'Em Off, Buchanan*, in 1982. Equally swift decline with two disastrous openings, especially *The Trial*, which closed on opening night. Reduced to directing dinner theaters and summer community theater, desperate for a comeback. Married and divorced three times. Accompanied to Broward's Rock by Tonelda Divine, an aspiring actress.

Annie pressed her fingers against her temples. "I feel like a mouse in a fun-house barrel. My head is swimming with intimate details about people I hardly know."

"Excellent mental discipline." Max was unsympathetic. "Anyway, Sam needs a success."

Annie recalled his plaintive pleas on the telephone Sunday afternoon. "I bet Sam needs cash, too," she said dryly. "And speaking of money, what about T.K.?"

"I thought about him," Max said agreeably. "Right from the first. He plays golf with Jenkins. But, so far as I can discover,

T.K.'s got plenty of money. He's been a member of the Million Dollar Club for years, the money keeps rolling in."

"Million Dollar Club?"

He grinned. "T.K. sells insurance. That means he's sold more than a million dollars in policies. Every time an insured pays a premium, T.K. gets his cut. The insurance business is one of the money world's best-kept secrets."

"The first rule of money — Them that has gets. So you don't think T.K. could be bribed by Jenkins, but he might help him out just one good old boy to another."

"Yeah." He didn't sound convinced. "But T.K.'s nobody's fool. Behind that old jock facade is a pretty tough customer. Besides, Freddy was their cat."

"Maybe T.K.'s mad at Janet," she suggested.

"Because of Shane?"

"Exactly."

"So he killed Freddy?" Max looked disgusted.

"We don't know what the Hortons are like, not really. And people can do nasty things." And she thought of Seeley's *The Listening House* and Slesar's *The Thing at the Door*.

Max tossed the printout on the table and

leaned back in his chair. "Okay. You're so keen on a psychological profile. *You* tell *me*."

She picked up the computer sheets and skimmed the Horton bins:

T. K. (THOMAS KINKAID) HORTON, B. 1948, Broward's Rock, South Carolina. Graduate of The Citadel, 1969. All-state football, 1965, 1966. Defensive lineman for The Citadel, 1967–69. Worked for Sampson Life Insurance in Atlanta for ten years after graduation before returning to Broward's Rock and establishing his own agency. Active in amateur theatricals in Atlanta, where he met Janet Kessler, a fine arts graduate of Emory. They were married in 1970. Daughter, Cindy, b. 1971. Successful Broward's Rock businessman, insurance agency owner, owner of The Shrimp Boat restaurant, controlling interest Broward's Rock Luxury Autos, part owner The Shipshape Launderettes. Past president Chamber of Commerce; active in Bible Study, First Baptist Church; director this year's United Fund Drive.

T.K. didn't need favors from Harley Jenkins. If T.K. planned the sabotage, it was purely for personal reasons, not financial. The Broward's Rock economy was booming, and the fortunes of the Hortons right along with it.

Harley didn't need money either — and he would never do anything to jeopardize the island's well-being because it would directly affect his own finances. Diverted, she lowered the printout and blurted, "Nope, Jenkins isn't behind it."

Max looked confused. "I thought we were talking about T.K."

If he were Jerry North, he would have understood, but she did deign to explain. "Because of Freddy."

"Freddy? What do Freddy and Jenkins have to do with each other?" he asked wildly.

"I know Jenkins is a rat. He's the kind of louse who probably likes to take potshots at cats, but not publicly. He wouldn't do anything that could possibly cut the tourist flow. When the story gets out about Freddy, it will make headlines from coast to coast. It's the kind of headline news editors can't resist. CAT KILLER PROWLS THEATER. FELINE DEAD ON DELIVERY. FELLED FELIX —"

"Down, girl. Maybe we can get you a job on *The Island Gazette*."

"I thought the phrasing felicitous."

"You have a point," he admitted grudgingly.

"So the sabotage isn't the product of a conspiracy headed by Jenkins," she concluded.

But Max wasn't ready to relinquish his theory quite yet. "He's such a clod, it probably wouldn't occur to him what a stink a cat-killing would raise."

"Clod, yes," she agreed. "Stupid, no."

Max looked mulish. "If it isn't Jenkins, who or what is it?"

It was up to her to uphold the tradition of thoughtful, *insightful* detection. Ah, the shades of psychiatrist-detectives Dr. Emmanuel Cellini, Dr. Sarah Chayse, Dr. Paul Prye, Dame Beatrice Bradley, and Dr. John Smith.

But, unfortunately, she wasn't teeming with insights at this particular moment. She frowned at the printout again.

Hmm. T.K. palled around with Jenkins, all right, but he was pretty much a home-by-eight fellow. "T.K. doesn't play the ponies — or chase shady ladies?"

"Not according to Vince Ellis, who covers this island like a fog. He says T.K.'s the original family man. As Vince put it, part of a vanishing species."

JANET KESSLER HORTON. Annie raised an eyebrow. Vince had dug up the dope, or unloaded it, on these two, if that was where Max had obtained his information. In addition to particulars (Janet, B. 1948, graduated Emory 1969), it described her as a sentimental sap, always looking for her Rhett Butler. Until this year, her flirtatious forays had always been discreet and presumably chaste. Then she had fallen for Shane Petree with a headlong abandon rivaled only by her own daughter's avid interest in the has-been actor.

Annie wondered briefly if the sweaty stallion had got a bit more than he had bargained for.

And she wondered, too, if Janet knew that Cindy had been spending some hot and heavy afternoons with Shane out in the bay aboard *Sweet Lady.*

If either Janet or Cindy was feeling slighted by Shane or angry with the other, they could be just feline and clever enough to plan the campaign. Or it could be T.K. acting out a jealous fury.

"But all of the sabotage hasn't been directed at Shane," Annie observed.

Once again, she could see Max scrambling mentally for the connection. Then he nodded. "Oh, sure. If it's T.K. If it's one of the Hortons, it reveals some depths to their psyches that I'd sure as hell rather not plumb."

"The person behind this is not going to be too lovable. But smart and calculating."

"That should clear Shane."

She understood his disdain, but didn't quite agree. "Actually, Shane's not dumb. He's just lazy and absolutely egocentric."

She scanned the information on him. Nothing much she didn't know. A beauty boy in a series of surfer movies. A skilled bodysurfer, excellent sailor, passable at golf and tennis. Quite the lothario around the marina. Spent a lot of time pampering his body. Insatiable so far as women were concerned. Always on the prowl. But his marriage to Sheridan seemed stable. Annie wondered who had what that the other wanted. A love match, she felt sure, it wasn't. The only surprise was his age. Forty-two. She had to hand it to the hunk; he didn't look it.

Shane's history primarily revealed total self-absorption. Would he plan and carry out the acts of sabotage? The annoying incidents might appeal to his warped sense of humor, but it all seemed like too much effort for him to bother.

"Okay. Not Shane," she agreed, although their reasons differed.

That left Carla, Hugo, Arthur, and Eugene.

"Whoever is behind this *is* taking a chance," she emphasized. "It takes a cool head, the ability to plan, steady nerves, and a compelling reason. And whoever did it has a nasty streak." She looked steadily at Max. "How about Carla?"

"Why Carla?"

"She sure isn't friends with anybody. Maybe she's more than unfriendly. Maybe she's damn hostile."

"That might be," Max said slowly. "You know, we've both tried to be friendly, and she just ignores us. I have a feeling she's been hurt a lot, and she isn't willing to open up at all. And something tells me that what she sees between us bothers her."

"Maybe," Annie agreed. "But she's obviously hungry for companionship or she wouldn't be active in the players."

"Right. So we make a full circle." Max shrugged. "She needs the players, wants to be a part of it, so why the hell would she destroy it?"

It didn't seem likely. Annie eyes dropped to the printout.

CARLA MORRIS FOUNTAIN.
B. 1951, Atlanta, Georgia. B.A., Vassar, 1972. Taught Latin September 1972 to March 1976 at St. Agnes Secondary School in Atlanta. Opened art gallery, Broward's Rock, April 10, 1976. Lives alone. Active in Broward's Rock Players. Apparently no close friends of either sex. Pleasant, but aloof. Not a mixer.

Annie sighed and flipped the page. Ah, Hugo, handsome Hugo. Unlike Shane, he married his women. Presently living with his third wife, Cory Lee, in one of the showcase homes of the island. Hugo's record was as exemplary as Shane's was mediocre: A Charleston native, Phi Beta Kappa at Stanford, Order of the Coif at Northwestern, a distinguished career as a plaintiff's attorney in Atlanta, long acclaimed as one of the South's most gifted actors, recently retired to Broward's Rock. An accomplished actor, race-winning yachtsman, celebrated hunter, scratch golfer.

As for Arthur Killeen, who was such a marvelous Dr. Einstein, nothing in his bio caught the eye.

B. 1929, Winnetka, Il. B.A., Northwestern, 1950, two-year tour in Korea as a lieutenant, Purple Heart (leg wound). Honorable discharge. M. Beatrice Simpson, 1952; two children. Pharmaceutical salesman, traveling Midwest, 1952–1982. Ret. to Broward's Rock, fall 1983, bought Cole Drugstore. The Killeens are active members of the First Baptist Church. He teaches a Bible study class. Members of Saturday Highsteppers Square Dancing Club. He is chairman of the County Republicans.

Finally, Eugene. Myopic blue eyes and an inexhaustible supply of TR anecdotes.

EUGENE FERRAMOND. B. 1934, in Broward's Rock. [Max had pencilled in: *A native, rara avis.*] Owner Shiny Brite Laundry and Cleaners. B.A. in history, Clemson, 1955. Two-year tour as a second lieutenant in Germany. Returned to Broward's Rock in 1957 to work in family business. Became laundry owner on death of father in 1979. Never married. Active in South Carolina Historical Society. An acknowledged expert on history of Broward's Rock, the Battle of New Orleans and Theodore Roosevelt.

Annie flung the printout onto the table. "You know what I think?"

"What?"

She reached out, touched his cheek. "I think there are more fun ways to spend a Monday night."

9

Cord grass, caressed by the early evening off-shore breeze, rippled away from her like a sea of silk. Annie welcomed the distinctive tangy scent of the marsh, a combination of salt water, chlorophyll exuded from the spartina grass, the decay of fallen plants and animals, and sulfur from marsh mud. She braced her hands against the wooden railing and savored the brilliant red splash of the setting sun.

Was there any lovelier place in the world? She swatted at a no-see-um and waved away a green-head fly which had taken a deeply personal interest in the sweet aroma of her hair spray, holding firm her early 1940s pageboy. (Opening night, of course, was still a week away, but it was never too soon to start work on her hair, which had a tendency to wave upward unless sternly disciplined.) She applauded the mating antics of a male fiddler crab, busily swinging his one large claw to entice a lady crab into his burrow. A variation on *autres temps, autres moeures.* He had plenty of fellows this lovely evening. From her perch above the marsh, she could see hundreds of the crabs and hear the crackle of their feet on the mud flat. Hidden in the five-foot cord grass, a hyena cackle emitted its distinctive call. The breeze rustled the spartina grass, and for a moment she was reminded sharply of prairie wheat in Texas, where she grew up.

Then she heard the swift tattoo of a horn and the roar of Max's Porsche. She hurried around the porch to the steps, waved, and started down. She couldn't suppress an ear-to-ear grin. Max was obviously already into his role, slouching cockily against the red leather upholstery. He was such a marvelous Mortimer. She ran toward the car. It might not be sophisticated, but she was alight with excitement and anticipation. In only a little while, the first complete run-through of the play would be underway — and despite everything, she just couldn't wait!

Carla, nervous as a brood hen, made last-minute adjustments to the set. Her face was grim and pale, whether from concentration or unhappiness Annie had no idea. When Annie smiled a hello and paused to compliment the set, Carla stared at her unresponsively for a long moment, then muttered, "Glad you like it," before turning away to check the list of props for Act I. Obviously, nerves weren't confined to the players.

Annie admired the perfection of the Victorian setting, the statuette of Minerva, Goddess of Wisdom, in the niche midway up the stair wall, the two three-prong silver candelabra atop the sideboard, and the substantial William Morris chairs, then headed downstairs to the dressing area. Although no one, of course, was in costume or makeup tonight (the first dress rehearsal was scheduled for the coming Sunday afternoon, the second for Monday night, and, hurrah, the opening for next Tuesday), Burt urged everyone to get into a groove with their timing and to use the greenroom between scenes.

The only access from the stage area was down the narrow, steep, creaky stairs that opened just behind the back curtain at upstage right, which was very convenient for this particular play with its offstage cellar, where Teddy dug those useful canals and, occasionally, trenches for yellow fever victims.

The below-stage area itself compared favorably with the Roman catacombs. The corridors, which branched off in unexpected loops and jogs, were ill-lit, musty, and, tonight, redolent with fresh coffee, mold, makeup, paint, plywood, and mosquito spray.

The greenroom opened to the right of the stairs. This was the area where actors awaited their entrances. Two sagging couches, an assortment of straight chairs, stools, and camp chairs were scattered the length of the long, narrow area. Burt had put a coffee urn on a table at the far end, along with a plate of cookies. A cooler on the floor held cans of soda.

The paint and wood odors emanated from the prop shop across the hall. Farther down the dim length of the corridor was the prop storage area, an enormous room with bays, ells, and innumerable nooks that contained stage trees, boulders, mock-ups of cars including a 1929 Ford, flags, fake suits of armor, trellises of paper flowers, and an unimaginable array of flotsam and jetsam from past high school productions. Across the corridor were the two large dressing rooms, plus two small ones with stars affixed to the outer panels. Men's and women's restrooms were at the end of the hall next to the dim cavern that was the boiler room.

It was terrific fun to see the whole cast assembled, including Sam and T.K. as policemen, and Burt as Mr. Witherspoon, the fussy superintendent of Happy Dale Sanitarium who arrives in Act III to accept Abby, Martha, and Teddy as new patients. (Except, of course, that Abby and Martha discover he is a lonely widower and perhaps there will be just time for a nice glass of elderberry wine before they depart . . .)

Burt stuck his head in the greenroom. "Ten minutes."

Henny Brawley grinned and gave a thumbs-up sign.

Eugene smiled genially at Annie. "Interesting, that."

More TR memorabilia?

TR's look-alike cleared his throat. "Of course, we wouldn't want the converse."

Annie looked at him blankly.

"When one of the emperors party at the Roman Colosseum gave a thumbs-down, it meant death for the gladiator."

Annie felt a stab of irritation. Eugene might be living proof of a little knowledge being a bad thing. At the least, he'd dimmed her pleasure in the moment. Then she decided she was being as superstitious as poor Sam. After all, Eugene couldn't help being a compendium of useless facts. Determinedly, she willed away her momentary unease.

"I guess we're all right," she said brightly. "No gladiators here," and she whirled away from Eugene to hurry upstairs. She wanted to see the opening scene.

To complete her pleasure, Annie found the crate of programs tucked near the prop table and filched one to admire. She settled in a front-row seat. (She didn't make her entrance until about seven minutes into Act I.)

ARSENIC AND OLD LACE
A Play in Three Acts
By Joseph Kesselring

Cast in order of appearance:

Abby Brewster . . . . Henrietta Brawley
The Rev. Dr. Harper
. . . . The Rev. Charles Donaldson
Teddy Brewster . . . . Shane Petree
Officer Brophy . . . . Vincent Ellis
Officer Klein . . . . Samuel Bratton Haznine
Martha Brewster . . . . Janet Horton
Elaine Harper . . . . Annie Laurance
Mortimer Brewster . . . . Max Darling
Mr. Gibbs . . . . Ben Tippett
Jonathan Brewster . . . . Hugo Wolf
Dr. Einstein . . . . Arthur Killeen
Officer O'Hara . . . . . . Eugene Ferramond
Lieutenant Rooney . . . . T. K. Horton
Mr. Witherspoon . . . . Burt Conroy

The houselights dimmed, the stage darkened, and Annie sat back to enjoy the play.

In the ensuing hour, she took the stage twice as Elaine. Responsible for keeping track of her own entrances, she had developed a fine inner clock that alerted her that her cue was nearing, whether she was out in front, downstairs, or taking a quick breather on the back steps outside the stage door. All the cast members moved about, except Vince Ellis, who settled down to a serious game of poker in the greenroom with Ben Tippet when they were off. At various times, Annie caught glimpses of Shane, who paced impatiently in the below-stage hallway between appearances; Hugo, who glowered at them all impartially when offstage, but whose performance was brilliant; Arthur, who smiled at her shyly, clearly excited by his participation; and Janet, who dashed down several times to dart into the ladies' room. Even Henny confessed to feeling a little parched, rushing into the greenroom once in search of her thermos of iced tea and shedding her warmup jacket to reveal a Spuds Mackenzie T-shirt.

But, most of the time, Annie stayed in the auditorium, because this was as near as she would come to seeing the production as a whole, and because she was out of the way of Carla and Cindy, as they changed props between scenes. Annie was, of course, faithfully on hand for all of Max's appearances as Mortimer. She didn't intend to tell him how superb he was. The man was quite conceited enough without her driveling like a fan letter. But, golly, he *was* wonderful!

After her stint as Elaine in Act II, when Jonathan tries unsuccessfully to imprison her in the cellar, she slipped down the stage right steps and returned to her familiar seat. A shadow moved in the darkness, and Eugene plumped down beside her.

"Going great, isn't it?" he whispered.

She didn't want to talk; she wanted to watch. But Eugene was due on as O'Hara in just a few minutes, so she would be patient.

"Sure is."

"Everybody's swell, aren't they? Henny's just a real star."

"Henny and Hugo and Max," she replied.

He gnawed at his lip. "Shane's learned his lines."

Now that, of course, qualified as noblesse oblige of the first order. Actually,

Shane had started off fairly well in the first act, but then he began to hurry his lines, and, when he was offstage, urged the others to pick up the pace. She even heard him telling Arthur, "We don't want to be here all night, old man." He didn't even have time for his nightly sweetie-feely session behind the backdrop with Cindy. Annie was amused to see Shane brush off the teenager when she rushed to give him a big hug after the first act and stood on tiptoe to whisper in his ear. He disengaged her almost roughly, saying irritably, "Not tonight, Cindy," and ducking down the stairs. Cindy had glared after him, her eyes hard. Shane's impatience irritated the hell out of Hugo, who snarled, "Slow down, or I'll slow you down permanently." The saving grace was that the other cast members were too professional to let Shane break their rhythm and, after all, Teddy, though a fun figure in the play, wasn't as critical to its success as were Abby, Martha, and Jonathan. Although if Shane kept up his rapid-fire delivery on opening night, it surely would detract from the others' performances. Sam, of course, periodically yanked at his fringe of hair and moaned, "This is not a friggin' express-way!"

Annie said dryly, "If Shane doesn't stop trying to stampede everyone, Hugo may break his neck." Then she added briskly, "But, overall, it's going great. And you're going to be a smash as O'Hara."

"I'll give it my best shot," he offered. He took a deep breath. "As TR once said, 'Far better it is to dare mighty things, to win glorious triumphs, even though chequered by failure, than to take rank with those poor spirits who neither enjoy much nor suffer much, because they live in the gray twilight that knows not victory or defeat.' " His blunt head turned toward her. "Don't you agree?"

"Oh, thoroughly."

She was saved from further comment when he added prosaically, "Almost my time. See you later, Annie."

And Eugene *was* superb as the hopeful policeman playwright assuring the drama critic that he has absolutely no idea what goes on in Brooklyn, while the critic is awash in a welter of corpses and crazy relatives. The remainder of Act II sparkled, in part because Shane had no more appearances. But acrimony broke out almost immediately at the end of the act, when Carla accused Cindy of misplacing Abby's and Martha's hymnals.

"I did not," the teenager screeched. "I haven't touched them!"

Carla ran out onstage, looked over the downstage left table, then whirled toward Cindy. "If you didn't spend every minute chasing after Shane, you could be of some help."

Cindy flipped her long blond hair angrily. "What's the matter with you? PMS? Or maybe you don't even have periods."

Sam bounced up on his sneakered feet, moving deftly between them. "Girls, girls, stuff it. Come on, Carla, put anything on. We'll find 'em later."

For the first time all evening Annie thought of the saboteur, then shrugged it away. Everything was going perfectly, and the misplacement of the hymnals was surely too minor to have been planned. Just one of those prop mix-ups. What was remarkable was what a fabulous run-through it had turned out to be. Except for Shane, of course. One and all, the principals were turning in first-rate-performances.

With substitutes for the hymnals finally slapped in place, the curtain opened on Act III. Annie slipped comfortably down in her seat. She wasn't due on until almost the finale, so she could thoroughly enjoy the complications of life at the Brewster manse. And she could smell success. Burt must be overjoyed. And Sam was surely visualizing a bright white trail leading back to Broadway. Annie grinned. It was fun to be part of something good.

Mortimer jousted with Jonathan over the disposition of the corpses (Mr. Hoskins belonged to Abby and Martha; Mr. Spenalzo was the contribution of Jonathan and Dr. Einstein). There was a rapid flurry of coming and going at this point, Mortimer off, Jonathan on, Abby and Martha off, Einstein on.

Jonathan demanded that Einstein bring up his medical instruments for use on Mortimer. Dr. Einstein refused, but Jonathan knew the medical bag was in the cellar and departed to find it.

And then, nothing happened.

Dr. Einstein, alone on the stage by the cellar door, finally twisted his head to look up toward the second-floor landing.

Annie leaned forward.

At this point, Teddy should burst onto the landing and raise his bugle, then Mortimer should frantically dash out and grab his arm, to prevent the bugle call.

There was a flurry of sound backstage.

"Well, where the hell is he?" Even the back curtain couldn't muffle Hugo's clarion, outraged tone.

The rehearsal slammed to a halt. Back-stage, Sam squalled, "Amateurs! God deliver me from amateurs!" Burt darted onstage and peered out over the lights at the auditorium. "Shane?" His voice quivered with irritation. "Anybody see him? Is he out there?"

Annie stood up and looked around. In a minute, the houselights flickered on.

Eugene, his mustache bristling officiously, poked his head through the red velvet curtains of the center aisle. "Haven't seen him," he called. "I'll take a look in the foyer," and his head withdrew.

Soon, the entire cast and crew were involved.

Five minutes later, after searching the restroom, the greenroom, the dressing rooms, and the parking lot, a dour cast and crew gathered onstage.

Max ducked back inside through the stage door. "His car's out there. No sign of him."

Cindy looked surprised. "His car's out there? But I thought maybe —" Then she stopped, but not quite soon enough.

T.K. looked at her sharply. "What did you think, young lady?"

His daughter gave a huffy little shrug

and refused to reply.

But Burt was too anxious to be politic. "What the hell did you think? You know what that jerk was up to?"

Cindy glanced at her father's reddening face, then said sullenly, "I don't *know* anything for sure. But he said he was going to be busy after the show." Fury flared in her eyes.

Max studied her. "You think he had a date with somebody?"

"Yes." Resentment and anger snapped her full moist lips shut.

"By God, this is the last straw!" Hugo slammed a fist against the stairs and they wobbled. "Now we know who's caused all the trouble throughout the rehearsals. Anybody who'd pull a trick like this certainly did the rest of it."

"But his car's out there," Max protested. "So he hasn't left."

"Unless someone picked him up. I'm sure there is a cadre of willing females lined up across the island," Hugo said maliciously, flicking disdainful glances at Janet and Cindy.

Their faces bore an uncanny, damning resemblance as both stiffened at the implication of his words.

"He certainly didn't hide the cat in the

window seat," Henny interjected, "so I'd say it's very questionable that this is a trick on Shane's part."

"Could he be sick?" Janet quavered.

"We looked in the johns," Burt retorted.

"How carefully did you search downstairs?" Max asked.

"He's not in the greenroom or the dressing rooms. He's not anywhere," Burt insisted.

"But if he's sick," Janet fretted, "he might have fallen somewhere. Oh, we'd better look again —"

"If he's sick, I hope it's terminal," Hugo snapped. "I for one did not come to the theater tonight to search for a half-assed actor. I will wait ten more minutes, and if he doesn't show up, I'm leaving — and I won't be back."

This galvanized Sam into a frenzy of action. "Quick, quick. Come on, now, let's give it a big try, boys and girls, downstairs and out in the lot, too. Get some flashlights. Come on, everybody, let's get with it. He has to be somewhere!"

Annie glanced down at her watch. It was almost ten-forty. Actually, the play had been almost on schedule until Shane missed his entrance. For the first time all evening, she felt tired and more than a little irritated. Obviously, Shane wasn't anywhere around. She didn't know whether his disappearance was part of the malicious mischief which had dogged the rehearsals or whether he'd taken French leave for his own purposes, but she was damn sure she wasn't interested in being part of the search party. However, Max was leading a pack out into the parking lot. She shrugged and followed Vince down the backstage steps. Tallyho.

Even with the huge flashlight from Max's car and a pencil-sized addition from her purse, they found no trace of Shane in the lot. Vince headed for the maintenance garage for school buses, while Eugene and Arthur climbed the steps of the baseball stands. Circling the track, Annie stumbled over a gopher burrow. As she limped back toward the light over the stage door, she was considering artistic ways of revenging herself upon Shane, starting with a hatchet buried in his thick skull.

Then, awkwardly, she began to run, ignoring the twinge in her ankle, because the sound that carried on the silky night air, though muffled and indistinct, was unmistakably a horror-freighted scream.

10

Vince Ellis (perennial winner of the island's annual triathalon) reached the stage door twenty-five yards in the lead. Annie was straining for breath, but she was right behind Max as he plunged up the steps. Eugene and Arthur were trailing far behind

Screams, sobs, and a hoarse flurry of shouts echoed up the stairwell from the basement.

Thudding down the narrow steps, they found a knot of shaken onlookers clustered around the open door to the boiler room.

Annie craned to see past Arthur's bony shoulders, then wished she hadn't.

Shane's pink cotton sports shirt bunched awkwardly across his chest, forming a depression. The blood trickling down from his pulpy face had collected in a dark, viscous pool. Once he had been handsome; now blood suffused the eye sockets, shards of bone poked whitely through torn flesh.

Annie drew her breath in sharply. "What did that to his face?" she asked, her voice high.

Arthur didn't turn but he answered her in a dull monotone. "Gunshot wounds. Several." And Annie remembered he wore a Purple Heart and an ill-fitting uniform every year in the Fourth of July parade.

It was Janet who found Shane, and Janet who screamed, but the wrenching sobs came from Cindy, who knelt on the gritty cement floor, holding a flaccid hand tightly between her own.

"Shane. Shane!"

T.K. shouldered past Annie, then shoved Arthur and Hugo aside. "Get up, Cindy. Get up." For once T.K. had no eyes for his wife, who sagged against a dusty pillar, her hands at her throat, her face crumpled in horror. There was both anguish and fear in his voice as he reached down to grab his daughter's arm.

"Leave me alone," she cried, twisting free. Cindy turned a grief-distorted face toward her father. "Don't touch me. You hated him. You know you did. Oh, leave me alone."

T.K.'s jowly face turned crimson, and he yanked the girl to her feet and began to shake her harshly. "Shut up," he shouted. "Shut your mouth."

Janet flung herself toward them. "Stop it! Stop it, both of you!"

Vince Ellis, the freckles standing out against his face, watched them intently. T.K., his jaw quivering as he stared at his daughter, never even noticed.

From behind her, Annie heard Sam murmur, "Oh, God, I'm going to be sick," and the sound of running footsteps.

Carla stood just inside the door to the boiler room, her arms folded tightly at the waist, her face a studied blank.

Hugo stared down at the body. "God, if the bastard doesn't cause trouble one way, he does another. Call the police, someone."

Eugene sighed and blinked his eyes owlishly. Annie wished he didn't remind her so forcibly of Teddy Roosevelt, certainly not with the other Teddy so grotesquely dead. She moved so that Eugene wasn't in her line of vision.

Henny Brawley's face was pale beneath her makeup, but she stepped forward. Resolutely ignoring the corpse, she took charge. "Max, go upstairs and phone Chief Saulter. Burt, you and Arthur stand guard over the body. And everyone else" — she raised her voice slightly — "move now to the greenroom. We will await the police there."

Annie wasn't the least surprised when

everyone did exactly as they had been instructed.

It was a dispirited group that waited, nervously avoiding each other's eyes, talking in disjointed and unconnected phrases.

Annie dispensed coffee from the urn, and Henny passed out the coffee cups and soft drinks. Sam came in, his pudgy face slack and pale, and miserably accepted a soda.

The Hortons bunched together in a far corner, but they might as well have been poles apart for all the comfort they offered each other. Janet ignored T.K.'s questioning looks, and Cindy's back was turned to her parents.

Carla sat stiffly in a straight chair, her knees tight together, and stared at the door to the hall. Hugo lit an outsized cigar and ignored all of them. Eugene paced up and down the middle of the room, his hands clasped behind his back.

As Max entered, everyone looked at him expectantly, then lifted their eyes to the ceiling as a siren sounded faintly.

Chief Saulter entered a few minutes later, accompanied by the two patrolmen who constituted his entire force. Saulter's shirt was rumpled, and Annie knew he must have dressed hurriedly. He glanced around the greenroom appraisingly. "Everybody stay put, please. We'll be talking to you as soon as possible." Then he hurried on down the hall. Max moved to Annie's side and took her hand. She gave his a grateful squeeze.

Arthur and Burt joined them in the greenroom. Voices murmured down the hall. Someone laughed. Flashes from a camera flickered steadily for some minutes. Janet whimpered once, eyes on the door. And they waited.

It was almost midnight when Saulter returned to the greenroom, rubbing the back of his neck wearily. He checked the notes in his hand. "Deceased identified as Shane Petree, forty-two, resident of Broward's Rock." He glanced over his shoulder. "Hey, Harry, you found his wife yet?"

A muffled reply.

Saulter nodded. "Let me know when you do." Then he turned back to them. "Murder by gunshot. No weapon found. Deceased shot several times in the face."

A gasp from Janet. T.K.'s mouth tightened.

For the first time Annie thought about guns and shots — and noise. How had none of them heard a gun go off several times? She opened her mouth. Max gently covered it with his hand. She looked up at him sharply.

"Quiet, sweetie," he cautioned softly. "Whatever it is, let it go for now."

She subsided reluctantly.

Chief Saulter completed a slow survey of the waiting faces. "Who wanted to kill him?"

Nobody said a word.

Annie passed the marmalade to Max. "I'd say the chief didn't make much progress last night."

Max munched the marmaladed English muffin and waved away a dragonfly, who zoomed up, regrouped, and made another sortie. "On the contrary," he said indistinctly, "he narrowed his circle of suspects comfortably." Licking his fingers, he ticked off the names. "You. Me. Henny. Janet. Hugo. Arthur. Eugene. Sam. Burt. T.K. Cindy. And Carla."

"That's not narrow," she objected. "That's a herd."

"Look at it this way. He's cleared Vince Ellis and Ben Tippett. They were playing poker during the critical period. Ben lost forty-nine dollars to Vince. And Father Donaldson had left the theater and was watching TV in his living room with his wife. Also — and this is crucial for those of us on that list — the chief's proved pretty conclusively that it had to be someone who was at the theater, because Cindy, who claims she perched on the rope platform except when it was time for a scene change, swears absolutely nobody came in or out of the stage door all night except one of us."

"Isn't Cindy a suspect?" Annie demanded.

"Oh, sure. But between Cindy and Carla, it's pretty clear no strangers came in. And you would have noticed any new faces coming through the auditorium. Ditto Eugene. That leaves only the basement entrance to the boiler room, and that was bolted shut. So," he pronounced with satisfaction, "you've got yourself a locked-room mystery, Annie Laurance."

"Not in the classic sense. A locked-room mystery is when a victim is found murdered in a locked room and there's no way anybody could have gotten in or out. Except, of course, there's always a trick to it. Read Dr. Gideon Fell's lecture in *The Hollow Man*. Then you'll understand."

Annie realized she had been singularly

lacking in tact, when Max shot her a highly offended look.

"But I see your point," she said quickly, trying to make amends. "Certainly the number of suspects seems to be limited to your list. But isn't it possible that somebody could have snuck in through a broken window in the basement —"

"And somehow enticed Shane into the boiler room, shot him, and escaped without anybody seeing or hearing him! Oh, fat chance."

Diverted, she demanded, "That's what I wanted to ask the chief last night. Why didn't anyone hear the shots?"

"Maybe the gun had a silencer on it. Maybe the boiler room absorbs noise." Max reached for another muffin. "And maybe somebody heard it and decided not to be a hero."

Annie mulled that over. "You mean somebody might have heard and decided to keep quiet?"

"Sure."

"But if they'd speak up now, it could help the investigation."

Max reached across the table and patted her with a sticky hand. "My love, not everyone is imbued with your generally helpful attitude toward the authorities. And, of course," he concluded, "the easiest assumption is that the sound didn't carry from the boiler room —"

"Why the boiler room?" she puzzled. "And how did the murderer lure Shane there?"

He finished his second muffin, drained his coffee cup, and poured a refill for each of them from her pink porcelain jug. He looked on top of the world, well rested, devilishly handsome, and quite pleased with himself. He did love to be asked questions. Annie complimented herself on her thoughtfulness in plying him with questions she could *easily* answer on her own. She merely liked to think out loud.

Max leaned back and pontificated. "Where was a tryst least likely to be interrupted? The boiler room, of course." Warming to his theme, he elucidated odiously, "As is obvious to even the meanest intelligence" (Did he think he was Poirot talking to Chief Inspector Japp?), "no one had any business in the boiler room, so where could there be a safer place to plan a murder? As for enticing Shane into the boiler room, that's easy," he declared with maddening confidence. "Say it's one of us — and you're going to have to give in on that point, sweetie — all the killer had to do was lurk downstairs 'til Shane came out of the greenroom, then give him a wave, and say, 'Hey, you've got a phone call and there's an extension down this way.' Hell, Shane wouldn't know where the phones are. And why should he be suspicious? So, the killer leads him like a lamb into the boiler room, shuts the door, then pulls out the gun, and lets him have it. Simple."

Annie still resisted the closed-circle theory. "Maybe Shane *met* somebody in the boiler room, unbolted the door, and let the person in."

"Who bolted the door shut?"

"The murderer," Annie said triumphantly.

"And how," Max asked sweetly, "did our murderer exit?"

She opened her mouth, then closed it. An unknown killer would then have had to negotiate the cellar corridor, go up the stairs, and leave through the stage door. Or, more impossibly yet, down the stage steps into the auditorium, up an aisle and out through the front foyer, without having been seen by either Cindy or Carla, who were backstage throughout the rehearsal except for brief trips downstairs, or any of the actors going on and off stage, or Annie and Eugene who spent most of the evening in the front seats.

If it wasn't a genuine locked-room mystery, it was a close relative. Like the passengers in *Death in the Clouds*, they knew who the suspects were. It was a chilling thought.

"But that's pretty dumb on the murderer's part," she said tartly.

"Why so?"

"Why do it at a rehearsal? Why not wait until opening night? Then there would be ushers, ticket takers, all kinds of extra people around. Why do it when it's limited to" —she flipped up her fingers — "twelve people. Ten, not counting you and me." She tilted her head. "*Surely* Chief Saulter's not counting us."

He slouched back in the comfortable plastic webbed chair. "On the theory that once innocent, forever innocent? I'm afraid I wouldn't bank on that."

"But he *knows* us."

Max chuckled at her outrage. "Saulter'd be accused of discrimination if he excluded us on a personal basis. Don't count us out, Annie."

"So we're murder suspects. Again." She shrugged. "Well, the chief may have to consider us formally, but he *knows* we're okay. I'm not worried." But Max had a faraway, thoughtful look on his face. "Hey, you're not worried, are you?"

"Huh?"

"About the chief suspecting us?"

"Oh, no. No, I was just thinking about what you said. About the murder occurring at the rehearsal. That's important, Annie. Don't you see what the murder accomplished?"

"It's put twelve people in a fix."

"The play. It won't open."

She hadn't given a thought to the fate of the play. "Oh, sure. I guess that goes without saying."

"Do you suppose Shane was killed to keep the play from opening?" he asked slowly.

She looked at him in horror. "That's too crazy. No one would murder someone just to keep the play off the stage, or to ruin the players' season."

"But the sabotage happened. Why? It can't be separate from the murder."

"Sure it can," she disagreed. "The sabotage — that was little stuff. Pranks. All except Freddy. And even so, killing a cat is far short of murder. No. I think it's coincidence."

"Coincidence? Oh, come on, Annie."

201

"Besides, we don't even know for sure whether the play will be called off. I mean, Eugene could play Teddy and Burt could do Officer O'Hara and we could make up Sam so that he could be Mr. Witherspoon, too."

Even as she spoke, a dreadful thought curled in the recesses of her mind. Could this just possibly be what Eugene would have assumed? He'd wanted that role so badly. . . . But that was too crazy, too. Eugene might want to be Teddy, he might be the world's very best Teddy, but he wouldn't kill a man over a role in a play. Would he?

Annie finished the last bite of her strawberry muffin and tapped her fork on her plate. "Motive. That's what we have to determine. We're talking in a vacuum until we consider motive."

He waited, expecting clarification.

"Look at it this way," she continued urgently. "Did the murder occur last night because it *had* to occur on Tuesday night? Or was the time incidental and the motive an outpouring of hate that merely reached its crest yesterday?"

He looked blank.

"Max, was he killed because of the play? Or was he killed because he was Shane and somebody hated him?"

"When we know that, we'll know who killed him," he said reasonably.

Annie was pouring fresh coffee when the phone rang. She hurried inside to answer it, and Max followed, bringing their plates to the sink.

"Hello."

"Annie, Burt here." He sounded very tired. "Saulter's put the auditorium off-limits for now. I decided to cancel all rehearsals until this weekend at least."

She couldn't mask her surprise. "Are you thinking of continuing with the production?"

"My God, we have to have something on the boards next Tuesday night," he snapped defensively. "I mean, the world can't come to a stop because Shane got himself murdered. Of course, I'm damn sorry and everything, but what the hell do you think I should do?"

She almost suggested delaying the opening of the season for at least a week, but she understood Burt's dilemma. A delay in opening would throw off the entire summer schedule.

"I don't know what's going to happen." He was aggrieved. "I've alerted the *Mousetrap* cast to be ready, just in case"

In case one of the *Arsenic* principals was arrested?

"If it all shakes out, we'll have a dress rehearsal next Sunday or Monday. We're almost ready to go as is. And Eugene will be Teddy, of course."

Oh, of course. So Eugene would have his role after all. Her spine prickled.

Burt sighed. "So I guess everything's going as well as could be expected. I told Saulter to go easy on everybody when he talks to them. I don't want the cast all nervy."

That would be a shame, all right.

"You've talked to the chief?" Annie let it dangle.

"Yeah. He sounded sour as hell. Apparently Sheridan frosted him some way. Guess she was pretty bitchy. I don't know what she'd said."

Annie pictured that smooth, arrogant face with the unreadable amber eyes. "No telling."

He sighed again. "Well, it could be worse. I'll let you know on rehearsal."

She hung up and turned as Max settled on the couch. He held out her coffee mug.

She sat down beside him and took the mug. "Burt's really put out. Very inconsiderate of Shane to get murdered and put a crimp in rehearsals, but, fear not, the players shall survive. Although rehearsals are canceled until Sunday." She hefted her mug. "The show must go on."

"Burt is a trifle single-minded," Max murmured.

Her mind skittered off in several different directions. She didn't need to hurry to the shop. Ingrid would arrive at ten and open. Why *had* the murder occurred at rehearsal? She'd bet Sheridan had given Chief Saulter an earful. Sheridan. Annie sat very still. Where was Sheridan when the murder occurred? By God, that was a good question. Maybe she'd finally tired of having a roving Romeo for a husband. Could she have slipped unseen into the theater and pulled it off? Appealing as Annie found that scenario, it wasn't too likely. If she had, she was a successor to Houdini. So far as Annie knew, Sheridan had never set foot in the theater. But, where was Sheridan when Shane was shot?

She turned to Max and demanded, "What about Sheridan? You know the old saw. *Cherchez la femme.*" Max was shaking his head. So, okay, that wasn't quite the original meaning, but, after all, she could take a fresh tack. "Okay, okay. I mean, who does a husband in? His wife. And vice versa. What the hell about Sheridan? She's a tough cookie."

"But not invisible," he replied mildly.

Annie glared.

"Same objection as to the unknown murderer. How could Sheridan have entered and left the basement without being seen?"

"A disguise?" Annie suggested. "Dressed like a man? If you just caught a glimpse, maybe you might think she was Vince or Sam or Eugene."

"Oh, let's see," Max mused. "She's about five foot two, built decidedly like a woman should be, moves like a woman —"

Annie reviewed them in her mind: Vince, redheaded and a burly six feet tall; Sam, pear-shaped and balding on top with that distinctive fringe of floppy yellow hair; and Eugene, portly with a bearlike chest.

The phone rang.

"I still like Sheridan," she said stubbornly as she reached for it.

"Hello."

"Annie, I *know* the police are off on the wrong foot. It's going to be up to us —"

A thunderous knock rattled her front door. Annie cupped a hand over her ear and gestured for Max to answer.

"— to ferret out the truth. I have no *doubt* that we can succeed. However dark it may look —"

Max opened the door. Somehow, Annie wasn't terribly surprised to see Chief Saulter, his thin face as creased as a bassett hound's. He looked discomfited, irritated, and upset. And he wasn't alone. A heavyset man stood behind him.

"— you can count on me and Talleyrand —"

"Henny, I'm sorry, but the chief's here. I guess he wants to talk to us."

Max stood back to let them enter, and the bigger man surged past Saulter.

"Although," and Henny's tone was clearly irritated, "that circuit solicitor from Beaufort is being extremely uncooperative. Even more difficult than Inspector Piper is at times. I shall prevail, of course," and the line buzzed.

Hildegarde Withers, no doubt about it.

Annie hung up, turned to face the new arrivals, and took an immediate, visceral dislike to the chief's companion. A good six inches taller and fifty pounds heavier than Saulter, he radiated a take-charge arrogance. He had bulging blue eyes, he was too heavy for his buttoned vest, and cinnamon after-shave emanated from him in a heady wave. His watery blue eyes fastened on her avidly. He reminded her unpleasantly of an osprey spotting an especially succulent catfish. He bounded toward her.

"Good morning," the stranger boomed. It was a courtroom voice, mellifluous, sonorous, and as contrived as a rock star's entrance. "Miss Laurance, I presume."

Annie nodded, but before she could speak, he swept on.

"I am Brice Willard Posey, circuit solicitor, and I've decided to assist the chief in his investigations." His eyes oozed speculation. "So *you* are the girl in the case."

Annie bristled.

Saulter, his voice carefully devoid of expression, inserted, "Mr. Posey came over this morning, as soon as he got some calls from the media."

Posey shot Saulter a sharp look, but the chief's corrugated face was bland. The circuit solicitor took a deep breath. "I intend to pursue every lead no matter where it takes me. I shall do my duty without fear or favor."

There hardly seemed to be an appropriate answer. Laurance temper rising, Annie gestured for them to be seated.

Posey dropped heavily into a chair and focused a hard stare on Annie. Interrogation intimidation look number two, she decided.

It wasn't lost on Max, of course. He shed

his usual air of amiability, raked Posey with a measuring glance, dismissed him, and turned politely to Saulter. "You want to talk to us, Chief?"

Posey flushed angrily. He leaned forward, his hands flat against his beefy thighs. "As circuit solicitor for this county, I have made a name for myself by my forthright battle against crime."

Chief Saulter sat in a wicker chair and watched, thin-lipped.

Posey's bulging blue eyes shone with self-absorption. "I have fought the good fight, and I'm not afraid to face the voters, now or in the future."

Annie knew she shouldn't, but some temptations cannot be resisted. "And you're running for office? Right now?" she asked, her voice light and innocent.

Posey's response revealed his respect for and interest in female voters. "A public servant is *always* running for office, Miss Laurance." He paused ponderously, hoping perhaps that she was capable of grasping this concept. "I have made it clear always that I will never be influenced by the wealth or social position of those who break the law." He nodded slowly in self-approbation. "And I cannot be seduced from my duty by the wiles of the so-called gentler sex." Those slimy blue eyes climbed over Annie.

"How admirable!" Max: proclaimed. "A bully position."

Annie hoped he wouldn't lay it on too thick. But Max had had enough of Brice Willard Posey. Once again, he turned toward the chief. "What can we do for you?"

"To tell the truth —" Saulter began.

"The truth reveals men and women as they are. In all their sickness of the flesh." Posey's inflection rendered the last word exceedingly nasty. "We know the truth about you, Miss Laurance. The stricken widow has revealed all."

Annie was trying so hard to envision Sheridan as a stricken widow that she missed some of his next speech.

"— shameless advances."

She stared at him blankly.

Max intervened. "Posey, you've been had. It was a joke."

"A joke?" Posey demanded, his voice rising. "How can you describe this woman's actions" — (Annie was fascinated by her new characterization. It put her right on a level with a hapless Perry Mason client.) — "as humorous? To flaunt herself as an object of sexual attraction to a happily married man, is that humorous? To

210

brazenly pursue this man, despite his continued protestations of disinterest, is that humorous?"

Sweat beaded Posey's face. He glistened with fervor. "And we know what can happen when *sex* is thwarted! It can corrode the soul, destroy human balance, lead a morally bankrupt individual to that greatest of all sins, murder!"

Posey breathed heavily in the following silence. Annie and Max studied him with the curiosity Sherlock Holmes might bestow upon a heretofore unfamiliar tobacco ash.

"A joke?" Saulter asked quietly.

Annie turned to him gratefully. "Yes, Chief. Shane made a pass at me. I told him to drop dead." She paused, realizing that her choice of words might be unfortunate. "I mean, I told him to get lost. It made him mad, of course. The great male ego. Anyway, when we got back inside that night at the party, he made this scene, pretending I'd been running after him and —"

"So you admit it!" Posey roared, jumping to his fee.

Her head swung back toward the circuit solicitor.

"You were outside with Shane, out in the garden of the man's very own house with his wife just feet away!"

"I wasn't with him," she objected. "I was —"

"You are tangled up in your own lies!" he thundered. "But I shall wrench the truth from you." Heavy face twisted in concentration, blue eyes glowing, he shook an accusing finger at Annie. "You, Miss Laurance, you must stand up and face the truth of your character, Home-breaker. Lustful predator. Wanton, whoring —"

Max lunged, fists doubled.

Chief Saulter and Annie moved at once.

And so did Posey. For a man of his bulk, he exhibited extreme agility, writhing side-ways to lunge behind Saulter.

Max stopped, fists raised, eyes blazing at the large cowering figure, and began to laugh. "As the Chinese say, paper tigers cannot bite."

Grateful that his sense of the absurd had saved her fiancé from perpetrating an assault upon an officer of the law, Annie joined in, more from nervous relief than amusement.

Posey's face turned an unhealthy ocher. Chest heaving, he glowered.

Saulter watched, his eyes flicking uneasily from face to face.

Posey pursed his fleshy lips and snarled, "You are a violent man, aren't you, Mr.

Darling?" The protuberant blue eyes glowed with hatred. "Violent. Impulsive. Loath to suffer encroachment upon your beloved."

Annie stiffened.

"Let us consider *you*, Mr. Darling. Engaged to a woman who has lost all control over her actions because of her lust for another man." Obviously, he had her confused with the female as depicted in hardboileds. Posey took his favorite stance, accusatory finger waggling in beat with his attack. "You have the strongest motive of all, the wounded soul of the lover cast aside." Posey leaned forward, though still well behind Saulter. "Isn't it a fact, Mr. Darling, that you had reason to be very angry with Shane Petree? Isn't it a fact that the woman you hoped to marry had lost her head over him? Isn't it a fact that Shane Petree rebuffed her advances publicly on Sunday night?"

This was too much. Unable to contain herself any longer, Annie erupted. "Wait a minute! This is ridiculous. This —"

"Ridiculous?" Posey bellowed. "Yes, it seems ridiculous that any young woman would be so foolish as to throw herself at a happily married man. But that is the fact. Mrs. Petree has told me all about it, how her husband said you chased after him, kept pestering him, even though he told you repeatedly that he wasn't interested."

"My God, it was a joke! Shane made it all up. He was such a —"

The circuit solicitor's knowing look didn't falter. "Mrs. Petree was reluctant to tell us, but you have to come out with the truth in a murder case."

At that, Annie exploded, even though Saulter shook his head warningly. "It was a lie! My God, ask around the island. That hot-panted lowlife was in and out of half the beds on Broward's Rock, but not mine. Now, you go talk to people and —"

Posey's glance dripped a stomach-curdling mixture of self-righteousness and pity. "Of course, Miss Laurance, you know the truth of it, better than anyone. And in your heart, you know that *you* are guilty of murder. *Your* licentious actions have led this man" — he gestured toward Max, who raised a mildly inquiring eyebrow — "to break that most solemn commandment which separates us from lower beings. You have incited murder," he intoned, "and you shall not escape the judgment of your fellows."

Gathering steam, Posey swung toward Max. Even Hamilton Burger was never this

214

obnoxious! "They tell me you stood there Sunday evening and *smiled*, Mr. Darling, when this woman's public humiliation occurred, but the festering began in your heart, you can't deny it. Outwardly, you appeared unmoved, but your devotion to this . . . woman, the woman you wanted to make your wife, can't be denied. Did you not even attempt to attack the *law* itself when her true character was described? It is transparently clear that your apparent unconcern was the product of a clever plan, the creation of a mind diseased by injury and determined to seek its insidious revenge. Are you going to pretend that you are so little a man that you would have stood by and let the woman you love fling herself at another man?" Posey shook his head in answer to his own question. "Events speak for themselves. Who is injured? Whose pride has been affronted? Who is accustomed at all times to deference because of his exalted social position? *We* know who," he concluded portentously.

Max folded his arms and grinned. "I'll bet you make a helluva stump speech."

Saulter sucked his breath in.

Annie flapped her hands, but Max ignored her. Good grief, couldn't he see that he was infuriating Posey? Lordy, did Max *want* to get arrested?

The phone rang.

Posey jerked his head imperiously at Saulter, but he never took his eyes off Max.

Annie didn't even have time to object. After all, it was *her* phone. But the chief answered and, after a moment's exchange, handed her the receiver.

"Hello," she cried abstractedly.

"Annie, my sweet, *I* will take care of everything."

Annie heard Laurel's dulcet tone and, louder and stronger, Posey's infuriated roar.

"I'm in touch with Mrs. Crabtree, and *everything* will be all right . . ."

"You think you're very, very smart, don't you, Mr. Darling. We'll see how —"

". . . crowning the veil with myrtle . . ."

"— know a motive when I see one and —"

". . . sweetest custom! Ten yards of sheeting wrapped round and round the bride!"

"You didn't like it one little bit, did you, Mr. Darling?"

"Really, the Irish have some wonderful ideas. Drench the fruitcake with brandy!

Of course, we can't let Uncle Waldo have any because . . ."

"Laurel," Annie shouted, "we've had a murder!"

There was an instant's pause. Posey's heavy head swung toward her in irritation.

"Oh, of course," Laurel cried. "I know all about it. That's why I rang up. I *know* how you and Max are, always *delving*. So put your mind at ease, Annie. I will take care of everything."

The connection broke.

"How's Laurel?" Max asked cheerfully.

Take care of everything. A thrill of horror shot through Annie. Where *was* Laurel? What in heaven's name was she *planning*? What would she do *next*?

"Darling, I'm not through with you," Posey barked.

"I rather think you are," Max observed with a distinct lack of interest. "You bore me."

Posey's face twitched with anger and vindictiveness. "You'd better listen, Mr. Darling. You think you can get away with murder because you're a rich man. You're used to having your way, everybody kowtowing to you. Well, I can tell you that Brice Posey doesn't kowtow." His eyes glittered. "Oh, yes, you have the strongest motive of all. You didn't want to lose Miss Laurance, did you? You made sure she couldn't belong to Shane Petree. You murdered him — and I'm going to see that you pay with your life."

"Are you arresting me?" Max inquired, without a quiver of concern.

The prosecutor's jaw bunched. "Not quite yet, Mr. Darling."

"Wait a minute. Wait *a minute*." Annie turned furiously toward Chief Saulter. "Can't you tell this — this *idiot* — anything? My God, Shane Petree's the last man in the world I would ever have been interested in. Max thought the whole thing was funny! He *knows* I'm not interested in anybody else — and certainly not Shane. Chief, can't you tell him?"

Posey shot a look of clear dislike at Saulter. "A good investigating officer *never* lets personal friendship interfere with duty."

Annie felt a chill. She could almost smell Posey's blood lust. Dizzily, she pressed her fingers against her throbbing temples. Max didn't shoot anyone — *couldn't* shoot anyone. . . .

"Can't you test for gunpowder residue?" she demanded. Scientific detection, *à la* Dr. Thorndyke, that was the ticket. "That will clear Max. A paraffin test. That will do it."

Posey's mouth curved disdainfully. "That's no longer done, Miss Laurance. It was not a reliable test. The modern police department — and certainly we pride ourselves upon our knowledge of and use of the most innovative techniques — relies upon neutron activation analysis, atomic absorption spectrophotometry, or scanning electron microscopy/energy dispersive X-ray analysis." He didn't stumble once. She wondered how he'd do with a pint of pickled peppers. "Unfortunately, in the instant case, we are too late. Many, many hours too late. As any skilled ballistics expert can attest, gunshot residue remains on the hands for up to six hours unless, of course, a suspect has the opportunity to remove any detritus with the application of soap and water. In our present situation, there was more than enough time for the murderer to remove all traces of his insidious act. If careful procedure had been followed in the extant case, we might have flushed our murderer immediately." His protuberant eyes focused on Max again. "But *I* am now on the case, and I will discover the truth — wherever it leads!"

He swung around, chest out, and strode

to the door. Saulter followed reluctantly. The chief flashed a look of sheer disgust over his shoulder.

Annie whirled toward Max, her eyes bright with alarm, her chin jutting out with determination. "Max, that odious circuit-whatever is lusting for your scalp. And you just egged him on!"

"I did, didn't I?" he agreed cheerfully. "Let him lust. The fat man doesn't scare me. Did you see him duck behind Saulter?" He chuckled.

"He who laughs last," she warned. A few more Chinese aphorisms, and they could share a Charlie Chan button. But, actually, if wasn't funny. Posey *meant* every word.

"Max, we've got to be serious. We're going to have to find the murderer ourselves. Like Nick and Nora Charles."

Like Nick and Nora? Hey, do I get a martini?"

11

Max proved to be about as tractable as Nick Charles. They argued all the way out to his car. Annie fumed, "Why are you so impossibly stubborn! So incredibly obtuse! So infuriatingly pigheaded!"

He wasn't even fazed. She didn't know which exasperated her the most, his refusal to cooperate or his winsome confidence that his attitude was the essence of reason.

"Annie, love," he said kindly. "You really do take life much too seriously indeed. In fact, Laurel and I were talking about that just the other day."

"You were?" He didn't even notice the dangerous edge to her voice.

"Yes. She *worries* about you. She's concerned that you are so wound up, so intense." His limpid blue eyes regarded her pensively. "She said, 'Max, my sweet, we must lift the burden from dear Annie's shoulders. You and I.'"

This dreadful prospect was almost enough to deflect her attention from the matter at hand, but not quite, though she lodged the worrisome phrase in her mind for later consideration.

As he dropped into the bucket seat, Annie made a last-ditch effort. "Max, this isn't a game. Posey wants your scalp — and Saulter can't do a thing about it. So we've got to get busy and see what we can find out." She bent down to peer at him. "What do you have to do today that's more important than saving your neck?"

"Oh, another engagement elsewhere." He put the Porsche in gear.

Annie clamped her hand onto the doorjamb. "You are avoiding my question."

He smiled winningly and blew her a kiss. "Have a good morning, honey, and —"

"Max, where are you going?"

"Here and there," he replied airily, waving his hand.

"Where?"

"Oh, roundabout." The car began to ease backwards.

Annie intensified her grip. "Max! Aren't you going to help me find out what's happening?"

"Nope. I am a private citizen. I am not responsible for the investigation of crime in Beaufort County. The duly elected officials of said county can pursue any and all investigations they like, but count me out."

"Posey's going to investigate you right into the county jail," she snapped.

"Annie, Annie, I'm afraid Laurel's right. We need to help you relax. The idea of my being considered seriously as a murder suspect is patently absurd."

She shook her head, then brushed hair from her face, as the Porsche, unleashed, jumped backwards. Max waved a cheery farewell.

She stared after the bright red car for a moment, then stamped her foot, and stalked toward her Volvo.

In the storeroom of Death on Demand, Annie hunched over a notepad. It had a few scrawls on it, notations which would be unintelligible to other eyes. But she knew that long, stick-of-bologna shape was Max's neck, which apparently she was going to have to save all by herself. The anvil-shaped appendage attached to one end was his bloated head, swollen out of proportion by an unsquashable self-confidence. A bulgy, gorillalike body repre- sented Posey. She, of course, was the robed figure with a happy smile, topped by a halo. The pen moved, and she added another haloed figure. The Saint, of course. What would Leslie Charteris's suave sleuth do, if transported across the Atlantic and faced with her problem? Probably bust a few heads and manage something spectacularly audacious.

But this wasn't the proper milieu for The Saint. He belonged behind the wheel of a racing car or scaling the side of a French chateau. No, she needed inspiration nearer home. Nero Wolfe was too cerebral, and besides, she didn't have an Archie since Max had disappeared upon some obscure errand. (For his mother? The thought terrified her.) Miss Silver's gimlet eye would soon pierce the veil of obscurity, but Annie's group of suspects wouldn't sit tamely in a drawing room to be gently questioned.

The storeroom door swung silently open, and Ingrid poked her head in. "Chief Saulter's coming up the boardwalk. Shall I tell him you've left?" Hilda Adams couldn't have been more ready to stand watchdog.

Annie had much to do. Most of all, she needed to think. But the chief might know something helpful. "No, thanks, Ingrid. Send him on back."

Nodding, Ingrid bustled to the front of the shop.

Inspiration. Well, she couldn't do better than Miss Marple. What was it the sleuth of St. Mary Mead always warned? Things are often not what they seem. Could that be the situation here? But how could she know what was real and what was show? What did the long series of malicious pranks have to do with Shane's murder? Nothing? Everything?

She turned when a tap sounded on the door. Saulter looked at her mournfully, like a hound dog left behind on hunt day. "Thought I'd drop by."

"Come on in, Chief." She waved him to the other straight chair in the cramped storeroom. It was wedged between the receiving table and the back door.

He pulled it out, turned it around, and straddled it. "Sure sorry about this morning, Annie."

"Not your fault," she said quickly.

Some of his gloom lifted. "Glad you see that. Nothin' I can do about Posey. He's running for reelection — and he sure hates rich folks. Thing about it is, Max is the kind of rich folks he hates most. Born to it. He sort of likes Harley Jenkins. He made all his own money."

"Chief, you don't think —" She swallowed. "He doesn't have enough to really go after Max, does he?"

Saulter scratched at his sparse topping of graying brown hair. "Hell of it is, Max is as good a suspect as anybody. I mean, nobody sticks out."

Annie sketched a dangling noose on her notepad. "What about Sheridan? Doesn't everybody look at the wife first."

His sallow face colored, and he stared down at the floor. "Don't let on I told you, but it looks like she's got the hell of an alibi."

"Alibis are made to be broken."

"Hers is Harley Jenkins," he mumbled. "They both swear they checked into the Crown Shore Motel before ten and didn't leave the room 'til it after midnight. And it checks out. Windows open onto a patio. Bartender on the patio says nobody came out that way. Desk clerk swears nobody poked a nose through the door."

"How long's she been sneaking around with Harley?" Annie sketched in a four-poster.

He lifted his faded brown eyes. "You think she set it up?"

"Fortunate for her, isn't it? Wouldn't *you* have looked at her pretty closely?" Annie added a row of hatchets for chopping cherry trees.

"I would have." He poked at a copy of H. R. F. Keating's *A Perfect Murder.* "Tell you what, Annie. I'll see what I can find out, let you know."

"You're all right, Chief," she said softly. He reddened again, then stood and returned the chair to its place. "Wish I could do better than that. I'd like to find the killer right under Posey's nose."

"Maybe we can, Chief."

"Now look, Annie. You be careful, hear? Don't go pokin' in a rattler's hidey-hole."

"I'll call you if I find anything at all." She reached out and gripped his gnarled hand. "I promise."

"You do that." He rubbed his chin. "You might be lookin' out for a discarded gun. We haven't found the twenty-two yet. Course it will take days to go through all the stuff in the prop storage area."

She hadn't thought about the gun and what might have happened to it. A .22. She sighed. They were easy to come up with.

He paused in the doorway. "I'll get back to you, if I find out anything to help Max."

And what was *she* going to do to help Max? Even if he stubbornly resisted help. And where was Max right this minute? She shook away the lingering feeling of uneasiness and glanced down at her notepad.

227

Was the jaunty figure of The Saint looking at her reproachfully? What was her plan of action?

The phone rang.

"Death on Demand." She and Ingrid answered simultaneously.

A crisp English accent announced, "Murder does not sprout overnight. As any half-wilted gardener well knows, a bloom is the culmination of months of germination. But I can dig up the truth. I intend to find out every germane fact in Shane's life. Even if it smells like a compost heap. I have succeeded in locating his best friend. Another womanizer, apparently. And I intend to wring the facts out of this young man."

Annie was impatient. She didn't have time for Henny's foolishness. She needed to *think!*

Henny didn't wait for an answer. "The seed of this crime shall be unearthed." The line went dead.

John Sherwood's Celia Grant, no doubt. Until now, Annie had enjoyed Henny's sleuthing. But nothing was very funny with that lout Posey lusting for Max's scalp. The fact that Max refused to admit his peril only made it worse. Even her storeroom was gloomy and somber. She'd always enjoyed working here in the mornings, with sunlight spilling in through the single high window, but now a thick bank of clouds presaged a storm and the air was heavy. She flicked on the overhead light. Several cartons needed to be opened. One was from a used book dealer in London and should include an autographed jacketed first edition of Michael Gilbert's *Smallbone Deceased*. Normally, that would have been the highlight of her morning. Now, she gave it a single, disinterested glance and began to pace.

Max was in trouble.

Well, if not actually in acute jeopardy at the moment, was approaching, as certainly as the coming storm. Thunder crackled in the distance, and the overhead light wavered. Okay, Max was at risk, and she had to figure out how to save him. Clearly, it was up to her to find the murderer of Shane Petree.

So, the important question, the question that had to be answered, was why?

Why was Shane Petree murdered?

And there were other questions that could determine the parameters of the problem:

Was the murder a culmination of the sabotage?

Was the murder intended to prevent the staging of *Arsenic and Old Lace*? Was it part of a conspiracy directed by Harley Jenkins III to ruin the theater company's season?

Did Eugene murder Shane to take his place as Teddy? Did Sam murder Shane so that Eugene could be Teddy, thereby enhancing the play's chances of success?

Was the murder independent of the sabotage?

Why did the murder occur at the rehearsal, when the number of suspects was so limited?

Could someone have slipped into the theater, killed Shane, and escaped again unseen?

Where was the gun?

And — fascinating to pursue — what was the point of shooting Shane during the play at all? Why not gun him down in his driveway or the parking lot of the Island Hills Country Club? Did this suggest an urgency to the crime, some reason that the murder had to occur at that particular time?

Annie paced away from the table. Every question only suggested another. And she still had no inkling of the answer to the most important question of all: Why did Shane die?

She whirled around, returned to the worktable, and looked down at her notepad.

The jaunty figure of The Saint rollicked near the top of the page.

She took it as an omen. What could she do that would be audacious?

It was the Trump Tower of Broward's Rock. A two-story waterfall cascaded down shiny blocks of quartz in a cypress-walled atrium. Black-stemmed ebony spleenwort sprouted from an oyster-shell mound, and six-foot royal ferns and saw grass recreated a low-country salt marsh. Tasteful gold-block letters along a foot-high marble wall proclaimed HALCYON DEVELOPMENT INC. On a sunny day, the water and stone glittered like diamonds, but this morning it looked more like a stream of pewter in the sullen, storm-bleached light. The clouds were building, darkening. It was going to rain soon, which, of course, always spelled increased sales for all the shops, including Death on Demand, as beach-banished vacationers milled idly among the tables and shelves, with gloomy glances at the rain-smeared windows. Normally, Annie would be scooting back to the shop to help Ingrid with the overload, but today Ingrid would have to manage by herself.

The peroxide blonde at the reception desk flicked her a bored glance.

Annie took out one of her cards. It was crimson with *Death on Demand* in black letters, an Italian Renaissance silver dagger as a logo, and the inscription, *Crimes For Every Taste.* In the lower right-hand corner, it read, *Annie Laurance, Prop.* On the back, she quickly wrote: *Could we visit about a matter of great interest to both of us? Annie Laurance.*

The receptionist took the card and moved languidly up the steps of the red-carpeted stairs. When she returned, a sparkle of curiosity lighted her vacant eyes. "This way, Miss Laurance."

Harley Edward Jenkins III's office was on the second floor, with a commanding view of the harbor through a window that filled an entire wall. He sat with his back to the panorama of anchored yachts and battened-down sailboats. The coming storm sent choppy waves rolling across the harbor to slap against the docks, creating a lace filigree of spume.

Holding her card between a beefy thumb and forefinger, Harley rose as the girl showed Annie in, then waited until the door closed behind the receptionist. Clearly, Jenkins was king of his domain. Everything was on a grand scale to match his overpowering physical presence: outsize leather club chairs, an enormous painting of duck hunters on a crisp fall dawn that filled the wall opposite the harbor window, a cypress coffee table with a five-foot diameter.

"Miss Laurance." His red-veined face was bland, but his cold blue eyes were wary. He waggled the card. "You intrigue me. What possible interest could we have in common?" A jovial smile curved his thick lips, though it didn't touch those watchful eyes. "But forgive me, won't you have some coffee? Or perhaps a glass of wine?"

She smiled, too. "No, thank you, Mr. Jenkins. I don't want to take up too much of your time."

He waved a meaty hand toward one of the red leather chairs near his desk. "My time is completely at your disposal, Ms. Laurance."

This kind of repartee was right up Judge Dee's alley. But Annie found it tiresome, so she didn't mince words.

"We do have an interest in common. I assume, sir, that you don't like to be hood-winked?"

He lowered himself into the embrace of his leather chair. "Nobody fools me."

"So you pride yourself on your ability to judge men. But can you be sure of judging women as well?"

He waited, regarding her with the unblinking, inimical stare of a mass-produced Buddha.

"When did Sheridan Petree start pursuing you?"

Slowly, his huge fist closed around her card, crushing it. His eyes peered out with reptilian coldness from their thick folds of flesh. "I don't care for your implication, little lady."

And I don't like you, buster, she longed to say. Little lady, indeed! But she wasn't here to slug it out over male chauvinism, she reminded herself. Max, the stubborn oaf, needed her.

"But she did pursue you, didn't she?"

Jenkins hunched at his massive ebony desk, unmoving as a granite mountain.

Finally, the words as crisp as fresh dollar bills, he threw it out on the table. "You want to prove she set up her alibi the night her husband was murdered."

"Right." Annie leaned forward in her chair. This could make or break Sheridan's alibi.

Jenkins rolled the cardboard ball that had been her card in his fingers, then dropped it in his ashtray and reached for his humidor. Ignoring Annie, he selected a round, fat cigar, snipped off its end, and lit it. The acrid fumes rolled toward her.

Finally, the calculating eyes lifted to her face. "Of course, Sheridan had to tell the cops about you and Shane." He took a deep draw on the cigar. Apparently nobody'd ever told him not to inhale. "So you have an ax to grind."

"I'd say it's important to both of us."

He leaned back and looked reflectively past her at the hunting scene. "I got to talking to Sheridan in the bar at the club one night. About a month ago." The heavy face was thoughtful. "Kind of on the spur of the minute."

"Is that a regular haunt of yours? Do you go to the club bar often?"

Once again he emanated alertness, like a tiger poised to leap. "Almost every night."

She was silent. Let him think about it. She smiled brightly. "So, if you're doing Sheridan a favor by saying she was with you last night —"

He made a chest-deep noise which she belatedly recognized as a laugh. "Young lady, I wouldn't do my mother that kind of favor."

With a sinking feeling, Annie realized that she believed him. Her disappointment was so acute her chest ached. Sheridan's alibi was real. She and Jenkins were pursuing pleasure at the very moment someone blew Shane away. Then inspiration struck. It wasn't much to salvage, but it was all she could see at the moment. An alibi for Sheridan was also an alibi for Jenkins. After all, wasn't that how it worked in *Death on the Nile*?

"How important was it to you that the players' summer season fail?"

Harley had no problem following the bouncing ball. "You thinking about the troubles you people had?"

"You know about them?"

"Sure. Sheridan told me. I thought they were pretty funny, 'til somebody killed that cat. That was shitty."

In Annie's opinion, gunning free-flying birds out of a November sky was equally shitty, but she said mildly, "You like cats?"

"Crazy about 'em. Got six. Abyssinians. And they're smart as the deuce." His tone was admiring.

Of course, Hitler loved dogs and Aryan children, too.

"Besides," Jenkins said easily, "Sheridan's convinced me I'm being wrong-headed about this theater stuff. I'm going to compromise."

"Really?"

"Sure thing. I've got a phone call in to Burt, and he's going to be pleased. Sheridan's going to donate the money to build a memorial theater to Shane. The Petree Theater, over on Marsh Road." He gestured in the direction opposite the harbor. "And to sweeten the pot for Burt, I'm going to find a restaurant to go into the spot here on the harbor. That will bring his little gift shop even more customers. So, you see, everything's going to work out fine."

And he had no earthly motive to sabotage the players' season. None, ladies and gentlemen. He was purer than Ivory Soap flakes.

Savagely, Annie wished she could read those marble-blue eyes better. Right now they glistened with false good cheer.

He rose, and she stood, too. He walked her to the door, his hand companionably on her elbow.

She gave it one last shot. "Was it your idea or Sheridan's to build a memorial theater?"

He quirked an eyebrow. "Sheridan's. Any

reason why she shouldn't?"

No. No reason, Annie thought. It was a graceful gesture on the part of the bereaved widow, and an equally graceful response by the real estate magnate. Just peachy for everybody.

"So, little lady, I guess if anybody was sabotaging your play, maybe they had it in for Burt or Sam."

She looked up at him sharply.

Harley smiled good-humoredly, a man with a rock-solid alibi.

As Annie turned up the boardwalk, the first large raindrops pelted down. The tourist bureau never stressed it, but June, July, and August were the wet months. How could one have all this lovely subtropical growth without the liquid gold of summer? At the steps to Death on Demand, she started to duck inside, changed her mind (Ingrid could handle everything), picked up speed, and ran, her steps reverberating on the wood. Dodging tourists seeking shelter, she crunched across the oyster-shell parking lanes, unlocked her Volvo, and flung herself inside.

Rain sluiced down. She stared at the opaque windshield and brooded. She'd started with the premise that Sheridan had used Jenkins to forge a fake alibi, and now toyed with the idea that Jenkins had used Sheridan for the same purpose. Jenkins's words had the ring of truth (and corroboration by a bartender and desk clerk), but the rock-solid alibi simply aroused her suspicions. Would either Sheridan or Jenkins support an alibi for the other for reasons of their own? It was possible. Not likely, but possible. And she knew Henny was even now scouring that room at the Crown Shore Motel for a hidden exit.

So, she wasn't quite ready to cross Sheridan and Jenkins off her suspect list. She kept them there along with, of course, the three Hortons, Burt, Carla, Sam, Eugene, Arthur, and Hugo. A purist would include Henny. But some things were possible, and some weren't. She'd just as soon believe she or Max had done it, as consider Henny.

She trotted out the motives, one by one, like obedient sheep.

T.K. — the wronged husband and infuriated father.

Janet — would she rather see Shane dead than share him?

Cindy — a determination to destroy what she might be losing.

Burt — the success-obsessed president

of the players. How far would he go to re-move the weak link from the play?

Carla — she was a loner, who took great strength from her community involvement. Had she decided Shane was an obstacle that had to be removed?

Sam — how badly did Sam want the play to succeed?

Eugene — had his obsession with TR passed the bounds of sanity?

Arthur — the charming, raffish Dr. Ein-stein. How important was the play to him? Or could he have some other reason for wishing Shane dead?

Hugo — an arrogant, determined man, who wanted a chance to succeed in yet an-other arena. Did he see himself and his goals as paramount?

The flood of rain eased into a softer pat-tern, and she began to discern the outline of two ragged palmettos and a hibiscus.

Annie beat an impatient tattoo on the steering wheel. She felt as if her mind were fuzzy and indistinct, that she wasn't seeing the true pattern of the crime. It was ob-scured by too many motives, too many emotions, too many suspects.

Maybe it was time to get back to the ba-sics and take a good hard look at the man who had been Shane Petree.

★ ★ ★

She followed the maid up a freestanding spiral staircase. Despite the rain-sheathed windows, the bronze balustrade gleamed like gold. At the top, the maid stepped back and gestured toward the end of the hall.

Annie's shoes clicked against the polished hall tiles. She paused at the open door.

Sheridan Petree looked up from a desk of glass and chrome. She sat in a butterfly chair with a black-and-silver cotton fabric. The floor was of pale pink Paros marble, and the walls were of brushed aluminum. Rain pattered against uncurtained windows. The only color in the study came from her dusty blond hair and the apricot sweats she wore. Designer sweats, of course. Annie suddenly felt hot and unattractive in her yellow slicker.

"What a surprise," Sheridan said coolly. "Do come in."

"I know this isn't a good time to call, but I felt you would share my concern." She pulled off the raincoat, spattering drops on the marble floor.

Sheridan put down a pen by an open notebook. Her smooth, unlined face was composed.

Annie perched on an angular aluminum chair, which was roughly as comfortable as resting on a pile of crowbars, and crumpled the damp raincoat in her lap. "I'm right in supposing you want your husband's murderer found?"

Unreadable amber eyes stared at her for a long moment. "I surely do." Her voice was musical. But did it have an undercurrent of amusement?

Sheridan flipped open a crystal box and lifted out a cork-tipped cigarette. She lit it, then said, "Oh, would you care for a cigarette?"

"No, thank you."

"You don't smoke, of course."

"No."

"You just do everything right, don't you, Annie?" Now, a clear tone of amusement. "Don't smoke. Try to solve murders." She blew out a plume of smoke. "Even going so far as to try and destroy the poor widow's alibi."

So Jenkins had warned her.

"I had to check."

"The police have already done so." Sheridan regarded her without warmth.

"The solicitor is a lot more interested in persecuting Max than he is in discovering the murderer."

242

"So you came to talk to me." Those amber eyes locked on Annie's face. "Are you still suspicious of my alibi?"

"I'm always suspicious."

Sheridan tapped a long ash into a marble ashtray. "Why, that surely does worry me." Sarcasm rippled like a snake gliding into water.

Annie felt a violent impulse to slap Sheridan Petree right across the face just as hard as she could. She clenched her hands in her lap. This woman was *not* going to provoke her.

"Look, Sheridan, so far as I can see, you aren't likely to throw yourself onto a burning bier in grief. And Shane did have his . . . proclivities. Maybe you got tired of him running around on you."

The smooth face remained placid. Then Sheridan laughed. It was a clear, chiming laugh that sounded like faraway temple bells. Her perfect, red lips curved. "I don't suppose I begrudge you that. After all, you've got real trouble. I mean, I hated to tell the police about you and Shane." Those tawny eyes opened wide. "But I just had to tell the truth, now didn't I? Of course, Shane was so attractive to women, I hardly blame you. Poor boy. Women just *threw* themselves at him. It was such a bore."

For a moment, a red haze obscured Annie's vision, but she managed not to fling herself at her tormentor. She controlled her breathing and merely said, "I'm surprised you believed that silly story. I would have thought you'd know Shane better than that."

The amber eyes suddenly, for just a vivid instant, burned with fury. Oh, yes, Sheridan knew better. She knew she was married to a womanizer, but she'd thrown Annie and Max to the wolves without a qualm. Not a very likable lady, Mrs. Petree.

They regarded each other unblinkingly for a long moment, then Sheridan stubbed out her cigarette.

Annie knew her time was almost up. She made one last, desperate attempt. "Who do *you* think killed him?"

The question, oddly, caught Sheridan by surprise. Annie could have sworn from the sudden flicker in her eyes that she hadn't even *thought* about it. That shocked her. She knew Sheridan and Shane were totally self-centered and predatory. But, for God's sake, didn't Sheridan care enough even to have wondered?

The rain beat against the windows in a soft, insistent tattoo.

Sheridan fluttered her hands helplessly. "Why, I don't know, really. It's all so strange." She gave Annie a puzzled look. "Shane always had women — and their husbands — mad at him. I suppose T.K.'s the logical choice." For an instant, ugliness quivered in those light eyes. "Or Max."

Annie gripped the metal sides of the chair to keep herself in place.

Sheridan reached out for another cigarette, lit it. "But it seems so strange to mix it all up with the play. I don't understand it at all. Actually, Annie," and she leaned forward, "I don't think it will ever be solved. It's one of those really weird murders." She drew deeply on her cigarette. "Maybe it was just something that got out of hand."

That was a unique description of murder. "Out of hand?"

"All those peculiar things that happened, that dummy in the attic and the cut curtain rope and that brown cat —" Sheridan said vaguely.

Orange, Annie thought, not brown. But Sheridan was repeating what she'd been told, so that showed anew how information could be garbled upon repetition. Just like "mess beetle" in Phoebe Atwood Taylor's *The Perennial Boarder.*

But she considered Sheridan's suggestion. Something that got out of hand. Then, sharply, almost angrily, she rejected it. Murder, unless a product of madness, was committed to achieve a particular goal. She must discover the *reason* for Shane's demise, and that meant focusing on Shane.

"This last week, Sheridan, did Shane do anything different? Anything unusual?"

Once again, surprise flickered on Sheridan's face. Surprise and wariness?

"Different?"

"Did anything happen to upset him?" That last night, Shane had been so impatient for the rehearsal to end. She remembered how mad they all were at him for rushing his lines. "Was he excited about anything?"

Sheridan smoked and considered the question. Finally, slowly, she nodded. "You know, he was in an exceptionally good mood. I mean, he was really up. Of course, I thought he was excited about the play. It had been a long time since he'd acted in anything." She ground the cigarette out and sighed. "I wish I could be more helpful. But I can't think of anything else. Poor Shane." The tawny eyes glistened with amusement. "He was in *such* a good humor."

Annie shivered. What a funny epitaph.

"Look, I know this sounds odd, but would you let me look at his room? Maybe at his desk?"

Sheridan hesitated, then gave a tiny, bored shrug. Annie followed her down the black-and-white-tiled hall to a room at the far end of the house. The door was closed. Sheridan opened it and let Annie precede her.

It was a massive master bedroom, but Annie knew the instant she set foot in it that this had been Shane's room alone. There was no scent — and Deneuve perfume wafted dreamily from Sheridan — and no life. Tweed-covered armchairs. A gray silk bedspread. Lacquered walls of dark orange. A glass-and-aluminum coffee table. It might have been an especially expensive guest suite in a southern California condo.

No books. No papers scattered about. No photographs. Nothing to indicate the last resident hadn't checked out weeks ago.

Sheridan leaned against the door as Annie crossed to the melon-colored desk. Tucking her rain slicker under her arm, she pulled open the drawer.

Several decks of cards. Some golf scorecards. A sheaf of papers. Annie poked at them. Maps of the intracoastal waterway. A Sony Walkman. The side drawers held neat stacks of *Sailing Magazine* and *Southern Boating Magazine.*

It didn't take long to look through the chest. It contained the usual: silk bikini shorts, waist size thirty-six, crew-neck T-shirts, sport and dress socks, polo shirts in an array of pastel colors, swimwear, tennis clothes. The contents of the closet revealed a taste for expensive and excellent sportswear.

Annie wanted, suddenly, to be out of this room and out of this house. If Shane had had any kind of life, he must not have lived it in these rooms.

Sheridan walked down to the front door with her.

"Are the services scheduled?" Annie asked.

"Services?" Sheridan opened the door. "Oh, Shane didn't believe in all that sort of thing. He'll be cremated."

"Oh."

"I'm having his ashes scattered at sea." She nodded. "Shane would like that. I'll ask one of his friends to take them out on his boat."

"Won't you go?" The question spurted out before Annie before Annie had time to realize how tactless it was.

Sheridan shivered. "No. No. I hate water."

Annie thought of all the boating magazines in that sterile room.

"Shane must have loved to sail?"

Sheridan's mouth twitched. "He certainly did. My God, he spent every minute he could on the water. But I just hate it."

The afternoon sparkled brightly, as though no rain cloud had neared the island. And it crawled by. Annie called Chief Saulter twice (he wasn't in), dropped over to Confidential Commissions three times (Max's secretary offered serenely that she *thought* he'd gone into Savannah, something to do with the wedding, she thought, then looked curiously at Annie as she stiffened as though poked by a cattle prod), paused once to look out over the marina at Shane's boat and wondered what tales it could tell, and even spent a fruitless half hour on the phone, trying to track down Henny.

When the phone rang at about four o'clock, she leapt for it.

"Annie?"

The amount of inquiry, interest, apprehension, determination, and excitement

projected in Laurel's husky pronouncement of her name triggered Annie's worst
fears. She was, literally, struck speechless.

"Annie, dear?"

She gripped the receiver and breathed
deeply.

"My sweet, do you have asthma?" Genuine concern spilled over the wire.

"No." Annie struggled for calm. "No,
absolutely not. Laurel, what have you been
up to?"

"I?" Innocence rang as sweetly as struck
crystal. "Everything and nothing," she
trilled. "Working, always working, though,
as you know, it is a labor of love, freely offered. Love for you and Maxwell. Love for
the world. Love for the beginnings of this
marvelous new age."

Annie waited, her hand cramping on the
receiver.

"Oh, well, I was just thinking about you.
I'll give a ring back later —"

"Laurel, I want to know —"

"I thought perhaps you were so over-
come with joy, you'd been unable to call,
but, obviously, Maxwell isn't back yet. Be
filled with the spirit of joy, love, and
charity, my dear."

Annie stared at the receiver, buzzing
with the broken connection.

She shook her head. If Laurel was now giving benedictions — Then a phrase neoned in her mind. *Maxwell isn't back yet.*

12

Henny was unemotional, matter-of-fact, when she rang up at six o'clock. "Subject exhibited change of manner in recent months. Less time in regular haunts. Friend glimpsed him with unknown redhead at The Red Rooster in Chastain. Not introduced, couple left upon sighting friend. Will pursue investigation." A California accent? Perhaps this was the methodical work of Sue Grafton's Kinsey Millhone.

At seven, Annie jumped up from a solitary dinner of nachos and a reheated chicken enchilada to grab her phone.

Saulter said morosely, "Posey spent the afternoon taking statements from people who heard Shane accuse you of chasing him at the Petrees' party Sunday night. He's laying the groundwork to show Max had a hell of a motive."

She could almost hear the clang of cell doors behind Max. "Chief, isn't Posey looking anywhere else? Isn't he finding out anything about Shane?"

"Posey's obsessed with Max. Dammit,

Max shouldn't have made him mad."

"Chief, Posey couldn't have arrested Max already, could he? Have him stashed in jail somewhere?" She explained in a rush. "Max dropped me off at the harbor this morning, and I haven't heard a word from him since. Nothing!"

Saulter's silence had a peculiar quality.

"Chief!" she demanded, with visions of Max held incommunicado in a window-less, hot room, hungry, ill-treated, and —

She realized Saulter was laughing. "You don't know where he is?"

"No." Simple, crisp, declarative.

"He's okay, Annie. Posey put a tail on him while he's on the mainland. But Max has spent the damndest afternoon! Well, better let him tell you about it. Anyway, I just called to let you know Posey wants everyone who was at the auditorium when Shane was killed to be there at nine tomorrow morning. Going to do a run-through of the play from the time Shane was last on stage 'til he was found. Give us a better time frame. See you then."

It was almost ten when Max called.

"Oh." She was casual. "How're tricks?"

"Now, Annie."

"Of course, I *know* too much communication in a relationship can be destructive.

253

I understand that each partner must retain independence. Certainly I support openness, freedom, autonomy." She drew her breath in sharply, then expelled it. "Max, where in the hell have you been?"

She was persuaded finally — after all, she was always willing to be reasonable; it was a hallmark of her character; everyone knew that — to meet him at the side entrance to the main reception room at the Island Hills Golf and Country Club.

Moonlight splashed across the shell-paved lot. Max hurried out to greet her.

She was friendly, of course, but reserved.

Max slipped his arm around her stiff shoulders, peered at her in the moonlight, then gave her a hug.

"This way," he boomed, like a tour guide en route to the crown jewels. At the side door, he paused and said reverentially, "Annie, you're going to be amazed." Implicit in this pronouncement was the suggestion that she might also be apologetic for her lack of enthusiasm.

He flung open the door.

She stepped into the darkened room.

"Lights," he cried, sweeping his hand against the wall.

The crystal chandelier glittered to life, and a hundred pinpoints of light shafted down on a table positioned beneath it.

Annie gasped.

Max was right in one respect. She was truly amazed.

The table was swathed in yards of shimmering, ice-white damask. In the center, in regal splendor, sat — Annie narrowed her eyes and warily approached.

"It had to be just the right color. That's what took all afternoon," he explained chattily, at her heels.

"It looks like —" She covered her eyes with her hands, pulled them away. "It looks like a wedding cake, with red icing, in the shape of a truncated pyramid. Topped by a live tree sapling."

"Carmine red." He glowed. Stepping back, he studied the cake critically. "Doesn't that red look smashing in contrast to the green of the fir tree?"

Roots in the cake. She recalled that fragment of his conversation with Laurel. She pointed wordlessly at the tree.

"Lovely custom," he declared avuncularly. "Bermuda. We can plant it and watch it grow, right along with our marriage." He sighed in satisfaction. "But it's the red that sets it off. I kept bringing swatches from the dressmaker to the bakery until they got it right." He beamed at her. "Mrs. Crabtree is a wonderful woman."

"A red wedding cake," she wailed.

CRIME SCENE
DO NOT ENTER

The bright yellow placard was taped to the closed doors of the center aisle. Annie and Max were the second to arrive Thursday morning. Sam greeted them like millionaire cousins, darting forward to grip Max's hand.

"Jesus, I'm glad you've come. This place is like a morgue." His fluffy fringe of blond hair was tousled. His right eye flickered with a nervous tic. "The cops called at dawn" — that was probably Sam's definition of eight a.m. — "said everybody had to get down here. I keep calling Burt, but his line's busy. No reason for this to louse up our rehearsals. Right? Eugene can play Teddy, and I'll take over O'Hara."

Obviously, he hadn't learned yet of Burt's decision to cancel rehearsals for the present, but continued to plan on opening Tuesday. "Sam, it's —"

"The play's ready. I'm ready. Everybody's a trouper. Right?"

"Relax," Annie urged. "It's okay, Sam. For now, everything's still go."

Sam clapped his hands in excitement, then hunched his shoulders and looked nervously around. "God, that's great," he breathed. "Course, I figured Burt would keep his head."

And had he also figured that Eugene was a good enough Teddy to vault the play to certain success?

The front door squeaked open. Annie turned in relief. Sam's good humor, under the circumstances, seemed more than a little callous.

Eugene lumbered inside. His face was appropriately presidential at a time of crisis, serious, steadfast, and somber.

Sam skipped eagerly toward him. "Eugene, listen, old man, you can go on as Teddy, can't you? I'll work with you all week. It's no biggie, right?"

Eugene forgot presidential gravity and beamed as he held up the blue-backed script. "Actually, I've been working on it. Got in a couple of hours this morning." He smoothed his brush mustache complacently. "Didn't want to let the players down."

Sam clapped him robustly on the shoulder. "That's a boy." He rubbed his hands together. "Now, when Burt comes, don't let him give us any gloom and doom. I mean, we can handle this."

She and Max exchanged pained glances, then her eyes widened in astonishment as she looked past Max at the opening door.

A figure, swathed in a brilliantly striped silk dress in which vermilion predominated, glided inside. The yellowish cast to the features, achieved by an artful application of makeup that included a subtle flattening of the eyes, made Henny Brawley look like a first cousin to the alligator Annie had spotted in a lagoon when they drove to the school.

There was no question of the role intended when Henny burst into a macaw-loud screech. "Wrongheaded, that's what the police are! And I intend to make sure there is no miscarriage of justice! It's the psychology that counts." This time, Henny was firmly cast as Gladys Mitchell's Dame Beatrice Bradley.

Vince Ellis strode into the foyer at her heels, his dark eyes alert and curious. Today, he carried a notebook, playing island reporter at the ready. He had nothing to worry about, Annie thought sourly. Saulter had given the all-clear to Vince, Ben Tippett, and Father Donaldson, who were alibied during the period when Shane was killed.

Arthur Killeen, his narrow face pale, slipped in and hovered unobtrusively at the edge of the circle around Vince.

Sam led the pack. "What's the deal? Have you heard anything? When can we rehearse again?"

Vince pointed at the police signs. "It may depend on when they release the auditorium."

Sam began to pace. "They can't stop us forever. This isn't Russia."

Annie moved a few feet away. She couldn't decide whether to be utterly disgusted with Sam or to appreciate his honesty. Obviously, to him, the only importance of Shane, dead or alive, was in relation to Sam's production of *Arsenic and Old Lace*. But did he have to be so appallingly single-minded?

Hugo arrived next. His icy gaze touched each person briefly. Annie felt chilled. Just so might the judge have surveyed the assembled houseguests in Christie's *And Then There Were None*.

The Hortons and Burt came in together, with Carla a few steps behind.

Sam stood on tiptoe to attract Burt's attention, but before he could open his mouth, Hugo announced brusquely, "Okay, here we are. Where's the law?"

Burt rubbed irritably at his high-bridged nose. "I presume the authorities are en route. I haven't had a chance to contact all of you, but, for right now, I'm suspending rehearsals at least until Sunday. We'll plan on opening Tuesday night, although I've alerted the *Mousetrap* cast — in case we have complications."

Hugo's rugged visage cracked in a humorless smile. "Life as a euphemism. You mean, if they arrest a cast member who can't be replaced." He glanced at Janet, then Max.

"Not very goddam funny," T.K. said levelly.

Sam bounced up and down on his sneakered feet. "Not to worry, everybody. Keep calm. Keep happy. Let the cops worry about Shane. Remember, girls and boys, Solomon Purdy's coming. He's looking for a director." Then, he added hastily, "And actors, actors, too, all the time. We have a shot at Broadway, boys and girls —"

"Who gives a damn about Solomon Purdy. Or you," T.K. exploded. "Goddamn, Shane gets bumped off, and all you can think about is yourself. And everybody knows you're through. You're washed up, a has-been."

Sam whirled on him. "I guess you're all upset about the murder? Sure you are — when he was screwing your wife and your daughter, I guess you just feel real —"

T.K. lowered his head like an enraged buffalo and charged. Sam ducked behind Carla. Annie and Max lunged forward, grabbing at T.K. Vince Ellis wrote furiously in his notepad.

Burt held up his hands and yelled, "Stop it! All of you, stop it!"

On this note, the doors opened and Saulter and Posey walked in.

You could have cut the atmosphere in the Broward's Rock High School auditorium with a carving knife and served it at an Addams family tea. To say the attendees of this reunion looked glum would be a masterpiece of understatement. The only cheerful face belonged to Brice Posey, who stood downstage center to orchestrate the reenactment, pitching his voice so it carried clearly to Vince Ellis in the first row.

Posey had shed his pinstripe coat, retained his vest. Patches of sweat stained the underarms of his blue oxford cloth shirt.

"Take your places." And Posey planted himself at downstage right, arms folded.

They started with Teddy's appearance (and Eugene was superb) from the Brewster cellar in Act II and stopped at the point when Teddy was supposed to enter, bugle in hand, early in Act III. It was a ragged performance. Having Posey's portly body stolidly onstage throughout didn't help anyone's concentration.

Posey looked inquiringly at Saulter, who held a stopwatch in his hand.

"Thirty-two minutes, eight seconds."

Sam yawned, frankly bored. Burt spoke in his precise voice. "That doesn't allow for the delay before the start of Act Three. We had a mix-up on some props that slowed us down. I'd add at least six minutes."

"Forty minutes," Posey boomed. "Now, what time was it when Petree made his last exit?"

After a good deal of discussion, the best estimate was approximately ten o'clock.

"So the murder occurred," Posey intoned portentously, "between ten and ten-forty." He gestured for everyone to come onstage, then stared searchingly at each person in turn. The cast members returned his gaze warily. Only Henny, a bizarre Abby in her bright dress, seemed undaunted.

Posey took a deep breath. Saulter, apparently forewarned, opened a notebook and waited.

"Where were you between ten and ten-forty last night?" Posey shouted at Arthur.

Arthur jumped, swallowed, and nervously smoothed the lock of dark hair from his eyes.

His answer, of course, paralleled that of all the cast members. Onstage and off. Backstage. Downstairs. In the greenroom. In the john. Out to the parking lot for a breath of air.

And nobody quite remembered when they'd last seen Shane. Or perhaps no one cared to be linked to him during the period when the murder occurred.

Only T.K. tried to establish total absence from below stage.

"I don't come on until the last part of Act Three, so I hung around out in the parking lot. A nice night."

Posey's thick lips curved in a tiny, satisfied smile. "You weren't interested in watching your wife act? She has a pretty big role, doesn't she?"

T.K. paused overlong before answering. "Sure, I was interested. I just happened to go outside."

Janet broke in eagerly. "He can see me act anytime. He just likes to be alone sometimes. And, see, that proves T.K. couldn't have done it."

"Ah, Mrs. Horton." Posey looked like a barracuda sighting a very slow-moving sea turtle. "Your defense is certainly evidence of *wifely* concern. But I'm intrigued. Why should I think Mr. Horton would want to kill Mr. Petree?" His voice rose disingenuously.

Janet's sheeplike face stiffened. "But that's *why* you're finding out where everyone was, isn't it? Because you think one of us shot him?"

"That's correct. *One* of you." The full voice caressed the damning word. "But why should you be fearful for your husband? Is there any reason why he, more so than anyone else here in this auditorium, should have wanted to put an end to Mr. Petree's life?"

Dumbly, Janet shook her head. "Oh, no, no, not at all." Her voice was so low it could scarcely be heard.

"It couldn't be that you feel a little

guilty, could it, Mrs. Horton?"

"Guilty? I haven't done anything. I was onstage most of the time."

Posey stamped heavily across the stage until he stood a scant foot from the cowering Janet. "Guilty about your sexual transgressions, Mrs. Horton!" he thundered.

Bastard, Annie thought. He didn't have to bare all this publicly. He could have talked to Janet and T.K. privately. Certainly he didn't have to bellow it out in front of everyone — including Vince Ellis. But the reporter wasn't taking notes now. Instead, he stared at Posey, not bothering to disguise his disgust.

It was utterly still. Janet nervously clutched at her throat and didn't look toward T.K. Her husband's face was a sick putty color. He stared down at the floor, his mouth quivering.

"Ah, yes, Mrs. Horton, guilt about your sexual transgressions." Posey raised a finger, pointed it. Annie recognized the stance. It must be his favorite courtroom histrionic. "Do you deny you had sex with Mr. Petree? Not once, but repeatedly?"

Annie wanted to cry out that this was indecent, brutal, vicious, but she stood as a part of that frozen circle.

Janet's pale face flushed crimson, then

the color ebbed, leaving her gray and shaken. Her chest heaved as she struggled to breathe, then, with the desperate courage of a cornered animal, she screamed, "T.K. was outside! He didn't do it. He'd never do it! And it wasn't the way you make it sound. I didn't . . . I wasn't . . . He just came after me, and I was such a fool, but I didn't care about him." She looked past her tormentor, her china-blue eyes full of pain. "T.K., T.K." Tears flooded her eyes, slipped unchecked down her face, smearing her makeup. "I love T.K.," she cried brokenly.

"Next best thing to Joan Collins," Cindy remarked acidly. The teenager stood with a hand on her hip, breasts thrust forward. Annie was sorely tempted to swat her rear and stick her in a corner. "She never could tell the truth. God, she doesn't know the difference between fantasy and reality. She chased Shane 'til he was sick of it."

"That's enough, Cindy," T.K. ordered hoarsely.

Janet swung on her daughter. "Shut up, shut up, you little whore!" Not jealousy, but fear burned in Janet's eyes. She knew full well — as did they all — that every word Cindy uttered increased T.K.'s peril.

Posey relished every minute of it. Annie

thought the salacious gleam in his eyes rivaled an X-rated film for sheer nastiness. "So Mr. Petree liked you better, did he?"

Cindy's smile was proud. "Sure. He laughed about her. Said she was a dry old stick. He — he was just wonderful."

Annie had had enough. "But you were sure ticked off with Shane that last night, weren't you?"

Cindy's eyes narrowed, and her face hardened in remembered anger. "I don't know what got into him. We always went to his boat on Tuesday nights, but he said he was busy. And I *know* he was going out that night. I saw him loading stuff on his boat in the afternoon." She added waspishly, her face sharp and foxlike, "I figured he had a date with someone else."

Posey's heavy head swung slowly toward T.K. "So how did it feel, knowing he was screwing both your wife and your daughter?" The ugly words stained the air like a poison.

Janet darted across the stage to stand by her husband. "Leave T.K. alone. He didn't kill Shane. He wouldn't do it, I tell you. I know who did it. It's all because of money. That's what happened. I knew when they took out those policies that Shane would die. I tell you, I knew it then."

"Shut up, Janet," T.K. said in a strangled voice.

But his wife was too overwrought to hear him. "You just find out where Sheridan was last night," she screamed at Posey. "That's what you need to do. You don't think she'd kill for a million dollars? And it's two million because it's death by misadventure. You can't tell me he was worth a million dollars to that string of computer stores they owned. Everybody knew they were going broke. You can buy computers for a nickel nowadays! They made them and made them and half of them are just a joke. And oil's down, way down. You just check and see how badly Mrs. Rich-and-Mighty Sheridan Prentiss Petree needed money."

Two million dollars. Two *million* dollars. Annie looked at Henny, whose lips were silently repeating the sum.

Posey rocked back on his heels, a look of immense satisfaction on his round face. If ever anyone looked like a dissolute pig, it was Posey. "Oh, I know my business, Mrs. Horton. I know it inside out. The first thing I did was inquire about the widow, especially since I understand she isn't a *grieving* widow."

Annie exchanged a thoughtful glance

with Henny. And Annie was reminded of Charlie Chan's famous saying, "Bad alibi like dead fish. Cannot stand test of time."

"That's right," Janet agreed eagerly. "She's bedded every man on the damn island at least once. Everybody knows that. And she could have sneaked in here. She could have come in by the stage door — or downstairs some way, just like whoever played all the tricks. You find out where Sheridan was last night."

"Oh, I already have." The tip of a pink tongue caressed his lower lip. "First thing I found out."

Even Janet, not-so-clever Janet, heard the lip-smacking undertone.

"Seems Mrs. Petree was busy last night between ten and eleven p.m. Very, very busy."

All eyes were on him. He wallowed in the attention.

Burt frowned, his thin mouth pursed. He made a movement, as if to intervene, then shrugged. Even the president of the players had no control over a circuit solicitor.

"Mrs. Petree was in room one-nineteen of the Crown Shore Motel at ten p.m. — and she wasn't alone. She was certainly not alone."

Obviously, it was a bombshell to most of

his listeners. Sam, of course, with no attention directed at him or his play, continued to look bored and fretful.

Eugene stared steadily at the floor. A red stain flushed his cheeks. Arthur studied Posey as if he'd just crawled out from beneath a rock.

Janet didn't give up easily. "It could be a fake. Some man she's persuaded —"

"Not just any man, Mrs. Horton. Mrs. Petree was with Mr. Harley Jenkins the Third, and he corroborates her every . . . movement." His watery blue eyes had a hot sheen. "The night clerk is well acquainted with Mr. Jenkins. He saw them go into the room. And stay there."

Saulter's face creased in a disapproving mask. Annie knew he was disgusted both by Posey's salacious insinuations and by his lack of professionalism, though Posey could point to a written transcript and demand to know what he had said that was objectionable. It was, of course, all in the way he had said it. He might as well have passed around porno photos of Harley and Sheridan.

Janet looked deflated, her thin cheeks sagging. Carla's patrician face was ostensibly indifferent, but the revulsion was clear in her large, violet eyes, while Hugo looked on sardonically. Annie would have given some zero coupon bonds for his thoughts.

Only Cindy seemed unaffected by Posey's performance. "Somebody sure could have come in downstairs. There are broken windows, lots of ways."

Posey looked at her cynically. "That's very convenient for you to say, Miss Horton. Are you suddenly trying to protect your father, too?"

"He doesn't need protecting," Janet protested.

"Perhaps he doesn't, Mrs. Horton," Posey agreed unctuously. "Because he isn't alone among men with motives to kill Mr. Petree." Posey whirled to point at Max. "*Is* he, Mr. Darling?"

Annie's heart began to thud and she knew then that, for all their differences, she and Janet were sisters under the skin when their men were threatened.

"Yes, we all know who had the strongest motive, don't we? Whose fiancée was throwing herself at Shane Petree? Who's used to having his way, a rich man, who can have what he wants, when he wants it?" Posey paused long enough for every eye to be riveted on him. "Who was the Long Island Skeet Champion four years ago?" He gave three judicious nods and pointed his stubby forefinger at Max. "Mr. Maxwell Darling."

Annie knew it was a performance, knew that every word and gesture was calculated to arouse. She knew it, but she couldn't stay quiet.

"You are a champion asshole," she announced loudly. "You wouldn't know a motive if you fell over it. Nobody in his right mind believes I would go after Shane! Why don't you find out who hated Shane? Somebody must have — and it wasn't Max. Max just *despised* him."

Max rolled his eyes helplessly and made a tamping motion with his hand. But Annie charged ahead. "Why don't you find out why the murder happened during rehearsal, and not during a performance? Where was Shane going Tuesday night? Why was he all excited? And he was! Ask anybody. And we've *told* you about the problems we had with the play. Somebody even shot the Hortons' cat! Max had no reason in the world to want to ruin the season, and obviously the sabotage must be connected to Shane's murder!"

Posey's jaws clenched. His pig-ugly eyes glared. "I'm not fooled by all the clever tricks that've been played. That sabotage didn't hurt a thing. If it's connected to the murder, Darling did it to confuse everybody. And," he concluded triumphantly, "it may not have a thing to do with the murder. The bullet that killed that cat didn't come from the gun that killed Petree. So, don't think anybody's going to play me for a fool, Miss Laurance. I'm taking Mr. Rich-and-Smart Darling into Beaufort to ask him some mighty sharp questions — and his money won't do him one bit of good."

As he hustled Max from the stage, Annie remembered another of Charlie Chan's philosophical asides. "If strength were all, tiger would not fear scorpion." And she pictured herself as a bright red darting scorpion!

13

Later, when it became important, Annie would calculate the time between the breakup of the meeting at the school auditorium and one forty-five when Saulter called her with the shocking news. But she wasn't thinking about time as she dialed call after call from Death on Demand. She was trying to make up her mind. Did she want to hire an establishment lawyer, an advocate in a Hermès tie from a ninety-man firm in Atlanta? Or did she want a blunt-spoken F. Lee Bailey, ready to scrap in the courtroom or out of it? Her personal taste ran to colorful fictional counselors like John J. Malone, who consumed far too much rye whiskey, and Donald Lam, who had lost his license. Perry Mason, of course, was busy in southern California. The smart money would opt for Antony Maitland or Horace Rumpole, but what she would give for the likes of a Dade Cooley!

She made a half dozen calls, culled through as many suggestions, and finally ran a whispery-voiced Jed McClanahan to earth in Columbia.

"You're the best criminal lawyer in South Carolina?" she demanded without preliminaries.

McClanahan's response was gratifyingly prompt. "Ma'am, I'm the best criminal lawyer in the United States of America."

On this encouraging note, she hired him to represent Max. "The circuit solicitor — the idiot — has taken him to Beaufort for questioning!" she fumed.

"Ma'am, would that be Brice Posey you're talkin' about?"

"It certainly would. Do you know him?"

"I can say I've made his acquaintance, and I'm pinin' to meet him again." If Annie had felt uncertain, the curl of derision in McClanahan's husky voice sealed her choice. "Now, you just relax there on the island and don't fret. I'll have Mr. Darlin' back across the water before you can shake a stick."

Annie felt an instant's unease. Did she really want a cliché-stuffed mind representing Max? But the deal was made. And at least he wasn't sanctimoniously quoting Scripture like H.C. Bailey's shyster, Joshua Clunk.

"How long do you think it will take, Mr. McClanahan?" She doodled on the phone pad, drawing a cell window with a white hankie flapping from it.

"Quicker than a Texas tornado, Miss Laurance."

After she hung up, she stared at the receiver in dismay. Had she bought a pig in a poke? Lordy, was it catching? "Damn," she said aloud.

The phone rang.

It would not be quite fair to say that, in common with white rats subjected simultaneously to a ring and a sting, she now exhibited an automatic response to the peal of a telephone bell.

She did quiver, and her eyes flared, but she was proud to see she picked it up with a steady hand.

"Death on Demand."

The macaw-sharp screech didn't bother with salutations. "It's clear as can be. And I'm working on it." So, Dame Beatrice Bradley was hewing to the scent. "I'm at the Crown Shore Motel, and they aren't going to put *anything* over on me."

"The Crown Shore Motel," Annie repeated blankly.

"Where Sheridan and Harley *claim* they spent the period during which Shane was murdered. Annie, you know your Freeman Wills Crofts. The real tip-off is an impregnable alibi. Well, just wait until I look it over. We'll see."

Annie hung up, and she couldn't help grinning. The Crown Shore Motel wouldn't know what hit it. Well, if there was anything fishy about that alibi, Henny would soon know. She drew a snaggle-toothed fish on her pad, a crouching lioness, and a fat toad, then settled in for a serious bout of thinking.

Finally, she wrote down three conclusions:

1. It was unlikely that further investigation of the suspects present when Shane's murder occurred would lead to additional information. Their motives were known, and, unless someone had remained silent about an incriminating action, there was no more to be gleaned from questions about the night of the murder.

2. The possibility of an unseen, unheard assailant from outside the school was extremely slim. Further, the two outsiders with motives (Sheridan and Harley) appeared to have an unbreakable alibi. Annie agreed with Henny that such a convenient alibi did seem suspicious, especially since the wicked widow was going to inherit an addi-

tional two million dollars.

3. Obviously, the true motive for Shane's murder was yet to be unearthed. (Could Celia Grant help here?)

All of which led inescapably to the conclusion, at least so far as Annie was concerned, that a great deal more attention must be paid the victim.

Why was Shane killed?

Why was he killed on Tuesday night?

Why had he changed the pattern of his life in recent months, according to Henny's informant?

Who was the redheaded woman with Shane at The Red Rooster?

Why did Shane tell Cindy he was busy on the night he was killed?

Why did Shane rush through his lines?

Why had he loaded his boat that afternoon?

Annie leaned against the railing that overlooked the Broward's Rock harbor. It was chock-full of pleasure craft this lovely summer day, almost every slip taken. A magnificent yacht (Fitzgerald was right; the rich *are* different) had tied up the night before and tourists gawked admiringly through sparkling windows at the slim, tanned young men and women lounging in the saloon. But Annie's eyes were focused on a sailboat at the far end of the harbor.

So Shane spent every possible moment aboard his sailboat. And he'd carried gear aboard Tuesday. Cindy saw him.

Cindy and Shane had often gone for midnight sails, and that's what she'd hoped for that night, but Shane said he was busy.

Why, then, had he carried something aboard?

What had he carried aboard?

Why was Shane excited and hyper at the rehearsal, champing to be done and gone?

Annie glanced toward the well-kept marina office. As usual, the owner, Skipper Worrell, was in residence. He ran a tight marina. Only ship owners were allowed on the docks. Tourists had to stay harborside.

He knew her, of course.

But he wouldn't let the Angel Gabriel board a boat that didn't belong to him. And Skipper knew what was going on around the island. He would know, as probably every newspaper-reading cretin in the county knew, that Shane had been shot dead Tuesday night.

So he wouldn't let Annie board *Sweet Lady.*

Annie cupped her chin in her hand and stared across the pea-green water. The harbor was shaped like a shallow horseshoe. On the spit of land to the south was the burned-out playhouse. After dark, it would be easy to slip into the water there unseen.

Hurried footsteps clipped across the wooden verandah behind her. Ingrid called urgently, "Annie, Annie, come quick!"

Holding hard to the telephone receiver, Annie made him repeat it.

But she'd heard the chief right the first time. "We found a gun, Annie. A twenty-two. Right on top of some wet towels in the clothes hamper in Max's bathroom." Silence. "You could've knocked me over with a whisk broom."

"Somebody planted it there. The *murderer* put it there!"

Chief Saulter sighed wearily. "Course, it'll have to go through ballistics to see if it's the gun that killed Shane."

"Oh, it did," she said bitterly. "You can bet that it did. Dammit, this makes me *crazy!* What time did you find it — and what were you doing searching Max's condo?"

"Look, Annie, I can't talk any longer.

I'm calling you from my car phone at the ferry dock. I've got to take the gun into Beaufort — and tell Posey."

"Chief, I'm coming, too!"

She flung down the phone and raced for the front of the store, calling over her shoulder to Ingrid, "Take care of everything. I've got to go to Beaufort."

She was at the front door when the familiar peal sounded again. Annie didn't slacken speed. She was at the end of the verandah when she heard Ingrid shouting, "Annie, it's Laurel. What shall I tell her?"

"Tell her . . . tell her the cake is . . . is lovely, and I'll talk to her later."

Much, much later.

Was it possible that a red wedding cake shaped like a truncated pyramid and topped by a fir sapling would satisfy Laurel?

Oh, dammit. Annie couldn't believe she was even thinking about the wedding with Max tied to the rails and a locomotive streaking toward him.

She drove like Modesty Blaise, but it didn't do any good. The ferry was pulling away from the dock as she slewed to a stop and jumped out.

Chief Saulter raised a hand in a lugubrious farewell. He looked as jolly as Mme. Defarge.

"Dammit, it was a plant!" Then, cupping her hands, she yelled, "What time did you go to Max's condo?"

The words drifted back to her, across the water. "One-thirty. Why?"

But she was walking swiftly toward the outdoor phone booth, calculating the time and reaching for a quarter. She had to make an important call.

The booth smelled of cigarette smoke, beer, and seaweed. It took five quarters to track the world's greatest trial lawyer to the Tell-It-to-the-Navy Bar and Grill in Beaufort.

"You can't keep him out of jail from there."

"What? What'd you say, hon?" The nail-scraping whine of a synthesizer pulsed behind the whispery voice.

Annie shouted, "You can't keep him out of jail from there!"

"Sweetheart, don't you worry your pretty head. If they arrest him, I'll get the best bail bondsman in South Carolina and we'll spring him in a New York minute. Now, I'm just takin' a break for a little sustenance, then I'll get right to it."

"They found a gun in Max's condo. It's the same kind that killed Shane."

"Found a gun? That might put us in a

pickle, all right." A pause. Did she hear the slosh of liquid? McClanahan burped quietly. "Now, let's see, Miss Laurance, tell me this: Does Mr. Darlin' ever have seizures of any kind, maybe little lapses of memory?"

Oh, God. The music, a dreadful combination of country and acid rock, ranged into the upper decibels. A dog would've howled.

Annie snapped, "No. He does not have seizures, mental lapses, emotional aberrations, or festering aggressions."

"Huh?"

"He is, in short, Mr. McClanahan, innocent. Now, you get the hell over to Posey's office and protect your client, and I'll figure out what's going on." She slammed down the receiver, bolted out of the booth, then stood uncertainly.

Brave words, indeed. She paced back to her car and stared out across the choppy water with troubled eyes. The ferry must be nearing shore now. Soon Posey would have the gun in his possession, the gun that a clever adversary had hidden in Max's condo. Yes, somewhere on this lovely island a dangerous and calculating intelligence was weaving a net around Max.

She knew only too well what it took to

convict. Means, motive, opportunity — and physical evidence.

The murderer had dropped the last one right into Posey's grasping hands.

When was the gun placed in Max's condo? And how?

Annie shook her hair back from her face, but even the ever-present sea breeze didn't refresh her. Her mind felt like a jellyfish left behind at high tide. When, when, when?

The gun was found in Max's clothes hamper. He would have showered this morning, before coming over to her tree house for breakfast. The gun must have been placed there after he'd left. . . .

Oh, no, she could narrow the time better than that, much better. Because no one knew Max was on Posey's list of suspects until the prosecutor went after Max during the grim session at the high school this morning. He'd taken Max in to Beaufort shortly after eleven. The murderer must have enjoyed Posey's attack on Max and seen a wonderful opportunity to tighten the net. That's when the decision must have been made. After eleven. And the chief searched the condo at one-thirty. So, the gun was put in place between eleven and one-thirty. Within a two-and-one-half-hour space, someone slipped into Max's condo with that damning evidence.

Max's condo didn't run to an alarm system. (Who needed an alarm system in a community on an island that had a single security-manned entrance-exit?) A good, healthy credit card would spring the front door. Max had a ground-floor condo with front walls around an entrance patio for privacy. Might as well have laid a red carpet for the murderer. But Posey would sneer at the claim of a frame-up.

Well, Annie had an advantage over him. She knew Max was innocent — and she knew — or could almost be certain — that one of those present at the high school auditorium that morning had put the gun in Max's apartment. Who else knew he was being questioned in Beaufort?

So she wanted to know the whereabouts from eleven to one-thirty of the members of that select group — and she had a few more trenchant and perhaps downright disagreeable questions to ask.

Cole Drugstore was an enclave from the past, with its original marble-topped tables and wire-backed chairs, revolving red Leatherette stools at the soda fountain, and lazily moving circular fans. The pleasant, musty dimness held memories of yesterday. For just an instant, Annie recalled long-ago afternoons and cherry phosphates with her uncle, the founder of Death on Demand. Then she hurried down the center aisle, shampoos and shaving lotions to her right, face powder and lipsticks to her left.

Arthur Killeen stood behind the cash register. He looked up with an automatic smile. When he saw her, the smile disappeared faster than a table full of Stephen King books at a science fiction convention. His hands pressed tightly against the counter top.

Annie wasn't sure just how she would approach each cast member. Should she appeal for help, mount a broadside attack, all guns smoking, or attempt a disarming ingenuousness?

Arthur's eyes flickered uneasily. His features looked pinched and tight. Odd. He had seemed, until now, a peripheral figure, the genial druggist who created such a diffident, appealing Dr. Einstein.

A mystery ploy flashed through her mind, that old saw of the telegram warning, "Flee, all is discovered."

She planted herself determinedly by the counter. "Arthur, you'd better level with me."

His shoulders sagged. "It was over years ago."

Annie waited, her face stern.

"It will kill her, if it comes out." His mouth twisted with bitterness. "Goddam, he was like a pig in heat. Why the hell did he want to go after Bea? She wasn't his type." He laughed mirthlessly. "But maybe that's why he did it, so he could chalk up a hit in the kind of circles he despised." His eyes reddened. "He laughed at her, you know. Told her she was a silly fool woman who thought she was better than everybody else, and he just wanted her to know she wasn't, then he walked out, still laughing."

Annie riffled through a dozen pictures in her mind, and finally, from a players' picnic the summer before, recalled Arthur's wife, Bea, a tiny blonde who wore her hair in a tight bun and only a smattering of pale pink lipstick.

"Where was Bea Tuesday night?"

"Oh, no, she's out of it, Annie. She was in Savannah with our daughter, who's expecting a baby."

So he was worried about Bea's reputation, not the possibility that she might be a suspect.

Or was he worried sick that Posey might

sniff out the affair between Shane and his wife and go after him?

"I guess you're going to tell Posey." A nerve twitched his cheek. "You'll do anything to help Max, won't you?"

"Max didn't do it."

"Neither did I." He started to turn away.

She decided on an oblique approach. "Arthur, you want to get this cleared up as soon as possible, don't you? I need to know where everyone went after they left the school this morning. Did you see anyone between eleven and one-thirty?"

His long pause might mean he had no idea of the purpose behind her question, or it might mean he thought very well on his feet. Finally, grudgingly, he said, "I went to the *Gazette* this morning to turn in some ads for the weekend. I saw Sam down there. I think that's — oh, I passed Hugo jogging as I drove back. He was on one of the bike paths next to the road. And Henny flashed by on her ten-speed near the bird preserve."

The Crown Shore Motel on the shore side of the island proudly offered a salt-water pool, in-room Jacuzzis, free continental breakfasts, and candy roses at bedtime. Jerry's Cabins on the marsh side of the island were the flip side of the coin, and offered very damn little. Rusted window screens, sagging wooden shutters, once-a-week maid service, and a half mile walk to Jerry's gas station, cafe, and roadside market for ice at 89 cents a bag were the extent of its amenities.

A rusted blue bike and an '86 Ford Falcon rental car with Georgia plates sat in the sandy ruts next to cabin seven.

Annie knocked on the door.

It opened at her first tap, and Sam burst out onto the wooden steps, with his finger to his lips. He softly closed the door behind him. "Tonelda's taking a nap," he cautioned. "Have you heard?" His voice radiated cheer, and Annie looked at him in surprise. His face blossomed with delight. Obviously, he didn't know about the gun being found at Max's.

Sam was prattling on. "Listen, we're hot. Really hot. AP called. UPI called. Cable News is sending a crew out from Atlanta. I've been down to the *Gazette* to talk to Vince. He says everybody in hell wants to know what's going on. Murder behind the scenes. Death backstage. Annie, you're not going to believe it, but" — he paused significantly — "the *New York Times* called."

"You've been to the *Gazette* today?

Around lunchtime?"

A look of thoughtful cunning flashed in his bloodshot eyes. "Later than that. I had to fix lunch for Tonelda. I was over to the harbor just a little while ago. Anyway," he went on impatiently, "this story has everything, a good-looking woman, a rich man —" He paused and stared at her, apparently thinking for the first time of his audience. His eyes shifted away. He gnawed on his upper lip, then said brightly, "But look, Annie, Max has money out the ass. They won't hold him. Even if they arrest him, I'm sure he can get out on bail in time for our opening. And it takes forever for criminal cases to come to trial. And no jury would convict him." He shook his head in awe. "Think about the free pub!"

So Sam did know about the gun. Of course he would know if he'd been to the *Gazette* offices. Vince would be the first to learn the astounding news of a search warrant sworn out for the home of a leading citizen. Vince was probably on Max's doorstep when the chief came out with the gun. But Sam would also know, obviously, if he put the gun in the hamper. And wasn't his claim of having been to the harbor area after lunch a clearly feeble attempt at an alibi?

She stared at him coldly, and even Sam must have felt the chill. He shot her a craven glance and reached inside his pocket to pull out a crumpled sheet of paper.

"Would you take a look at this? I'm going to see how much Vince will charge to run it as an ad. What do you think?"

not
even

M
U
R
D
E
R

can stop

"arsenic and Old Lace"

DIRECTED BY

Samuel Bratton Haznine

coming
June 9
Broward's Rock Players

She looked at it briefly.

"What do you think?" He couldn't disguise his eagerness.

"I think it's remarkable," she replied dryly. It was remarkable for its insensitivity, gall, and callousness. She stared up at his plump face, with its straggly halo of thin blond hair.

"Gee, that's great." Sam beamed at her. "Well, I'd better hurry, get it down to Vince. He's about to lock up this week's edition. I'd better hurry." He started down the steps toward the rental car, then turned. "Uh, Annie, if I can do anything to help about old Max, you let me know."

She watched him thoughtfully as he backed out of the rutted drive. Sam had one aim in life, to regain his place on Broadway. She had no doubt he would scratch, bite, kick, and knife his way past any obstacle.

But would he shoot Shane? And frame an innocent man for murder?

She wouldn't be at all surprised. She turned and began to pound on the weathered door.

"Jesus, knock it off!" a high voice called.

Annie continued to knock. Louder.

The door was yanked open. The spiky hair drooped sideways and makeup was smudged on Tonelda's sleep-heavy face. "What the hell do *you* want?"

Annie felt a stab of compassion. What the hell did Tonelda want? What had happened in her short and obviously traumatic life to land her in this seedy cabin with a man at least twice her age? But the dark eyes peering out from mascara-laden lids looked like old stones, discouraging sympathy.

"How long have you been asleep?"

"Jesus, you some kind of crazy government survey? What the hell difference does it make to you?" The door began to close.

Annie grabbed the doorknob. "When did Sam get back this morning from the meeting at the high school?"

For the first time, interest flickered in those eyes. "You're in the play, aren't you?"

Annie nodded.

"You got the rich boyfriend."

"Yes."

"So you're not after Sam, huh?"

"No, Tonelda." Her voice was gentle. "I'm not after Sam. Not that way. I just need to know where he was around lunchtime."

Reassured that her meal ticket wasn't endangered, Tonelda yawned. "I slept late.

He was gone when I woke up, and then he was late gettin' back. I was hungry. He didn't fix lunch 'til almost one."

So Sam hadn't come directly to the cabin from that session at the high school.

"And you went back to bed after lunch?"

Those old eyes stared at her. "What the hell is it to you, lady?" and the door slammed.

Back in her car, she headed for the entrance to the resort area. The guard waved her through the checkpoint (a yellow-and-black sticker on her windshield identified her as a resort resident). She hesitated at the fork. If she turned right, she would take the quicker route back to her tree house, then sweep by her turnoff and drive on to the condos that overlooked the sound. Max lived there, and so did Carla. If she turned left, she would head for Hugo's palatial beachfront house.

Carla obviously didn't like Shane. But Hugo, like Sam, harbored overweening ambition. Thoughtfully, Annie weighed dislike against ambition and turned left.

Unlike most island residences found at the end of dusty gray roads bordered by live oaks, Hugo's home was hidden from view behind a curving stucco wall painted lime green. A white-lacquered louvered gate barred entry. As Annie coasted to a stop, a green button glowed on a communications box atop a stand at car level. She stared at the wire-meshed box. A smooth male voice requested politely, "May I help you?"

"Yes, please. This is Annie Laurance. I'd like to talk to Mr. Wolf. He'll know what it's about."

"Just a moment, please."

The silvery green tunnel beneath the interlocking live oak limbs pulsed with the musical whir of chiggers, the buzz of green-head flies, the rustle of the glossy live oak leaves. Annie swatted at a mosquito and recalled what she knew of Hugo, a Charleston native, graduate of Stanford and Northwestern, an acclaimed trial attorney in Atlanta, a man who had retired to Broward's Rock to indulge his passions for yachting and acting. Married three times. And one tough customer.

A tiny buzz preceded a mellifluous announcement from the communications box. "When the gate opens, Miss Laurance, please drive through, then turn right at the fork. It will take you to the exercise area. Mr. Wolf is at the jai alai court."

Before the speech ended, the gate began

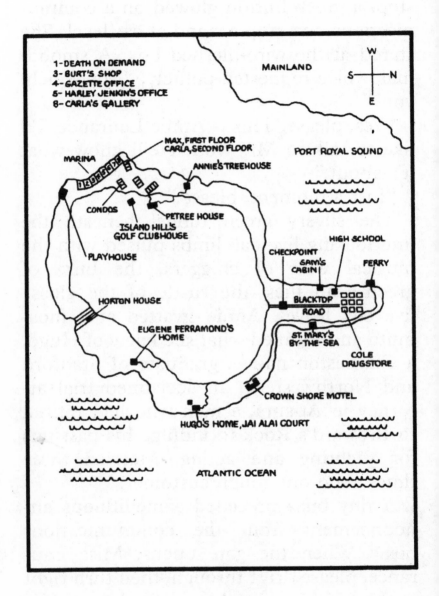

to swing inward. Annie nosed the Volvo through the entrance. The car cleared, and the gate automatically began to close. Turning at the fork, she glimpsed through a stand of yellow pines a two-story mansard-roofed house. French doors opened out onto tiled terraces decorated with huge blue, Chinese porcelain pots containing calla lillies. A lime stucco wall curved to embrace the landscaping of snowy white and pink azaleas, golden Peruvian daffodils, and brilliantly purple bougainvillea. The right fork ended in a circular drive flanked by a four-stall garage and the jai alai court, a long, rectangular two-story stucco building.

Hugo, wearing gray gym shorts, his body covered with a sheen of sweat, stood waiting there, a white towel slung over one shoulder. His impressive physique didn't surprise her, but she realized anew what a very magnificent male animal he was. He might be in his fifties, but men half his age would envy his strong legs, flat stomach, and muscular chest with its thick mat of iron-gray hair.

His craggy face was unsmiling as she hurried up the steps, and his dark eyes watched warily. He looked about as approachable as Dr. Jekyll at nightfall.

"I appreciate your seeing me, Hugo."

Her attempt at civility evoked no response. Instead, he jerked his head toward the door. "Cooler inside." And he held the door for her.

He led the way down a corridor that fronted on the court to an elevated bar overlooking a twenty-five-yard pool. He picked up a terry-cloth robe, slipped into it, then stepped behind the bar.

"What would you like?" He was barely civil.

"Oh, club soda, thanks."

He clunked ice into a tall glass, poured the soda, handed her a drink, then uncapped a bottle of imported beer.

She was accustomed to viewing him through a particular lens, as an actor and one not thrilled with his companions. Now, she saw a different facet of his personality. He was always impressive. Here, on his own turf, he was almost overpowering. It made her realize how little she knew of her fellow players. She was aware of segments of their lives and only what they chose to reveal. While she was seeking information to help Max, their lives continued with joys, fears, and pains of which she knew nothing.

But she knew enough of Hugo to realize

she was dealing with a subtle and sophisticated intellect, so she opted for frankness. Of a sort.

"The police have found a gun hidden in Max's condo." She ran a hand through her thick blond hair. "Of course, it will turn out to be the gun that killed Shane — and I don't suppose I have to tell you it was planted."

He listened impassively, using an edge of the towel to pat at his formidable face. "So the cops found a gun." He tilted his bottle, drank, then asked bluntly, "Why do you want to talk to me?"

She could be blunt, too. "Where were you between eleven and one-thirty?"

For an instant, anger burned in those dark eyes, then, slowly, derisively, he began to smile. "Here and there. After our instructive meeting at the school, I went for a jog. Actually, I suppose I must have passed Max's condo — but — sorry to say — I didn't see any suspicious characters lurking about. Damn shame I didn't have on my deerstalker hat. And then, oh, yes, then I came back here and had lunch with my wife." His eyes challenged her. "My very delectable wife, who will certainly corroborate my recollection. Then I came out here."

Her eyes glanced from the pool to the jai alai court.

He quirked a sardonic eyebrow. "You think it's a trifle excessive, perhaps? Annie, you do reflect your middle-class up-bringing so clearly." He rubbed the towel against his chest, swiped again at his face. "I believe in enjoying myself, and I don't let anything deflect me from what I want."

"You wanted Shane out of the play," she said flatly.

His full lips twisted into a smile. "Oh, yes, I did, didn't I?" His mocking tone dared her to make something of it.

Annie gripped her glass tightly, resisting the impulse to fling its contents into that flushed, arrogant face. Was Hugo deliberately baiting her?

She forced a conciliatory smile. "Hugo, I *know* that someone of your brilliance couldn't possibly be crazy enough to commit murder. But I thought, of every-one involved, you have the keenest mind, the best intellect, the most perceptive in-stincts." She paused, wondering if she were overdoing it. But he was nodding compla-cently. "Hugo, I need your help. I don't know what to do to help Max."

"Ah, yes, Max." His silvery black eye-brows drew down. "Frankly, the premise that Max is a murderer is absurd, but that doesn't lessen the seriousness of his situation. Unfortunately, a certain kind of mind — such as that possessed by Posey — is quite incapable of understanding or appreciating the absurd."

Hugo's chilling assessment frightened her almost as much as the discovery of the gun in the condo.

The retired lawyer nodded. "You're wise to start looking yourself."

She leaned forward against the bar. "Hugo, what do *you* think happened?"

"I am puzzled," he said slowly. "Granted, Shane was an unappealing lout. But he's been that ever since he's lived here. He was involved with the two silly Horton women. But he's been involved with them all spring. Why should T.K. suddenly turn murderous? It doesn't seem tenable to me to cast T.K. as the villain. Yet he's the only person who has even a reasonably strong motive."

"How about Harley Jenkins?"

"Jenkins?" He drank some of his beer. "I thought he and Sheridan alibied each other."

"I have trouble with that," Annie exclaimed. "And yet, he's so convincing. I wondered if he and Sheridan could be in it together?"

"Oh, my dear! To satisfy love's young dream?" Hugo laughed robustly. "I think not. Harley enjoys flesh, but he'd scarcely put himself in jeopardy — and Sheridan's flesh isn't even that attractive."

"There's no accounting for taste."

He shrugged. "True. And I'd never attempt to account for Harley's. Still —"

"He loves money more than anything."

Hugo finished his beer. "Right. That's his mainspring."

"So maybe he and Sheridan planned the murder together. Kill Shane, she gets two million, and they live happily ever after — or at least until one of them needs more money."

Hugo pensively rubbed his hawklike nose. "Hmm." Then shook his head. "I've been in some deals with Harley, and I'll grant that he's a class A, numero uno greedy bastard. He'd screw his mother out of her last Social Security check, if he needed the cash. But the trick is, Annie, he doesn't need cash. I couldn't begin to estimate the pile he made in the last bull market. He's got so much money, he could carpet Broward's Rock with it. Now, I'll admit, nobody loves money like the rich — but Harley runs more to greenmail, fudged records, and fiscal intimidation. Murder?

No. Not for a measly two million." He moved a shell filled with pepitas her way, then took a handful. As he popped several into his mouth, he chewed and added positively, "No. Besides, it's Sheridan who needs money. I've heard a rumor or two recently about her computer stores. That's her big investment outside of oil. As for oil, face it, the oil billionaires have shrunk to millionaires, and the millionaires have shrunk to bankruptcy court. But you can scratch Harley as the provider of a fake alibi. He wouldn't do it for love — or money. So you'll have to look elsewhere." He yawned, obviously losing interest. "Too bad the cops are after Max."

He picked up his towel, draped it over his shoulders, and stepped out from behind the bar. "Shower time for me." It was a dismissal. "Hope you have some luck in your researches."

Smoothly, he had her by the elbow and was walking her to the door. Annie shot one last question. "Did you see Shane when you were downstairs after his last exit?"

Hugo's face hardened. "I made every effort to avoid the sorry bastard. I don't like second-raters. I don't like to be associated with second-raters." Hugo's mouth closed in a cold, implacable slash.

At the door, she asked softly, "How much does it mean to you, Hugo, to be a Broadway star?"

He stared down at her and gradually the taut face relaxed. "On a scale of ten? I suppose it might slide in at a nine." His eyes gleamed sardonically. "But I don't have to resort to murder to triumph, Annie. I *always* have my way." He leaned back. The thick iron-gray hair fell away from his face as he laughed. "Ask my first two wives about that."

As he held open the door, he added wryly, "They both irritated me a good deal more than Shane. And, so far as I know, Martha's still photographing wildflowers in Vail — God, what a boring woman — and Genevieve is sculpting in Florence."

The sound of his throaty chuckle followed her down steps.

Her next departure from the island-circling blacktop was down a rutted side road and across a low dip that still held a couple of inches from yesterday's rain. At road's end waited a house far removed in time and spirit from Hugo's palatial residence. The Ferramond house had stood on Broward's Rock since the early 1800s and was once the center of a sprawling Sea

Island cotton plantation. Driving through the stone pillars to the land-side entrance, she studied the massive front portico, its upper story graced by curved segmental arches, framed between a corridor of majestic live oaks.

Eugene's dark blue Cadillac was parked in the circular drive. Annie pulled up behind it. She was walking up the broad bricked steps when an uneven rat-a-tat brought her to a stop. She thought at first it was an island woodpecker, but the taps were too irregular. She turned back down the steps, knowing where she would find Eugene. She followed an oyster-shell path through a grove of willows to the ruins of what had once been the slave quarters, and climbed whitewashed steps to knock at the open door of a rebuilt overseer's house. The scent of wood shavings, turpentine, and paint mixed with the sweeter perfume of honeysuckle from the vine that enveloped a nearby trellis.

Eugene looked up from his worktable, put down his hammer, and hurried forward to open the door. "Come on in, Annie. I'm just finishing up."

She'd seen Eugene's exhibits at the county fair, and several of the island shops carried his woodworking. He specialized in scale replicas of famous South Carolina mansions, including Drayton Hall, Middleton Place, and Mulberry.

But it wasn't a Southern home that he was finishing today.

He beamed at her.

She managed a smile in return, but she could hardly look away from the authentic — from the redbrick chimneys and green-painted trim to the sharply pitched roofs — rendition of Sagamore Hill which stood on Eugene's worktable.

He mistook her fascination, and bustled around the table to point out the piazza — "Teddy was standing just about there when he received official notification of his nomination for governor of New York in 1898" — and to indicate the Gun Room on the west end of the house on the third floor — "Here's where he wrote *The Rough Riders*. The Gun Room's real interesting. There's a suit of Philippine armor on the east wall and a cattle-horn chair near TR's desk. . . ."

"I guess you're really excited about playing Teddy?" she asked, abruptly.

He made a tiny adjustment to the miniature green-and white-striped awning above the ground-floor windows to the right of the piazza, then glanced at her reproachfully. "That's not the right way to look at it, Annie. Of course, I'm dreadfully sorry that anything should have happened to Shane. But, on the other hand, I feel it's my duty to do my best for the players." He bent, blew away a wood shaving. "I've been reminding myself that destiny plays a large role in every man's life. Certainly it did in TR's. And," his voice reverberated with quiet pride, "it's always been my role. One rehearsal and I'll be set."

If there were a cloud on Eugene's horizon, she couldn't see it. His satisfied demeanor jarred her. So she made no attempt to cushion her words.

"The police found a gun hidden in Max's condo."

If she wanted an effect, she got it.

His blocky face sagged in shock and distress. "Annie, I can't believe it! What's happened?"

As she told Eugene what little she knew and what she surmised, she watched him carefully. He tugged at his bristly orange mustache and kept muttering, "Oh, this is shocking news. Shocking. Most unfortunate." Then he sighed, patting her on the shoulder clumsily. "Obviously a dreadful mistake." He peered at her earnestly. "It will turn out to be a mistake, my dear. We all know Max couldn't be responsible."

And, apparently without seeing any significance to her question, he artlessly revealed he'd been in his workshop ever since coming home from the morning session at the school. He shook his head dolefully. "To think while I was immersing myself in pleasure that such horrible things were happening."

He reiterated his horror, concern, perplexity, and so on with touching earnestness as he walked Annie back to her car. His last words, before she pulled away, were, "Now, Annie, I'll do anything I can to help. Call on me at any time."

As she pulled away, she glanced in her rearview mirror at his substantial, respectable figure. Eugene was certainly not her picture of a murderer.

But, she reminded herself, like everyone else on her list, Eugene was also an accomplished actor.

The Hortons' rambling wooden house was in one of Annie's favorite developments. Here along the seaward side of the island, all the streets were named for butterflies — Swallowtail Circle, Monarch Drive, Viceroy Lane, Queen and Zebra streets, Sulphur Road. The Horton house was on Painted Lady Lane. The island is home to more than two hundred species, but these are some of the most abundant. A butterfly fan, Annie knew how to find her favorites because each family likes only certain flowers. Monarchs prefer milkweeds, swallowtails opt for sassafras, bay, and magnolia, viceroys lurk by willows, queens hover over butterfly weed, zebras cannot resist passionflowers, and sulphurs hustle to wild peas. Painted ladies, Annie knew, take their pleasure with thistles. Butterflies have a great deal in common with mystery fans, who are drawn only to their particular favorites, be they cozies, thrillers, romantic suspense, science fiction, hardboileds, softboileds, or historicals. She grinned as she pictured Henny Brawley with monarch wings, hovering over the comedy-caper shelves.

The Horton home was a typical two-hundred-thousand-dollar Broward's Rock house, built on several levels with lots of two-story glass panes, projecting porches, and assorted bay windows. The distinction of number six Painted Lady Lane was its landscaping. Ninety-foot yellow pines embraced the house. Artfully distributed patches of wildflowers created a natural garden, bright with redroot, cattails, yellow leopard's bane, purple bachelor's button, and blue hydrangea.

A single car was in the two-lane drive. Annie parked behind the Lincoln Continental. As she slammed her car door, Janet hurried around the side of the house. She wore a sun hat, dark glasses, dirt-stained shorts, and a terry-cloth top. She carried a trowel. Her outsize gardening gloves made her arms look foreshortened. Despite the shadow cast by the hat and the opaque glasses, her expression of stricken disappointment was unmistakable. Then it was gone, replaced by a stiff and not especially welcoming smile.

"Annie." She stopped by the edge of the drive and waited.

They stood in a pool of mid-afternoon heat. The drone of bees in the honeysuckle and the singsong of the katydids reminded Annie of lazy summer afternoons when there had been nothing more important to do than decide among reading the latest Victoria Holt, or taking a swim, or pedaling leisurely to Cole Drugstore for a cherry phosphate. The easy cadence of summer made an odd backdrop to her own sense of urgency and Janet's palpable unease.

"I wondered if I could talk to you for a minute?"

"Yes?"

"Is T.K. here?"

"Why? What do you want with T.K.?" Janet demanded sharply. "Look, I'm sick of everybody going after him. He hasn't done *anything*. He wouldn't shoot anybody. It's absurd." Her voice rose with each sentence.

Oh, but he might have, my dear, Annie thought, *and you know it, too, that's why you're so frightened.* Once again, she felt uncomfortably enmeshed in other lives, other emotions. Her own quest, to clear Max, was central to her, irrelevant to others. But she must take time to understand and respond, or she'd receive no help at all.

She made her voice soothing, reassuring. "God, I know, Janet. Posey's such a *fool*. And somebody hid a gun in Max's condo, so Posey's still questioning Max."

"A gun. The gun that killed Shane?" She reached out and grabbed Annie's arm, and the rough fabric of the gardening glove pressed unpleasantly against her skin.

Annie stared at the suddenly animated woman. Was this an artful performance, guaranteed to project innocence?

"Is it the gun that killed Shane?" Janet

cried again, her grip tightening.

"It's being tested, but obviously it is. It's a twenty-two and why else would anyone hide it in Max's place?"

"So Posey thinks Max did it!" Sheer joy rang in her voice. "Then he isn't after T.K.!" Tears began to roll down her cheeks, from behind the opaque glasses. She jammed the trowel into a baggy pocket, dropped Annie's arm, then slipped off her gloves and wadded one to use as handkerchief. "Oh, my God, I've been so frightened. Annie, I've been terrified!"

How Annie might feel hadn't yet occurred to her.

When the sniffles began to subside, Annie asked, "Is T.K. here? Or Cindy?"

The tears started again. "We were going to have lunch and Cindy wouldn't come down. When T.K. said she had to, she ran out of the house and slammed into her car. Then T.K. cried. Oh, God, he cried, and when I tried to tell him he shouldn't even care, he left, too. And neither one's come back all afternoon. Oh, Annie, everything's just gone to hell!" Janet raised her splotched, tear-streaked face. "I hate Shane more dead than I did when he was alive."

The short drive from the Hortons' to the

harbor reminded Annie just how small the island was, and how quickly any of her suspects could reach the condos. The harborside was jammed, and she pulled into one of the last parking spaces. It was a little early for dinner, even for the young families, but the hot-dog and ice-cream stands were busy, children raced to the far side of the marina to climb up into the lighthouse, and all the shops were open. She poked her head into Death on Demand. There was a crowd here, too, at the cash desk. Normally, it would have thrilled Annie to see all those books en route to new admirers. She scanned the titles — *The Spy Who Got His Feet Wet*, *The Villains*, *The Rosary Murders*, and *I Should Have Stayed Home*. Her eyes telegraphed a question to Ingrid, who soberly shook her head, then mouthed, "But Laurel —"

Annie hastily backed out and started up the boardwalk. So, no word on Max. God, what was the best lawyer in the United States of America *doing?* (She refused to permit her mind to entertain any thoughts at all on what Laurel might be doing.)

So far she hadn't eliminated anyone from this deadly sweepstakes. Any of them could have hidden that gun in Max's condo.

Two teenagers on skateboards careened past her, barely escaping a tumble over the heavy chain to the docks below. Annie looked out over the water. *Sweet Lady* rode quietly at her mooring. What exactly had Shane taken to the boat Tuesday? It was going to be damn disappointing if she went to all the trouble to board the boat illegally and found nothing but a stinking bait box. But he wouldn't have loaded bait for a midnight sail.

The sun was a fiery ball on the western horizon, gilding the boats a mellow peach. Nine o'clock. That's when she'd make her move.

She suddenly felt very tired, tired and more than a little afraid. If the gun checked out, Posey had physical evidence. But the gun couldn't have Max's fingerprints. She knew that. And that would be a strong argument that he hadn't hidden it. Besides, no one but an idiot would hide a murder weapon in his own house. Surely McClanahan was even now making that argument. Jesse Falkenstein would.

However, it was all too easy to look ahead and picture Posey's arm-pumping assault on a jury. "Ladies and gentlemen, we are dealing here with *arrogance*. The arrogance of the very, very rich. Mr. Darling was so sure of himself, of his wealth, of his position in the community —"

Gag.

Annie gripped the chain between the harbor stanchions. The pleasant breeze off the water stirred her hair. Was there any point in talking to Burt and Carla?

Yes. Talking to the other suspects was the only game in town right now. And she had to know whether they, too, had equal opportunity to secrete the gun. Turning, she looked at the plate-glass windows of Burt's store, Stuff 'N Such. It was perhaps a two-minute walk from here to the condos where both Max and Carla lived.

Talking to Burt was infinitely preferable to enduring the achingly slow passage of time and worrying about Max. What were they doing to him?

Annie lifted her chin and crossed to Stuff 'N Such.

Burt's store gave Max the heebie-jeebies, as he once elegantly phrased it.

Heebie-jeebies? Annie had asked.

It was a phrase coined in the forties by an American cartoonist, whose work Max's first stepfather had collected. To Max, it had always seemed a perfect description of physical discomfort similar to the prickle of your spine when nails screech down a chalkboard.

She understood Max's feelings. Stuff 'N Such was crammed from ceiling to floor with anything and everything that Burt hoped tourists might purchase, including a junky display of relics from past merchandising eras and a wondrous assortment of carved wooden shorebirds. Tins in a rainbow of colors advertised Melrose Marshmallows, Fertax Cream Mints, Necco Peach Bars, Blumenthal's Sweet Milk Chocolate Raisins, and Bunte's Fine Confections. An old oak icebox was opened to reveal several milk bottles from Sunny Hill Dairy and Borden's. Shelves on an opposite wall held perhaps fifty carved waterfowl. Every shorebird imaginable was represented — a great egret, a yellow-crowned night heron, the American bittern, the wood ibis, the oystercatcher. And throughout the long narrow shop rose the cloying scent of a half dozen potpourris and several dozen perfumed candles, ranging from bayberry to root beer.

Annie squeezed past two matrons whom it would be gracious to describe as portly, almost entangling herself in a bristly profusion of dried flower arrangements.

Burt exuded geniality as he bent near a

lanky tourist in a wildly clashing floral-patterned shirt. "Now this is a once-in-a-lifetime opportunity. As you can see, I not only have the Ivory Watch Charm ad, I actually have one of the charms." He held up the matchbox-sized replica. "It even has the gold ring on top." He looked past his customer at Annie, and his smile skewed sideways.

Annie mouthed, "Can I see you for a minute when you're free?"

The smile disappeared entirely, but Burt jerked his head briefly toward the closed door at the back of the shop.

In the office, Annie perched on the side of the worn walnut desk and waited. Burt came soon enough, but he stood just inside the door and didn't sit down in the kitchen chair behind the rickety desk. "Hell of a day. You want to see me?"

"The police found a gun in Max's condo."

"That's what I heard." No offer of concern. No protestation of Max's innocence. Nothing more than the bald reply, and an unfriendly face.

"It's a plant, of course." Her tone challenged him.

"I heard on the radio that it tested out to be the death weapon."

317

Annie tensed. For Posey to have already released that information to the media didn't bode well for Max.

Burt cleared his throat. "The sooner this is all cleared up, the better it will be for the players."

"Cleared up? What do you mean, cleared up? For God's sake, you can't think Max shot Shane? You know Max better than that!"

He threw up his hands. "Somebody did it. Somebody who was there. Who am I supposed to pick? Hugo? Carla? Henny? Hell, I can't believe anybody'd do it — but they did. And it's up to the police to solve it. They don't question people without reason."

Annie controlled her fury. There was nothing to be gained by telling Burt what an absolute louse she thought he was. Gritting her teeth, she asked, "Where did you go after you left the school this morning?"

"My God, it's June!" he exploded. "Where do you think I'd go? I came here. I've been here all day. I'll be here until ten o'clock tonight. Now, if you don't mind, Annie, I've got customers waiting and —"

"And you need money, don't you?" she demanded sharply.

A nerve twitched in his cheek. "What's that supposed to mean? Sure, I need money."

"And it's damn important to you to prevent Harley from putting in another retail store on the site of the playhouse, isn't it?"

He didn't answer. He opened the office door and held it for her, his face stony.

The wooden boardwalk was jammed now. Couples walked hand in hand; children, dogs, and bicyclists swarmed. The setting sun splashed crimson across the harbor, across sunburned faces and peeling noses. Boaters relaxed in deck chairs, gin and tonics at the ready. Strauss waltzes echoed merrily, if a little tinnily, from the harborside sound system. Annie eased through the crowd, passing the Proud Palmetto Design Shop and the Great Blue Heron Haberdashery, to stop in front of the Grand Strand Gallery.

A CLOSED sign hung inside the front door. A single painting, a small Klee, sat on an easel with a silver-gray satin backdrop. The lights along the walls were turned off; only the gilt frames could be seen in the dusky interior. In common with the other shops in the summertime, the

319

Grand Strand Gallery was open until eight every evening Monday through Saturday. But not tonight. She glanced at her watch. Just after seven.

A friendly voice called to her. "She's not there, Miss Laurance. Maybe's she's sick. The shop's been closed all day."

"I said *three* dips," a shrill young voice objected.

The cheerful girl behind the ice-cream stand waved to Annie and returned to her duty.

Turning toward Death on Demand, Annie walked swiftly. Carla hadn't been sick that morning.

So where was she?

Annie passed her bookstore, broke into a half run. It was only a block or so to the condos. Carla lived in the same unit as Max, on one of the upper floors.

The bell pealed. And pealed.

Annie kept pressing.

Where was Carla?

Then the doorknob rattled. Slowly, the door swung open.

There were no lights on inside. She could scarcely see the dim oblong that was Carla's face and the faintly darker outline of her body.

"Annie." Carla's husky voice was oddly flat, but she drew out the name like a comet's tail. "L'il Orphan Annie. But that's all right, folks. 'Cause she has Prince Charming." The shadowed face nodded with great dignity. "That's right, folks. Cinderella herself."

Carla was very, very drunk.

She turned away from the door, wavered, put a hand against the wall, then drew herself up and walked with drunken precision into the living room.

Annie felt, in quick succession, anger, relief, irritation, disgust, and pity. Damn. If only she'd come here from Sam's. Was there any point in trying to talk to Carla now? Hell, in this condition she probably didn't even remember Tuesday night!

Exasperated, Annie pulled open the door and stepped into the foyer. She flipped on a light. Carla paid no attention. She was walking with the eggshell particularity of a drunk through the living room to the open French windows and onto the balcony overlooking the sound. Annie hesitated, then followed. The light spilled into the living room, whose decor reminded Annie of the sand and gold of New Mexico, austere yet lovely. Annie paused at the French window.

Carla sat down in a white wicker chair.

There was a cut-glass decanter on the patio table, a half-filled tumbler beside it. She looked up.

"You still here? Cinderella?" The sodden face twisted in a semblance of a smile. "Not fair. You have a lover, don't you? But good girls always do. That's right. Good girls get the love — and bad girls —" She shook her head and her straight black hair swung softly in the twilight. "I thought I had a lover. Yes, I thought I did."

Shit. Once again, Annie felt herself confronted by the subterranean currents in other lives, buffeted by emotions she couldn't deflect.

Tears slid down Carla's face. She paid them no heed. Her hand moved out to pick up the decanter and pour the amber fluid into the tumbler. When she replaced the decanter, she misjudged the distance and the decanter rapped into the glass, then wobbled on the tabletop. She watched it intently, her brow furrowed, but it didn't tip.

"Carla."

The patrician profile turned slowly toward Annie.

"Do you remember Tuesday night? Do you remember Shane being shot?"

Carla lifted the tumbler and took a dainty sip. "I am not drunk," she said clearly. "Do I remember? Hard to forget. Very hard to forget. It was strange. I felt so weird. Like the weird sisters. They always knew when dreadful things must happen — and that was the question, you know, whether they *had* to happen. There we all stood, and he was dead. 'False face must hide what the false heart doth know.' " She began to laugh. "The old boy had it down right, didn't he? A false face. Oh, God, that's so funny. A false face."

"Who wore the false face, Carla? Do you know?"

But Carla only smiled.

"Were you here all day?" Annie demanded.

Carla lifted her glass and drank.

"Your apartment, it's right above Max's. Did you see or hear anybody down there between eleven and one-thirty?"

"Eleven and one-thirty?"

"Somebody hid the gun that killed Shane in Max's apartment. Would you know anything about that?"

"Ah, no. No. That's silly. That's very silly."

"Posey may arrest Max because of it."

Carla put down her tumbler. She began to shake her head. "No. You're lying, Annie. You're lying, aren't you?"

Annie turned away. It was pointless. Poor Carla. She was past comprehending.

Carla lurched to her feet and stumbled after her, clutching the wall for support.

The last words Annie heard as she ran down the outside steps were slurred and furious. "You're lying!" Carla cried behind her. "Aren't you?"

14

When the whirring tape on the answering machine emitted only a faint hiss, Annie knew she'd heard all the messages, and there was nothing from Max, nothing from the best criminal lawyer in the United States of America, nothing from Chief Saulter. Two calls from the *Atlanta Constitution*, one from AP, one from the *New York Times*, one from Ingrid ("Annie, I can't find out anything about Max!"), one from Vince Ellis ("Does Max have any statement for the press?"), three from Henny Brawley, and a dulcet-toned reassurance from Laurel that left Annie quivering with apprehension.

The first time Henny called, she was disgruntled and sounded as grouchy as Bertha Cool. "All right, all right, dammit. So there's only one way in and one way out of room one-nineteen. Thought there might have been a little money dropped into the right hands. But — bartender a Boy Scout leader and desk clerk studying for priesthood. Don't like to be foxed, but admit I am stymied. Will continue to investigate. Over and out."

In the second call, the accent was genteelly British, and the voice was soft and almost apologetic. "I know if I could think of a village parallel, it would all come clear."

And in the third message, "Things," Henny exclaimed sturdily, "are seldom what they seem to be. However, I see my way clearly now and, from this point forward, the guilty party shall not escape my view."

Annie arched an eyebrow. Actually, Henny was a bit off in the last characterization. Miss Marple engaged in thought rather than action, though, to be sure, she certainly participated actively in the denouement of *A Caribbean Mystery.* Hopefully Henny wasn't contemplating any drastic moves. But she should be safe enough since she stubbornly persisted in stewing over what even she now perceived to be an airtight alibi.

Then she listened twice to Laurel's melodious voice: "Annie, my sweet, do you realize the ceremony is but three months away? There is so much to be *done.* It's time to compare our guest lists, order the invitations and your personal writing paper, make a *final* decision about the color scheme for the wedding" (Was there a note of hopefulness here?), "begin shopping for your trousseau, arrange for the photography and the bridal portrait, consult with the florist — and I do have some tiny suggestions here, it's so *lovely* that bachelor's button means hope and jonquils represent affection returned, oh, there are so *many* possibilities." A light shower of laughter. "But I mustn't go on and on, I just want you to rest assured, dear Annie, that the wedding preparations are in good hands while you are preoccupied with crime. Of course, the idea of Maxwell as a murder suspect is *so* absurd, but with your background — the store, dear — you can scarcely be expected not to be a little bit concerned. You may free your mind of fear. *I* am in charge."

Annie flicked off the machine. She had a throbbing headache. But she had to think, keep thinking. (Only not about Laurel and the wedding. What did Laurel *mean*, I am in charge?) With every ounce of will, Annie refused to think further about what damage Laurel . . . It was essential to concentrate on finding *something* to help Max. She turned on every light in her tree house and wished she could find a similar switch in her mind. In the kitchen, she absentmindedly studied the contents of the refrigerator, rediscovered some pepper-speckled salami (at least she hoped it was pepper) which she anointed liberally with Dijon mustard and stashed between two pieces of rye bread. Settling on the wicker divan in the living room, she gnawed on her sandwich, which tasted a little peculiar, and drank a bottle of Dad's Root Beer. Max would hate this repast. Dear Max. Had he had dinner? The county jail would run to ham hock and limas. Were his captors shining bright lights in his eyes and shouting at him? This possibility was always a worry for a Mary Roberts Rinehart heroine. But this line of thought was dithering.

Had she accomplished anything in her afternoon forays? Her mind felt buffeted: Arthur's fear of exposure, Sam's blind ambition, Eugene's absorption in a life other than his own, Hugo's arrogant lust for success, the tragic unravelment of the Horton family, Burt's willingness to jettison anything and everything for himself or the players, Carla's unhappy love affair . . . It was as dismal a list of miseries as any found in a Mary Collins novel.

Annie finished the sandwich and tried to decide what she'd learned. Any of them could have hidden the gun in Max's condo. She frowned. Except Carla. Unless that final angry shout had been a master-piece of guile, Carla believed Annie was lying about Max's predicament. If Carla had hidden the gun, that certainly wouldn't be her response. Unless, of course, she was acting — but Carla was too drunk to act. Wasn't she? Or had that entire episode been staged? Slowly, Annie shook her head. No. Carla was drunk. So, scratch her from the list of possible gun hiders.

A full afternoon of work and only one name stricken from the list.

Annie felt a moment of panic. She'd spoken so grandiloquently to Jed McClan-ahan, blithely instructed him to get Max out of Posey's clutches while she herself single-handedly uncovered the identity of the murderer. She wasn't one step forward that she could see. And now it looked like the only remaining hope was the faint pos-sibility that something on Shane's boat would point to his murderer.

It wasn't much to look ahead to.

But it was all she had.

She squared her shoulders. Eve Gill would be raring to go.

Max leaned back in the straight chair,

his arms crossed on his chest, one loafer-shod foot draped casually over the opposite ankle. But his good humor was beginning to fray. Posey was such an ass. And so obsessed with Max as prey.

"And how can you explain the presence of the murder weapon in your home, Mr. Darling?" The pudgy forefinger waggled a scant foot from Max's nose.

This question, or some variant of it, had been hammered at him for much of the afternoon. Max had given up trying to reason with Posey. Instead, he watched Posey and Jed McClanahan, who marched right alongside the big circuit solicitor, matching florid phrase for florid phrase.

"My client," McClanahan intoned, and it was an impressive noise from a little fellow whose balding head came level with Posey's elbow, "has the constitutional right to remain silent. And I object to this continued flood of verbal abuse as unwarranted harassment. The writ of habeas corpus extends from sea to shining sea, Mr. Posey, and we shall not be deprived of its protection." The scrappy lawyer rolled up his shirtsleeves, but he looked not so much like Clarence Darrow at the Leopold-Loeb trial as the "before" model for a bodybuilding course. Even Donald

Lam would outweigh him.

Posey shook his head like a bull irritated by a gnat. "Do you deny, Mr. Darling, that you showered this morning in your bathroom?"

Pleased at a fresh question, Max opened his mouth —

McClanahan leapt to his side, a tatty leprechaun to the rescue. "My client has no comment. No comment." He bent to Max and whispered, purveying a strong scent of hair spray and bourbon, "Can't tell where he's going with that one. Don't say a word." McClanahan needed a shave and his blue eyes were bleary, but, right now, he was having a hell of a good time. He gave Max a manly cuff on the shoulder.

Max looked from the combative McClanahan to the apparently inexhaustible Posey, and decided he'd had enough, both of the prosecutor and of the best criminal lawyer in the United States of America. (*Where* had Annie found McClanahan?) It was time to get some legal counsel that would put an end to this farce, although he hated to hurt the little guy's feelings. But Max had no intention of spending the night in the Beaufort County jail, and it was long past dinnertime. And worse than his occasional hunger pang was the bubbling uneasiness when he thought about Annie.

Because he knew his Annie. She was stubborn, hot-tempered, determined — and on his side come hell or high water. She would batter down all opposition in her efforts to free him.

Unfortunately, that meant she was now hot on the trail of a clever and merciless killer, who was quite pleased to deliver Max up as murderer-in-chief.

Max rose. Posey and McClanahan swiveled to look at him.

The phone rang.

Posey picked it up, then began to frown. "What the hell . . . I don't see what concern it is of yours, Miss Fontaine, but yes, Mr. Darling is being questioned about the murder of Mr. Petree, and we did find the murder weapon in his —" Posey's face darkened. "What do you mean we couldn't have? We did. The ballistics —" He paused, then interrupted harshly, "Sounds to me like you've had a little too much to drink, lady, and I don't need to talk to you about Mr. Darling or the case!" He slammed down the phone.

He turned toward Max. "You got another lady friend, Darling."

Max smiled complacently.

"The broad that did the sets. Carla Fontaine. Not making much sense." He cleared his throat. "Now, as I was saying . . ."

Max started walking.

He ignored Posey's bellow and his lawyer's caution, pausing at the door only long enough to announce, "Arrest me, or I'm leaving."

Then he hurried down the hall, worry nipping at his heels. What was Annie up to? There was no telling what she might be doing — and what kind of danger she might be facing.

Fortunately, the Merchants Association of Broward's Rock liked the romantic look, opting for a string of varicolored lights that twinkled around the harbor at night, glowing a warm pink, yellow, and aqua, and providing only faint illumination. There was good, strong, piercing light, of course, at several points around the docks, but the far end of the harbor — where *Sweet Lady* rocked at anchor — was mercifully dark. Another plus was the cloudy night. A minus was the water, which only fish would consider comfortably warm.

Annie executed a steady breaststroke and knew she'd give a curious porpoise

heart failure if they came face-to-face —
because she lacked a face. The soggy wet
wool of a mothballed ski mask clung to her
skin and tickled her nose, but she was dark
from head to foot, wearing the hood, a
long-sleeved navy cotton pullover, and
black rayon slacks. She paused, treading
water, at the harbor entrance. Another
twenty yards to *Sweet Lady*. She remembered Max had once told her she swam
like an accountant tallying debits. Fast and
stylish she might not be, but she got there.

She wasn't even breathing hard when
she reached the side of the boat away from
the harbor lights. She put a hand on a
barnacled dock piling and silently tred
water. The boats anchored nearby were
dark and empty, the only sounds the slap
of water against the hulls, the squeak of
mooring lines through bow chocks, and the
mournful resonance of Willie Nelson on
the harbor sound system.

Annie eeled up over the stern like a
frogman in an Alistair MacLean thriller to
flop facedown on the deck.

No alarms. No shouts. No problem.

But when she had her breathing under
control, a sound raised the hair on the
back of her wet neck. Something was
scratching behind the closed hatch. It took

every ounce of will not to bolt upright and jump right back into the water.

Somebody or something was in *Sweet Lady*'s cabin.

Well.

She swallowed hard, pulled her water-proof flashlight from her pocket, knowing full well it lacked pizzazz as a weapon since it was rubber-sheathed, and yanked open the hatch before she could dwell any longer on the possibility of facing a killer, armed only with the tiny light.

The flurry of movement startled her enough that she switched the flashlight on briefly, just long enough to see the luminous eyes and magnificent gray coat of an immense Persian cat. Her thumb jammed down the switch. Darkness descended again. She waited for her heart to stop hammering. *Just a cat,* she kept saying to herself, *just a cat.* But why a cat on the sailboat? Did Shane always keep a cat here? Was the cat an intruder who'd been accidentally trapped?

She heard the click of the cat's claws as he descended the steps to the cabin. An irritable meow wafted up to her.

Only a cat, she reminded herself firmly, and edged down the companionway. Once in the cabin, she flicked on her flashlight again. The cat twirled around her ankles. Obviously, he recognized a cat person and just as obviously he was no stranger here. The flashlight beam passed over a plastic bowl that held water and another that was empty. Clearly, her furry companion wanted food.

The light from the flash danced over the bunks, the galley, the door to the head, then returned to the port bunk, which held a collapsible rubber life raft, a plastic cat-carrying case, and a blue vinyl gym bag. A very suggestive trio. A man in a hurry, and all the accoutrements of flight stowed aboard his boat.

Annie peeled off the soggy ski cap and stuffed it in a pocket, then caved in to the feline entreaties, opening a packet of dry food. The cat hunched over the bowl and began to eat voraciously. From her other pocket, Annie pulled out a pair of rubber gloves and slipped them on.

It didn't take long to empty the gym bag, and she knew she'd hit a jackpot:

A change of clothing, gray slacks and a yellow knit shirt

A roll of bills (five thousand dollars in twenties)

A man's travel kit packed with toiletries

Two Delta Airlines tickets to Atlanta, departing Savannah at 7:10 a.m. June third, with a connecting flight at 9:40 to Los Angeles.

And a sheet of notepaper with a checklist and some haphazard doodles.

In the left-hand corner was a list: cash, carrier, tickets, charts. Each word was checked off. On the right-hand side was a drawing with the descriptive phrase, *abandoned lighthouse,* three slash marks, the words *3 flashes* and, the numbers *0100*. A capsized sailboat rode some waves. There was a scrawled telephone number and, finally, an unexplained, unchecked list: *$1,000,000, LAX, Amer., Gate 17, 1600, 9/6/87.*

Annie studied the plane tickets. June third. Wednesday, the day after Shane was killed. So he'd had plans, all right. She looked at the manifest. The tickets were in the name of Mr. and Mrs. Bill Ford.

Mr. and *Mrs.?*

The cat leaped through the air to land on the bunk with a resounding thump. Annie's heart lurched. She stroked her new friend, who was offended by the rubber gloves, then carefully repacked the contents of the bag, and replaced it next to the cat-carrying case and the collapsible raft. She refilled the big cat's food and water bowls.

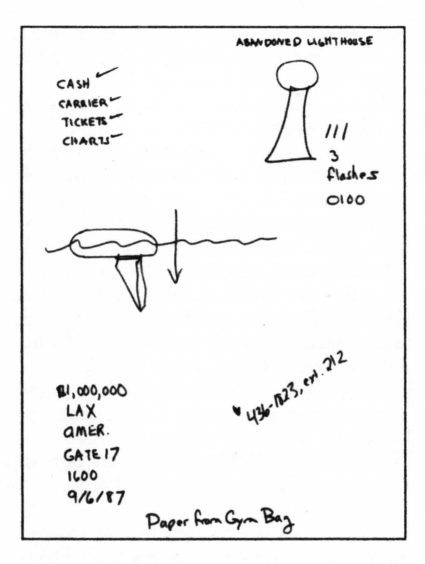

Paper from Gym Bag

Now — how could she bring the boat's contents to Posey's attention?

Sea water dripped on the floor of the phone booth. It was the sole phone booth in the harbor area. Annie had no reason to suppose the line to Death on Demand was tapped, but she wasn't taking any chances. She dialed.

"Hello?"

"Chief Saulter."

"Oh, hi, An—"

"No names, please," she whispered. "This is an anonymous phone call. A tip."

There was an instant's startled pause, then a quick, "Are you all right?"

"Just fine. Kind of wet and cold right now. But listen to this, Chief — Shane was up to something funny. Get a search warrant for his boat as fast as you can. This may blow the whole investigation wide open. It looks like he was planning a surreptitious exit from this island — and maybe somebody didn't want him to go. Can you check on it?"

"Will do."

She switched the Volvo heater on high, but she was still shivering when she turned up the dark, rutted road leading to her tree house. A hot shower. A cup of decaffeinated cappuccino and —

Her car lights illuminated the dark red Porsche parked in her drive. Slewing her car to a stop, she erupted out the door, shouting, "Max! Max, where are you?"

He met her halfway down her steps, and

suddenly she wasn't wet or cold or tired any longer. He grinned and held out his arms, obviously her same old insouciant Max. Though God knows he should have sense enough to look a little worried. In the midst of their embrace, she managed a muffled, "Max, you'll never guess —"

He held her at arm's length. "Practicing for the wedding relays?"

"Relays?"

"Yeah, I just got off the phone with Laurel. She called you. She was sorry to have missed you but said she'll be back in touch soon. Anyway, she and I thought it would be terrific fun to have our own version of the Olympics and . . ."

Her skin glowed a cheerful pink from the hot water and a brisk rubdown. She slipped into seersucker shorts and a T-shirt, gave her hair a brisk brushing, and hurried into the living room.

Max was draped comfortably over the wicker couch. Her heart flipped cheerfully at the sight of him, his sturdy, solid, *nice* body just where it should be.

He looked up, and she saw the beginnings of distraction in his appreciative blue eyes. But not now. Now, she wanted to concentrate on murder and its nefarious handmaidens: lust, greed, hatred, and fear.

"What do you think?" she asked quickly.

"I think you look very, very —"

"About the murder." Sternly.

He didn't bother to stifle a yawn. "Annie, I've spent a long day, a very long day, listening to Posey bellow about nothing else. I don't want to talk about Shane, think about his demise, or concern myself in any way with a problem which rightfully belongs to the duly constituted authorities of Beaufort County."

"But, Max —"

He rose, and now the gleam in his dark blue eyes was unmistakable. "Murder has its charms," he admitted, "but no charms to compare with yours." He held out his arms.

How could any red-blooded American girl resist that declaration? And Annie was patriotic to the core.

A good evening begets a good morning. As Annie poured Max's third cup of coffee, she gauged his humor. A-one. So —

"I'll bet the chief's hot on the trail."

Max lifted his blond head from the morning paper. "Hmm?"

"You know. The stuff I found on Shane's boat."

"Ah, yes, in your daring swim through

the perilous waters of the harbor."

Well, she *was* rather proud of her exploit.

Max grinned and dropped the paper beside his crumb-filled plate. "Okay, sweetie. It was great." His eyes crinkled thoughtfully. "You know, I wonder if he was running cocaine?"

Annie carefully refrained from whooping in triumph. She'd finally lured Max back to talking about the case. She did pop up and dart into the living room to return with a pad of paper. Quickly, she sketched a copy of the sheet she'd found in Shane's gym bag.

"Drugs," she repeated speculatively. Max was so smart sometimes.

"That's the only thing I know — besides rock music — that pays on the order of a million bucks."

"But if he was running drugs here, why a payoff in the Los Angeles International Airport on September sixth?"

He took the pad from her. "Maybe the payoff is *here* and that's just a reservation to go somewhere."

She munched on a muffin. "I thought the drug runners around here had their own operations. I mean, why would there be an L.A. connection for cocaine coming in here from Colombia? I thought the L.A.

people were tied up to the pipeline from Mexico?"

"Not being privy to the latest intelligence from the drug smugglers, I haven't the least idea." He shrugged and dropped the pad on the breakfast table, then swatted at a mosquito. (That was the only hazard of eating breakfast on her deck, but Annie considered fending off insects a small price to pay for the delight in watching the sun spread gold across the marsh.)

Max drank deeply of his coffee, then sighed happily, at peace with the world. "Well, Saulter can nose around and find out."

Annie was a little miffed at this abrupt dismissal of her gloriously garnered information. Who had gallantly braved jellyfish and damn cold water? And it was all so intriguing, the sums of money, the airplane tickets —

"Max, what if Mrs. Bill Ford was going to be Janet? Or Cindy? My God, talk about motives for murder!" She grabbed the pad and flapped it wildly in rising excitement.

Max was unimpressed. "Look, we can *imagine* scenarios from here to Hollywood. What matters are *facts*. Let's see what Saulter comes up with."

It was like being deprived of a brand-new toy. She wanted to sniff and scratch at every possible interpretation of Shane's list. But Max had a point. "You're worse than Sergeant Joe Friday," she groused.

"Actually, reason and not guesswork solves crimes," he abjured, taking the pad, flipping to a clean sheet, and scrawling rapidly.

She decided to ignore the implication, in order to facilitate premarital harmony.

He handed the pad to her with a flourish. "Here's a *reasoned* approach."

MOST LIKELY IN ORDER OF
DECREASING PROBABILITY

T.K.
Sam
Eugene
Cindy
Carla
Burt

LEAST LIKELY IN ORDER OF
INCREASING PROBABILITY

Henny
Janet
Hugo
Arthur

"Uhhm," she began doubtfully.

"Why, Annie, it's obvious." Max was supremely confident and just short of insulting. (It reminded her why she was not enamored of Sherlock Holmes.) "Look at it," Max instructed. "Who had the most free time? The people on list number one. They could easily wander downstairs for a soda or go to the john, wait until nobody was noticing, and get Shane's attention. Ergo, they are the most probable. Then flip the coin. Why would Henny, for example, who is offstage only twice, try to murder Shane during that period?"

"I've never suspected Henny."

He was impatient. "I know. That's just an example. I mean, by a stretch of the imagination, Henny could just possibly have managed physically to commit the crime, although we certainly don't have a motive for her. But the probability is small. You have to consider the odds."

Following Max's reasoning would put Hugo Wolf low on the suspect list, and Annie didn't buy that at all. "Hugo is smart. I can see him figuring this out, then committing the murder so that it would look difficult for him to be guilty."

"Well, he is a cool customer," Max conceded.

Annie began to get that old familiar mouse-in-a-barrel feeling. "Hmm. I understand what you're saying," which was kind of a white lie, "but it seems more important to me to figure who's most likely in terms of motive." She picked up the pen and made her own list.

MOST LIKELY IN TERMS
OF MOTIVE

T.K.
Janet
Hugo
Sam
Eugene
Arthur
Burt
Cindy
Carla/Henny

Max pointed at the last line.

"So what motive do they have?" Annie asked. "Carla didn't like him, but that doesn't seem to be enough. And Henny doesn't appear to have any motive at all. Besides, I'm sure Carla didn't hide the gun in your condo, so that clears her, and I'd just as soon suspect myself as suspect Henny." She grinned. "Oh, that Henny.

She's trying like a beaver to break Sheridan and Harley's alibi, and she's getting nowhere. Now, *they* both have juicy motives."

"But how could either one of them, assuming Henny breaks the alibi, have managed to get in and out of the school unseen?" Max demanded.

Annie nodded disconsolately. Either Cindy or Carla should have seen a nonplayer, because both spent most of the evening in the wings at stage right.

"Carla would have seen anyone who came through the stage door," Max said. "But Cindy was so busy watching the great lover, I doubt if she would have noticed the entrance of a draft horse."

"So, Carla's the only one who might really know."

"Carla," Max said thoughtfully. "That's funny. She phoned Posey yesterday evening. Apparently she was drinking and wanted to talk to him about me or the gun at my place. He hung up on her."

"I'm not surprised," Annie said. "She was drunk out of her mind last night."

"You saw her?"

It was a memory Annie didn't cherish. She hated even to tell Max. "She was — I think somebody dumped her. Something like that. She was so hostile to me."

"Why hostile to you?" He looked affronted.

She patted his shoulder. "Because we're happy," she said quietly. "Oh, Max, I felt so *sorry* for her. She was so bitter."

"Oh, well," he said easily. "She probably won't remember what she said. It'll be okay."

"People are funny, aren't they?" Annie knew that profundity ranked on a par with the exchanges on a late-night talk show. She shot Max a quick glance and saw his mouth curving into a grin.

"Speaking of funny people," he said genially, "wherever did you find the best criminal lawyer in the United States of America?"

"He got you out, didn't he?" she demanded defensively.

"Actually —" he began, then he grinned. "Actually, I find him quite fascinating on a personal level, but I'm glad I don't have to look to him for real representation. It isn't the distinct odor of bourbon and branch water that worries me, it's his habit of muttering about the McNaughton rule."

Annie didn't feel quite so certain Max could afford to be relaxed, despite her discoveries the night before. Persisting like a dog at a bone, she asked worriedly, "Do you really think Posey will pay any attention to the stuff on Shane's boat?"

He stretched and she took time to admire the pull of his polo shirt across his chest. "No sweat, Annie. We'll raise so much hell he'll have to. I'm not the least bit worried."

But Annie couldn't share his sense of well-being, despite their cheerful breakfast and idyllic surroundings. It was already in the eighties. She loved summer. The mud flats were steaming, emitting their unmistakably pungent smell. The *chit, chit, chit* of a frog-hungry marsh hawk and the hyena-like cackle of hidden rails eddied in the quiet morning air.

But she was ready for action, action that would clear Max. An odd sense of urgency pressed her. She pushed back her chair determinedly.

"Now, Annie . . ."

"I'm going to call Saulter."

Max gathered up their breakfast dishes and followed her inside, but she knew he was curious, too, because he put the dishes in the kitchen, then draped himself comfortably, across the couch as she dialed.

"Chief. Annie. Have you . . ."

"Oh."

That mournful monosyllable chilled her.

"Chief, you've checked out the boat, haven't you?"

"No can do. Posey says there's no way he's going to authorize a request for a search warrant on the basis of an anonymous tip. 'Specially not one from you." He hastened to add, "I didn't tell him it was you, but he's not stupid."

"Chief! This is important! It could break the case. Shane was obviously getting ready to skip town."

But her entreaties were to no avail.

"Do you mean Posey's going to ignore all of this?"

Silence.

"Chief, is Posey still after Max?"

"Posey thinks he has a good case —"

"A good case! Does he think Max is an idiot? Why would he hide the gun in his own condo?"

"I don't know anything for sure," the chief said mildly. "All I know is, Posey's got men with photos of Max checking every gun store in a radius of a hundred miles." He paused. "And now he's wondering what kind of info that Fontaine woman might have. He's going to talk to her later today."

Annie banged down the receiver and turned to Max. "What are we going to do?" she fumed.

It didn't help matters for Max to be so unconcerned. He lifted down from the wall an ornamental palm frond and fanned her. "We are going to relax," he crooned. "Annie, I worry about you. Laurel and I . . ."

It was perhaps a good thing for their forthcoming marriage that Annie was, at this point, too apoplectic to talk. At least, it prevented her from revealing her complete and total lack of interest in any joint strategies devised by Max and Laurel for her relaxation.

Wrestling the frond from him and flinging it to the floor, she announced in no uncertain terms: "All right. If those lousy — lousy . . ."

Max held up his hands.

Annie swallowed, lowered her voice. "If the duly constituted authorities refuse to do their duty, why then, we shall take over."

"Oh. What are we going to do?" He was mildly interested.

Annie spread her hands. Dammit, *she* didn't know. But somehow they had to learn the meaning of Shane's scrawls, and also — Why had Carla called Posey? What did Carla know?

"Carla!"

Max touched his hand to her brow in concern. Pettishly, she shoved it away.

"Why did Carla call Posey? Max, we'll start there."

Max whistled cheerfully as he drove the Porsche with his usual flourish, the live oak trees blurring as they flew past. His refusal to recognize the peril he was in astounded her. Even Colonel Bantry, though he tried to put on a good face, was terrified to the core in *The Body in the Library*.

He reached over and pinched her cheek. "Smile, Annie, smile."

She managed a grin, but her heart wasn't in it. Max could perform the most glorious ostrich act this side of Ringling Brothers, but Posey wasn't going away.

Maybe it would turn out that Carla knew something. But would she help them, even if she did?

The adobe-colored condos gleamed like rich cream in the June sunlight. Max pulled into the dappled shade beneath a spreading live oak. "Let's leave the windows down." It was that time of year.

He insisted on stopping first at his

ground-floor apartment. As he unlocked the front door, he said over his shoulder, "Obviously, this lock was no challenge to our murderer." He stooped and picked up the mail that had fallen through the front-door slot, skimming it quickly.

Normally, Annie loved Max's apartment. The living room was a cheerful eclectic mixture of art deco, southwestern Americana, and Danish modern. If it had no central theme, it did have a light, airy brightness and a casual elegance. But today she stood in the archway to the living room and wondered what alien step had sounded in this hall yesterday. The thought cast a cool shadow over the familiar warmth.

"No love letters," he mourned, dropping the lot, including magazines and bills, on a table. "So I guess we can run on up to Carla's."

"You were expecting love letters?"

"Sure. I get rafts of them. Course, you might want to look at this letter." He fished out one and offered it to her.

Annie had received a number of missives in recent weeks with delicate looped handwriting on pale apricot envelopes. She took Laurel's letter and firmly returned it to the pile.

She followed him through the front patio and out a side door to the outdoor steps leading up to the second and third stories, wondering how Carla felt today. Glancing at her watch, she saw it was almost ten a.m. If Carla was up, she probably had a monumental hangover.

Max poked the bell.

They waited. The roar of a motorboat in the harbor drifted up to them, mingling with the buzz of a blower tidying pine needles from the walks.

Max pressed the bell again, this time keeping his thumb on it. The sharp ring grated against the pleasant summer sounds.

Annie moved closer, lifted her hand and knocked, and the door swung slowly in.

"Carla?"

As they had been last night, the French windows to the balcony overlooking the sound were open wide. The breeze swept in, stirring the curtains, and rippling the long black hair that dangled over the edge of the couch.

15

"Max."

But he had seen, too.

"Stay here, Annie." He stepped into the foyer, and walked toward the couch and its grisly burden. As usual, Annie disregarded his warning and followed him.

They stopped several feet from the couch, rooted by shock.

The breeze rustled the newspaper lying on the glass coffee table and eddied the silky strands of Carla's long black hair, spread over the back of the couch. Carla's head was bent back at an unnatural angle. Her face was scarcely recognizable. A leather belt was drawn tightly around her throat. Death had not come gently to Carla, and its imprint was hideous.

Annie made a noise deep in her throat. Max swung around, pulled her close.

"Come on." His voice was harsh.

"Max, we can't leave her!"

"You can't help her now. We'll call from my place."

At his door, he paused. "Annie, I want you to go home. You can take my bike."

It was the very last thing she would have expected from Max. Did he think she was some kind of weak-kneed hysteric?

"Oh, now, wait a minute," she began combatively.

"Annie." He gripped her arm tightly. "Annie, the hell of it is — that belt around Carla's neck . . . it's mine."

She didn't stop to think. Her response was automatic. She tried to turn back to the stairs. "We've got to get it. My God, let's hurry! We've got to get it."

He held tight. "We can't do that, for God's sake."

And he wouldn't let her go.

Posey swaggered around the condos like Lt. Hanson in Phoebe Atwood Taylor's *Octagon House*. He ignored Annie, who had, of course, stayed, and directed all his venom at Max. "What did Fontaine know, Darling? Why did you have to shut her up? What did she have on you? Did she see you in the wrong place Tuesday night? What's the deal?"

Max said no. He said it loud and soft, over and over, and still Posey marched and gestured, keeping his back to that grotesque form on the couch. "So that's *your* belt? Suppose you tell us how it got around her neck? Can you tell us that?"

All the while, Chief Saulter, his weary face creased by worry, directed the investigation, the sketching, the photos, all the careful, patient, and orderly moves to record Carla Fontaine's final moments, her violent end in what had been a serene and lovely room.

In vain, Annie kept trying to interrupt Posey's harangue. Finally, when he paused for breath, she attacked. "Wait a minute. You've *got* to listen to me. I talked to Carla last night. She wasn't interested in Max until I told her the gun had been planted in his condo."

Posey's bulging blue eyes fastened on her with a distinct lack of enthusiasm. His fleshy lips drew back in a sardonic smile. "Loyalty is an exemplary virtue, Miss Laurance — except when it's misplaced. I advise you to tell the truth. This man" — and he tilted his heavy head toward Max — "isn't worthy of your devotion. He is a cold, calculating, vicious killer."

Annie felt her face flush. "I am not," she snapped bitingly, "a jury of cretins. I have every intention of telling the truth. My concern is your inability to *recognize* the truth. Now, why don't you shut your mouth for five seconds and *listen?*"

Max kept making down-girl gestures, but she and Posey glared at each other, hands on hips. Unfortunately, Posey was louder, bigger, and he was in charge.

As one of the policemen, at Posey's direction, grabbed her arm, she challenged, "And how about Shane? Why did he have *two* tickets for L.A.?" As the policeman edged her toward the door, she raised her voice: "And I keep telling you — Carla was dreadfully upset. She was drunk out of her mind, and she was furious with a lover, absolutely in despair. That's what was wrong with her yesterday. She didn't even *believe* me when I said the gun had been found at Max's. She wasn't interested in Max —"

The door closed in her face.

In the last instant, before the panel swung to, Chief Saulter mouthed, "Later."

Annie stood in the outdoor corridor, sucking in deep gulps of air, trying to control her fury.

Then she turned and raced down the steps to Max's condo. But she was still telephoning, hunting for Jed McClanahan, when Posey passed by the open door, his fat hand gripping Max's elbow. As Posey hustled him toward the police car, Max called, "Annie, for God's sake, don't do anything crazy!"

So Max was worried about her. Well, he needn't be. She'd be careful, but she certainly had no intention of sitting around and twiddling her thumbs until he got out of jail again — if he got out of jail again. Oh, she knew it was all a mistake. Or, no, that wasn't right. It was no mistake. Patently, it was a trap, ingeniously constructed by the real murderer. Well, what had been designed surely could be divined — but would anyone listen?

She finally ran McClanahan to earth at the Tell-It-to-the-Navy Bar and Grill.

"You've got to get Max out of jail."

"His belt?"

She tried to be patient. "Obviously the murderer stole it when he was hiding the gun in Max's place yesterday."

"Maybe Darling lost the belt somewhere," McClanahan mused.

"Don't think," she ordered briskly. "Get a bail bondsman and leave the thinking to me."

But when she hung up, she felt an instant of panic. "What in the *hell* was she going to do?"

Then she thought of Amelia Peabody

Emerson, who always felt equal to any occasion. What would Amelia do? Well, for starters, she wouldn't sit on her fanny worrying. She would be up and about.

Annie jumped to her feet. It was time to get back to the basics, and, as Hercule Poirot always pointed out, murder begins with its victim.

Why had Shane spent less time in his usual haunts the past few months?

What was the significance of the doodles on that sheet of paper she'd found aboard *Sweet Lady*?

Who was going to travel as Mrs. Bill Ford?

Who was the woman at The Red Rooster that he didn't introduce to his friend?

She swung back to the telephone.

It was midafternoon when Annie reached 915 West Ribaut Street in Chastain. It was her first visit to that genteel town since the memorable events of the annual house-and-garden tours in early April, but she didn't spare time remembering her unpleasant moments with Police Chief Harry Wells. Her every thought focused on the down-at-heel apartment house in front of her. As she walked up the warped wooden steps, she wondered just what she was going to say to Sue Kay Conrad.

Routine investigation had produced this address, just like the everyday procedures followed by Lt. Luis Mendoza of the Los Angeles Police Department. Her first move had been to call the telephone number scrawled on Shane's sheet of paper. The number belonged to the Buccaneer Inn on the outskirts of Chastain, a half mile from an abandoned lighthouse. Annie nosed around the lighthouse first. The door was ajar. Someone — vandals? or another? — had broken the padlock. Inside, footsteps showed on the dusty treads. At the motel, Annie obtained the description of a woman who had registered there the night of the murder. The desk clerk had noticed her car leaving about midnight. The car had returned at two a.m. Annie took the description to The Red Rooster, a neighborhood bar in Chastain. On a midafternoon in summer, it was drowsy, smelling of years of beer on tap. The tightly muscled bartender was impassive and uncooperative. Mendoza could have flashed his badge. Annie spread three twenties and two tens like a full house.

Now she walked up a dim stairway (the bulb on the landing was burned out) to apartment five.

Annie knocked firmly.

For a moment, she thought there would be no answer, then footsteps sounded on the other side of the thin door.

When it opened, the woman framed in the doorway stared at her with red-rimmed defeated eyes, and Annie knew she had the right place.

"I want to talk to you about Shane Petree." Annie's voice was gentle.

Tears welled up in Sue Kay's eyes. Wearily she gestured for Annie to enter.

Sue Kay Conrad. Late thirties. Divorced. Dyed red hair. An ex-teacher. Lost her job after being charged with possession of marijuana. Worked as waitress, bar girl, food demonstrator in supermarkets. But she loved to sail. Sacrificed every other luxury to keep her catamaran. And that was how she met Shane.

"He was wonderful. Oh, God, we had so much fun. And he was so *nice* to me."

Annie hid her surprise. Who was she to pigeonhole Shane as an all-time loser? Maybe with this woman there had been a flowering of true caring. Maybe with Sue Kay he found an honesty that his life had lacked. At the very least, here was someone who grieved for him.

"What was supposed to happen Tuesday

night?" Annie asked.

That produced another freshet of tears. But, finally, Sue Kay began to speak in a husky, sometimes defensive voice. And when she finished, Annie knew that somehow, in some way she didn't yet understand, she'd found the motive for Shane's murder.

"Do you want to help me catch the person who killed Shane?"

The weary face firmed. Sue Kay leaned forward. "I'll do anything in the world to help."

Annie and Sue Kay waited for two hours before Posey agreed to see them. Once in the small anteroom with its dark green walls and odoriferous cuspidor, Sue Kay turned and asked nervously, "Will they send me to jail?"

"No." Then Annie realized she actually couldn't promise that. Sue Kay and Shane had certainly planned to break some laws. Could she go to jail for planning a crime? Quickly, Annie pressed the older woman's arm. "I don't know, but I promise I'll get you a lawyer." And perhaps not the greatest trial lawyer in the United States of America.

When they were finally ushered into

Posey's office, Annie took one look at his face and knew she was in trouble. But surely he would listen.

Annie nodded toward her companion. "Mr. Posey, this is Mrs. Sue Kay Conrad, and she wants to make a statement about the murder of Shane Petree."

Posey tapped a pen impatiently against his shining desktop. "Ms. Laurance, I don't have time to waste. And as far as I'm concerned, the case is closed, so —"

"Mrs. Conrad is a citizen with information which she believes will be helpful to the state of South Carolina in prosecuting the murderer of Mr. Petree. Are you going to refuse to take her statement?"

Posey snorted like an exasperated hog, but he'd spotted Annie's hand poised with a pen over a pad of paper. And it was, after all, an election year.

"All right, Mrs. Conrad," he said wearily. "Let's have your story."

Sue Kay Conrad didn't look at anyone as she spoke. Her eyes were fastened on a point above Posey's head, but Annie knew she was looking back at days that would never come again.

". . . used to sail every day that we could. And we" — she flashed a defiant look —

"we fell in love. His wife . . . Oh, I know how the other woman always says a man's wife didn't understand him. But, she *didn't*. And she didn't care about him, not at all, and that's why he was always running after other women. But Shane and I — well, it was wonderful."

She paused. Her hands gripped her purse straps tightly. "I don't know when we first talked about it. I mean, it was kind of a dream we had, that we could run away and be happy with each other. Then one day, it was in April, he was real excited, and he asked me if I really would go away with him, just disappear without a trace, and start a new life somewhere under new names. Start all fresh." For an instant, memory glowed in her green eyes, then dimmed. "I said sure. I mean, what the hell? I had nothing here. And nobody. Nobody gave a damn whether I walked through a door or said hello or good-bye. But he wasn't kidding. It was all worked out. You see, they needed money, Shane and his wife, and they came up with this idea, that Shane would capsize his sailboat and drown. Of course, he wouldn't really drown, that was the neat part. He would disappear. They worked it out. He would turn over the boat, swim to shore, and disappear, go to a different town. They decided on L.A. and next fall, after the insurance money came through, Sheridan would meet him in the L.A. airport and give him a million in bearer bonds."

Posey planted his elbows on the desk and rested his porcine face in his hands. He didn't say a word.

Annie glared at him. If he wasn't going to ask any questions, she would. "Did Sheridan know about you?"

"Oh, no. No. Part of the deal was that he and Sheridan were through. No, she didn't know about me." For just an instant, humor flashed in Sue Kay's eyes. "From what Shane said about her, I don't think she'd have liked me being part of it."

Posey rolled his eyes ceilingward in disgust. "Ms. Laurance," he was long-suffering, "my department has thoroughly investigated the whereabouts of Mrs. Petree. There is no *doubt* where she was at the time her husband was shot. Now, I won't question your motives in trying to help the state of South Carolina, but this is a mighty convenient story you two have cooked up — and it isn't going to do you a damn bit of good!"

Forever afterward, she had no memory

of her return to the island. She pulsed with fury. That obtuse idiot! That bulging-eyed imbecile! That brain-dead buffoon! It was only when she screeched to a halt in her driveway, having hurtled across the island like Asey Mayo at the wheel of his Porter, that she became aware of her surroundings. The sun was setting and the sky to the west flamed a splendid red-gold, but, too busy for once to enjoy the beauty of the island, she raced up her steps, slammed inside, and began to pace. Otherwise, she would have exploded

"Easy does it," she warned herself aloud. She had to cool down. But she did have to hand it to Posey, he'd certainly concentrated her attention wonderfully. She was alive with determination to outwit him. By God, she would get to the truth — and she would rub Posey's nose in it!

She paced by her bookcase. The shining red glow spilling through her west windows brought faded bindings to life. Some titles didn't reassure. Unjust imprisonment was a fact in life as in fiction. Wretched Edmond Dantès in *The Count of Monte Cristo*. And in *Lady Molly of Scotland Yard*, it took Lady Molly years of effort to prove her husband's innocence and free him from Dartmoor.

If that oaf Posey . . . She turned, marched in the opposite direction. Okay, she had to stop wasting her energies fuming about Posey and put her mind on the problem. That always worked for Sir John Appleby.

And she knew her afternoon's work was significant. From the first, she'd questioned the timing of Shane's murder. Why that particular Tuesday night? Now, it seemed clear that —

The phone rang.

News about Max?

She sprang across the room and snatched up the receiver.

"Annie, dear, I've been calling all day." Laurel was much too good-humored to complain, but there was a faint note of distress in the golden voice.

"It's so regrettable," the liquid tone continued, "to have the wedding timetable interrupted like this." A thoughtful pause. "Annie, do you suppose it would help if I called that Posey man and explained that we have *responsibilities?* That it is our glorious privilege and duty — yes, our duty — to focus our energies upon this once-in-a-lifetime opportunity to become a part of the outpouring of human emotion that will crest in 2012? Annie?" A wealth of inquiry in the gentle enunciation of her name.

"Uh, Laurel, Max . . . Max . . . Max . . ."

"I do hope it isn't drafty in that jail. He catches cold so easily, and really it's absolutely necessary for Max to be in the pink. I've made the appointment for him to be measured for his black tailcoat. Now, it must be tailored properly. And I was thinking that it would add such a gay, *international* note, in keeping with our glorious theme, if I ordered tiny flags of as many countries as possible to be sewn into the satin trim of the trousers. Annie, what do you *think?*"

"You *know* that Max is in jail?"

A surprised pause. "Annie, don't you listen to the news? Dan Rather featured it."

"Laurel." Annie tried to keep her voice even and untroubled; it was important not to disturb the obviously precarious balance of Laurel's mind. "I can't talk about the wedding now. I don't even know if we can have a wedding —"

"Why ever not?" That Laurel was prompted to interrupt showed how much that statement shocked her.

"Max is in jail. He's going to stay in jail if I don't figure out who the murderer is."

"Annie, Annie, I can see I've caught you at a busy time. I shouldn't have bothered you with my concerns. I truly will take care of everything. Do rest now, my dear. Night, night."

Annie carefully replaced the receiver. If Posey ever met Laurel, he'd never believe Max was innocent.

Annie hurried into the kitchen and brewed strong, strong coffee. When it was made, she carried a steaming mug into the living room and settled on the wicker couch with the computer printouts on the cast and crew of *Arsenic and Old Lace*, Max's list of probabilities, her list of motives, and a fresh notebook.

First, she reread the printout. Then she turned to her notebook and carefully recreated the conversations she'd had with Harley, Sheridan, Arthur, Sam, Hugo, Eugene, Janet, Burt, and Carla. Finally, she added the probable timetable for the secretion of the gun in Max's condo and Carla's murder.

Why did Carla have to die?

Carla must have known something that placed the murderer in extreme jeopardy. What could —

The phone rang.

She stared at for it a moment, but answered on the third ring.

"Annie." The chief's voice was as mournful as a bloodhound's bay. "You did some good work today. Too bad Posey's such a damned fool."

Annie's blood pumped rapidly. Fool was scarcely descriptive enough.

Saulter continued, "I know it's all true, 'cause I went out to talk to Sheridan." A ruminative pause. "Posey's mad enough to skin me alive. Anyway, old Shane's lucky he's dead. When I told Sheridan about Sue Kay Conrad, I thought she was going to bust. I never *seen* a woman that mad. The look in her eyes would scorch hell. But she denies it all, of course."

"And Posey still refuses to listen?"

"Listening isn't Posey's strong point. But he's going to have to pay some attention to the autopsy report 'cause it raises some funny questions."

Her hand tightened on the phone. Autopsy. That conjured up unpleasant images. But surely the method of Carla's murder was obvious. Horribly obvious.

"Carla was already dying when she was strangled," the chief said quietly.

Annie practically stopped breathing. "What do you mean?"

"Carla was drunker than a hoot owl, all right, but she'd taken a couple of dozen Valium to boot. She was probably in a stupor when the murderer came in. It must have been as easy as pie to slip up behind her and drop the belt around her neck. That's why she didn't struggle. Usually, in a strangling, the victim's hands are all bunged up, but Carla just lay there."

Drunk. More than drunk. Drunk and *dying.*

"How did she ingest the Valium?" Annie asked crisply.

"It was in the dregs of her last drink. And only her prints are on the glass, the decanter, and the plastic prescription bottle."

With a pang Annie remembered the despair in Carla's eyes. "Do you think it was suicide — or did someone else drop the pills in her drink?"

"Two murderers? Hell, I'd say anything's possible in this case."

Annie worked it out "Okay, let's think two murderers for a minute. Murderer A arrives, sees she's blotto, finds her Valium, dumps it in her drink, watches while she finishes the whiskey, then departs. Murderer B arrives, finds her passed out, whips out Max's belt, and strangles her." Once again Annie recalled Carla's last evening, the tears, the despair. "No, Chief. Not two murderers. Suicide and one murderer."

She shivered. "Our killer is just a tad too efficient. Carla would have saved him some trouble. Damn whoever it was." Her voice shook with anger.

"Steady, Annie."

"If you'd seen Carla that night . . . Oh, Chief, she was so terribly unhappy. I don't suppose she left a note?" But Annie wasn't hopeful. Carla had been *so* drunk.

He was silent a shade too long.

"Chief?"

"No-o-o. Look, Annie, don't tell *anybody*, but there were some scrawls on the pad by her telephone. Looks like she'd talked to somebody. It doesn't make any sense, a bunch of X's and 'no' written over and over in capital letters — and Max's name."

Annie felt like she'd been kicked in the chest. Another link to Max.

Saulter continued gruffly, "Now, Posey thinks Carla saw something that linked Max to Shane's murder but she couldn't believe it and she wanted to talk to him before she went to the cops. He says maybe she was in love with Max and kept quiet to protect him, then decided she couldn't stick it out."

"That's the silliest damn thing I ever heard!"

Saulter began gingerly, "You don't suppose she —" He paused, tried again. "Could she have fallen for Max, one of those one-sided things? I mean, I know he isn't interested in anybody but you. . . ."

"Carla wasn't in love with Max." She spoke with such absolute certainty that it almost surprised her. Because, after all, why shouldn't everyone — including Carla — be in love with Max? He was fun and handsome and sexy and — She swerved back to the point. "Nope. And, Chief, I'm not saying it because I think it helps Max. I'm saying it because it's so. I've got antenna out to the wall as far as Max is concerned. I can calibrate another woman's interest in him to the millimeter. It's not that I'm jealous, nothing like that, but I always know when the signals are flying — and Carla didn't emit a beep in his direction. He might as well have been a horseshoe or a weeping willow for all the interest she exhibited. And besides, when I went to her place yesterday, she said she'd had a lover and she was so bitter, so unstrung. It sure wasn't Max."

"Well, she wrote down Max's name, that's all I can tell you," Saulter said gloomily. He didn't have to add that Posey would use it to his advantage. "And there's

374

the belt." The chiefs voice sank another notch. "No doubt but that it's Max's. Has his initials on the back. He bought it last year at some place in New York City called Ferragamo or something like that. His fingerprints are all over it. He says it was hanging in his closet, claims whoever planted the gun must have nosed around and taken it. Posey gives that the horselaugh."

"Chief, nobody in his right mind would use his own belt with initials and *fingerprints* on it to commit a murder!"

Saulter cleared his throat. "Posey says it happens all the time. Course, a good trial lawyer can make some time with the jury, I'd think."

Annie flopped down in the wicker chair by the phone. "Oh, God!"

"Yeah. And," and the momentary surge of vigor in his voice fled, "it sure doesn't help that Carla called Posey and Max overheard it and she got murdered that night."

"What time do they think she was killed?"

"The M.E. estimates time of death between six and ten last night. Course, we know she was alive 'til eight-ten. That's when she called Posey. Max claims when he got back to the island he went directly to your place and waited for you. But who's to prove it? Posey said he had plenty of time to kill her and get back before you arrived."

Posey. Posey. Posey. His every effort was venomously directed at finding evidence against Max — and all the while the truth was out there somewhere, but if they didn't start looking for it, time and obfuscation would bury it as deeply as in Patricia Moyes's *Johnny Under Ground* — and she couldn't wait twenty years for the mystery to be unraveled.

"Chief, are you trying to find out more about Carla? What she did yesterday? Who she might have talked to?"

"I wish I could. So far as we can discover, she went straight home from that session at the high school and started drinking. She didn't eat any lunch. She just sat there and drank all day, and — if we're right in figuring suicide — laced her last drink with Valium."

"Dear God, why? What happened to her to make her do it? If we can find that out, we may discover her murderer."

"You aren't thinking it might be separate from Shane's killing?" he asked slowly.

"I don't know. I don't know anything.

But we have to find out why she was so upset."

"Posey says it was because of Max."

"No. I was there, and I know it wasn't because of Max. Oh, if only Posey would listen!" She sighed. "Poor Carla. She must have been so terribly unhappy. And then to be killed in such a dreadful way." She swallowed. "Have you notified her family?"

"Yeah. But nobody seems to give much of a damn. We got in touch with a sister in Atlanta. Well, she was shaken up, like you'd expect. When she kind of settled down, I told her it would be Monday before we could release the body and where should we send it? So she got quiet and thought for a minute, then told me she'd call back. Okay, so about an hour later, she calls and this is the deal: They don't want the body. Told me to arrange a closed service here and have her buried in the Island Hills Cemetery. No expense spared or anything, but nobody will be coming, and the stone's just to say Carla Morris Fontaine, and her birth date and death date."

"*They* don't want her? Who's they?" Poor, poor Carla.

"Yeah, I got that. Her parents are alive. Mr. and Mrs. C. T. Fontaine. I got the address and everything, but the sister told me not to call them, they wouldn't talk to me. Said they didn't recognize Carla as their daughter."

"Oh, Chief."

"Yeah. Tough."

"What's the sister's name?"

He hesitated.

"Chief, please. I keep remembering her, how aloof and formal she was. She didn't try to be friends, you know. But she must have been so hungry for people to know. That's why she was in the players. She was a wonderful carpenter, did you know that? She could make or fix anything. But who was she? Why was she all alone? What had happened to her before she came here? Chief, I have to find out."

He sighed. "I'll probably end up in jail right alongside Max. I will for sure if Posey ever finds out I'm feeding stuff to you." He took a deep breath. "But I honest-to-God don't think Max could ever kill anybody, not in cold blood. Now, I'm not so sure about you, Annie, but I'd bet on old Max. So," and now his tone was brisk, a to-hell-with-Posey tone, "the sister's name is Mrs. Whitfield Cherry." And he gave Annie the address and phone number in Atlanta.

"The Cherry residence." The voice was

soft, Southern, and female.

"May I speak to Mrs. Whitfield Cherry, please?"

"May I ask who is calling?"

Annie hesitated. Her own name would mean nothing to Carla's sister, and, at this time, Mrs. Cherry would be loath to talk to strangers. "Please tell her that a good friend of her sister Carla needs urgently to speak to her." If that weren't quite true, she did hope to help track down Carla's murderer — and perhaps that could count as friendship delayed.

"Just a moment, please."

As she waited, Annie glanced around her living room, at her softball trophy atop the nearest bookcase, and she thought of all the good beer and fun players she'd known. And there was a snapshot of Ingrid among the many tacked to her bulletin board. Such a good friend, with her understated comments and staunch support. Her friends, many of them older, in the Altar Guild at St. Mary's. The friends she'd made in the Broward's Rock Merchants Association. Her tennis chums at the Island Hills Country Club. So many friends. And there, in the center of the board, smiling at her with a glint of devilment and his incomparable air of insouciance was Max, the best friend of all. Poor, poor Carla.

"Hello." The voice was clipped — and angry.

Annie was startled, but she began her spiel. "Hello. I'm Annie Laurance. I live on Broward's Rock and —"

"I don't know what you think you can gain from calling, but I want to make it very clear that we aren't going to give you any money at all. And if you try to bring some kind of palimony suit, we'll fight it every step of the way — and we have plenty of money to do it."

Annie had expected distress, perhaps a voice numb with grief, but not anger. "I don't —" she began.

The receiver slammed into the cradle.

So, there was a story there all right. But how was she going to get it?

Annie riffled through the computer printout, and reread the brief section on Carla:

Carla Morris Fontaine. B. 1951, Atlanta, Georgia. B.A., Vassar, 1972. Taught Latin September 1972 to March 1976 at St. Agnes Secondary School in Atlanta. Opened art gallery, Broward's Rock, April 10, 1976. Lives alone. Active in Broward's Rock Players. Apparently no close friends of either sex. Pleasant, but aloof. Not a mixer.

Palimony. Images floated in her mind, none of them savory. Wasn't that when a party to a sexual liaison tried to get money or proceeds from an estate on the basis of a long-term relationship not recognized by law?

Mrs. Whitfield Cherry had broad-jumped to a conclusion. The conclusion was wrong, but suddenly Carla's life, her loneliness, her aloofness, began to make some sense.

Annie made several more calls, before she tracked down Mrs. Harriet MacKenzie.

"Mrs. MacKenzie, I understand you were the headmistress at St. Agnes in the seventies."

"Yes." The voice was cultured, cheerful, and friendly. "What can I do for you?"

"Have you heard of the murder of Carla Fontaine?"

The pause was prolonged. "Yes. What a tragedy for the Fontaines. Are you a friend of Carla's?"

This time, Annie decided to avoid any possibility of a misunderstanding. "My fiancé and I knew Carla through the community theater here on Broward's Rock —

and that's why I'm calling you. The police have arrested Max, that's my fiancé, but I know the evidence against him has been manufactured. And I wanted to talk to you about Carla. I think it's very important to find out everything I can about her past."

"I doubt if I can be very helpful. I knew Carla as a teaching colleague and not very well at that because of the difference in our ages." The desire to end this conversation was very apparent in the brisk finality of the statement.

"Tell me, Mrs. MacKenzie, is St. Agnes on the quarter or semester system?"

"The semester."

"And how does the spring semester run? From January to May?" Annie waited tensely.

"Why, yes." She was puzzled, but unsuspecting.

"Will you tell me why Carla quit teaching in mid-semester?"

This time Annie knew she'd rung the bell. The silence was absolute.

"Please, Mrs. MacKenzie. I promise I won't spread this information around, but I think it is relevant to what happened here."

"How can it be?" The woman's voice was troubled. "This was an incident that happened years ago. What could it have to do with Carla's death?"

"Carla was involved with someone here — and I think you can tell me whether her lover was a man — or a woman."

The seconds ticked by, then Harriet MacKenzie sighed. "I hate talking about it. Miss Laurance, do you promise you won't repeat it unless absolutely necessary — and I *don't* intend to give you the name of the student."

"So Carla was involved with a student?"

Another weary sigh. "Yes. A very outstanding girl. And, of course, her family was wild, absolutely wild, when they found out. But do you know, Miss Laurance, I always suspected that the girl made the advances, then told some of her friends simply out of malice, and that it was Carla who was victimized. This girl went on to marry several times, and I've heard rumors of other entanglements. I always felt she took advantage of Carla, not the other way around. But, of course, Carla was older; she should have known better. I had no choice but to ask her to leave."

"And Carla's family?"

"Carla's family." The former headmistress's tone was noncommittal, then she said quietly, "It's hard not to be judgmental, Miss Laurance. And, of course, it's always so easy to see the other person's faults. But I've always felt that Carla's parents were so self-righteous, so obsessed with appearances, and so terribly cold. They felt that she had disgraced them, because the story went the rounds, you know. Everyone knew." A small laugh. "Of course, not literally everyone, but everyone who mattered to the Fontaines."

"So Carla left town, came here, and opened her gallery. Did they never have anything more to do with her?"

"I don't know about that. I think Carla had income from a trust fund. I never heard of her being back in Atlanta, but I can't tell you for certain." Mrs. MacKenzie hesitated, then said, "You won't tell them I told you, I hope."

"No. I don't see any reason to talk to them."

The retired headmistress heard the disdain in her voice. "It is a tragedy for everyone, Miss Laurance. And perhaps you are wrong, perhaps none of this has anything to do with her death."

"To the contrary, Mrs. MacKenzie, I'm afraid it has everything to do with it."

Carla was distraught because her lover had betrayed her. Did this mean she was upset because a woman she loved had been involved with Shane, and that she had murdered him and expected Carla to maintain silence? That would be enough to destroy Carla's faith in her lover, wouldn't it? So Carla put Valium in her whiskey, but her lover — the murderer — didn't know that and came to kill Carla.

What a muddle of crossed purposes and broken dreams.

But how had Carla known that her lover was the murderer? What had Carla seen? And who had been her lover?

There were only four other women at the theater the night Shane was shot: Cindy, Janet, Henny, and Annie herself. Obviously, it wasn't Henny.

Cindy. Nothing in Cindy's demeanor ever indicated the least bit of interest in her own sex. She was so vigorously lustful about Shane that it seemed unlikely.

Janet. Janet still seemed to Annie the acme of middle-class respectability, a woman who had slipped into an affair with Shane and was bitterly regretting it and hating even more his involvement with her daughter.

Annie shook her head in bewilderment.

As she considered Janet's and Cindy's involvement with Shane, Annie remembered anew just how loathsome Shane had been. Carla had *despised* him. That was clear, right from the first day of rehearsal, from her occasional glance of distaste, her incredulous disgust when he didn't even recognize the most common quote from *Macbeth*.

Annie paced into the kitchen and poured another mug of coffee. She felt supercharged, a mixture of energy, determination, and intense concentration. But she also felt a quiver of worry. Something didn't jell here. She was right, wasn't she, about Carla? Carla was depressed to the point of suicide by the actions of her lover. And her lover had to be a woman. That was clear as clear. And her lover was the murderer.

Cindy. Or Janet.

Was it conceivable that Carla was involved with one of *them?* But it had to be, unless Annie was absolutely off target.

Carla. It all came back to her — her likes, her dislikes, her loves and hates. Carla had seemed much as usual when they gathered at the school to hear Posey. Subdued, of course, as were they all. But she'd left there to go home and drink —

Annie put down her coffee mug untasted.

Carla seemed fine when she arrived at the high school auditorium Thursday morning. But after the session there, she'd returned to her condo and started to drink heavily. And it had upset her dreadfully when Annie told her the gun had been hidden in Max's condo. Annie thought about that morning's interrogation and Posey's loud, obnoxious behavior. She thought about the gun being placed in Max's apartment.

And, quickly, like the meshing of gears, it all came together in her mind.

There were so many pointers.

The maliciousness of the sabotage, especially the shooting of Freddy.

Shane's last-minute mastery of his lines.

The timing of the murder.

Carla's distress after the session with Posey at the high school.

And it all came down to a single fact. It wasn't what Carla *saw* that caused her suicide attempt — or her murder.

16

"Hello." His voice was thick with sleep.

Annie glanced at the clock and realized with surprise that it was almost midnight, but what she had to say couldn't wait. There was no time to lose.

"Chief, I know who the murderer is."

"The hell you say." Now he was wide awake. And eager.

Obviously, the chief *cared* about Max. Annie felt a warm rush of affection.

"What's happened? Where are you, girl?"

"Oh, I'm here. At home. And I haven't done anything yet. I called you first. I need your help. Now look, Chief, this is how I see it."

She laid it out for him, and, after a first shocked exclamation, he said slowly, "By God, it all fits . . . Jesus, what a bitch."

"Yes. I agree."

"To set somebody up like that! She's a monster, isn't she?"

Yes. A cool, calculating, manipulative monster, feigning love, instigating murder,

388

then brilliantly covering her tracks. Annie felt her throat tighten. And all they had against her was a reasoned judgment. Nothing concrete. Nothing to take to Posey and say, "Hey, look at this! She's the one!"

Chief Saulter, too, saw the problem. "Damn, I think you're right, only I don't see how we can ever prove it."

But Annie had an idea there, too.

"It isn't going to be easy. But, with your help, I'm going to raise a ghost."

She rode her bicycle through the night. Saulter had offered to pick her up, but there must be no public connection between them from this point on. As she pumped past the marsh ponds with their night sounds, the hoot of owls, the gurgle of water, the splash of scavenging raccoons and cotton rats, she realized anew how easy it was to get around Broward's Rock. It was just a few minutes' bike ride to any point. She would bet that was how the murderer came to Carla's condo last night, waiting until the fall of darkness and depending upon the anonymity of a bike rider, dressed perhaps in a navy-blue warmup, a scarf, un-remarkable, unremarked. When Annie reached the condos, she dropped her bike behind a sweet myrtle. Her shoes crushed fallen leaves and a spicy bay rum scent rose in the humid night air. She slipped from shadow to shadow and ran lightly up the outside steps to Carla's door. She knocked twice, softly and quickly, and the door swung open. For just an instant, she had a hideous memory of that morning, then she reached out and gripped the chief's strong brown hands.

"Her tape recorder's on the shelf above the TV." He turned his hooded flash briefly to his left.

That was the first requisite.

Then she explained the second. "Can you get the postmaster to cooperate?"

"Sure. You want to mail a tape and have it stamped with Thursday's date and delivered tomorrow morning. Right?"

"Yes. Otherwise the murderer will know Carla couldn't have mailed it. Everything hinges on that."

"No problem," he said softly. "The timing works fine. Carla could've mailed it late Thursday and that would account for delivery on Saturday instead of Friday morning."

Now, all Annie had to do was put on the best performance of her life.

Annie drew the curtains and turned on a

single floor lamp. In the dim light, she paced back and forth in Carla's living, room, glancing occasionally at the couch. She was remembering her visit with Carla, every word Carla had said, every intonation, that careful, particular, enunciated speech of the very intoxicated.

Because Carla must have called her murderer at some point, must have telephoned and said she knew that Max was being questioned and the gun had been found in his condo. Carla must have warned that she wouldn't be a party to a frame-up.

Carla meant that she had reached the end of her complicity, that she intended to die, but the murderer took it as a threat and so the murderer came.

By then Carla was sunk in her final sleep. Death was coming, but it came sooner than called. At least she hadn't suffered.

Carla's voice, its sound and substance and resonance.

Annie closed her eyes and pressed her hands to her face. In her mind, she could hear Carla: "L'il Orphan Annie. But that's all right, folks. 'Cause she has Prince Charming."

She dropped her hands, opened her eyes, and crossed to the tape recorder. When she turned it on, she began to speak and it was Carla's voice, husky and low, with its undercurrent of sadness and alienation, that hung in the quiet air:

"I will be dead when you hear this. But you won't care, will you? You never really cared for me at all. It was a sham, wasn't it, when we made love?"

Annie paused. She stared unseeingly across the night-shadowed room so dimly illuminated by the brass, onyx-based floor lamp. She let the tape roll for several seconds, because she was Carla and she was very, very drunk.

"Cinderella came. I told you that. You hid the gun at Max's. That was wrong. Dead wrong." A soft, hiccoughing laugh. "Dead wrong. Just like I'm going to be. But I won't help you do it. I was such a fool, listening to your lies, and all the while I think I knew. It's always been the same. I love, but nobody loves me. But that's not —" a pause and the very careful articulation of two syllables — "germane."

Silence again. Two seconds. Three.

"I hated Shane." The ghostly rendition of Carla's voice became harsh. "I hated him. To know he had touched you — And you convinced me he'd been so dreadful to you. But that wasn't true, was it? No, you

392

had such a long-range plan and you and I would enjoy the fruits together. What a laugh. God, what a laugh," and the word ended in a sob.

Carla, vulnerable, betrayed, exploited.

"Maybe it all went wrong because we called up the weird sisters. That's what they thought, you know, in Shakespeare's time. If you called up the forces of darkness, they would overwhelm you — and they did. They did. Remember what the first murderer said: 'I am one, my liege, Whom the vile blows and buffets of the world Hath so incens'd that I am reckless what I do to spite the world.' That's how I felt, but the agony of the act won't go away, so I'm going to sleep forever. I don't want to keep remembering."

Another pause. The longest pause.

"I don't know why I'm sending this to you." A brittle laugh. "But that's a lie. I know. I'm so angry. But I still want to give you some time. Perhaps you'll join me. That might be the easiest answer. You see, the world is going to know *everything* that happened. I've sent a tape to Annie, too. I told it all. Every ugly word of it."

A final pause. Annie clicked off the recorder and wiped away the tears streaming down her face.

★ ★ ★

Annie slept restlessly. Frightful images kept creeping out from the dark recesses of her mind. Finally, she lay quietly, watching the sun edge into her room, turning the shadows to gold. Saturday morning. The tape would be delivered to the murderer about nine-thirty. As on all Saturdays, Annie would be at Death on Demand.

Everything was in readiness, Ingrid sent to Beaufort on an errand to keep her out of harm's way, Annie equipped with a hidden microphone, and the back door unlocked so that Chief Saulter could slip inside to hide behind the coffee bar.

At nine-thirty, the telephone rang.

It had to be answered, of course, though, of all days and all hours, this was the very worst time for Laurel to call. But she was, after all, Max's mother.

"Death on Demand."

The tone was upbeat, feisty, and bright. "Leave it to me, Annie. Rebecca Schwartz knows where to hang out and when. The suspect won't give me the slip."

So Julie Smith's Jewish-feminist lawyer-heroine, or at least Henny's version of her, was hot on someone's trail. Annie would have grinned, but right now she was having a hard time breathing.

Shortly before ten, the postman and two sunburned, middle-aged tourists entered Death on Demand.

Annie nodded good morning at Sam Mickle, who didn't look big enough to hoist the large leather mail pouch slung over his shoulder. He plopped down a thick batch of circulars, magazines, bills, and — yes, there it was, the small padded envelope with the Death on Demand address penned in handwriting copied so meticulously from Carla's address book.

Sam paused, cleared his throat, and bent close to her, speaking softly so he wouldn't be overheard. "Miss Laurance, just want you to know, I think this arrest of Mr. Darling is a bad thing. A damn bad thing."

Annie felt as jittery as a second-story man perched on the sharply tilted tile roof of a French chateau. Lord, if there was ever a moment when she didn't want to be spotted in confidential conversation with her postman, this was it. She was aware of a shadow at the used-book window. If the murderer saw this . . . "Thanks, Sam. It will be all right." She stepped back. "Sorry, I've got customers."

He nodded and turned away.

Annie forced herself to look pleasant as she turned toward her unwanted customers. "Yes, can I help you?"

But if she felt thwarted, how must the murderer feel, peering through the window, and seeing the telltale envelope lying on the cash desk?

The husband, a skinny six-footer with thick-rimmed wire glasses, a nose smeared with sun block, and a querulous look, confided, "I'm always on the lookout for books about codes."

"Codes?"

"Cryptanalysis. You know, pigpen ciphers, chronograms one-time pads, vigenère ciphers." His peeling brow wrinkled in irritation. "You do realize there is a subgenre of mysteries based on codes?"

"Oh, yes, yes, of course. Right over here."

"And I don't have all the Elizabeth Peters. Can you help me?" his wife chirped.

Annie had never helped anybody quite so quickly. In less than eight minutes, she was ringing up her sales and shepherding them out the door, the man clutching *Spy in the Room*, *The Cipher*, *The Spy and the Thief*, and *Code Name Sebastian*. His equally sunburned wife carried *Crocodile on the Sandbank*, *The Curse of the Pharaohs*,

The Mummy Case, The Jackal's Head, Borrower of the Night, The Copenhagen Connection, and *Die for Love.*

And they were out the door and on their way wondering perhaps why they hadn't browsed a little longer.

No more customers, Annie prayed.

The doorbell sang.

Annie looked up and panic flooded her.

Oh, dear Lord, she should have known. She should have *known.* There hadn't been a phone call since last night.

Laurel swept inside, a slender, ethereal blonde in flowing blue . . . draperies. And that was as near as Annie could come to a description of her gown, which, exotic as it was, shimmered with elegance and style. She held out both hands, beaming, her blue eyes filled with a childlike warmth and delight.

"Annie, my, dear child, I am here!"

Another figure slipped in behind Laurel, moving swiftly to disappear behind the True Crime section.

Annie rushed out from behind the cash desk and gripped Laurel's arm.

A faint fragrance of lavender swirled in the air like mountain mist.

"Laurel." Annie's voice was breathless. What could she say? How could she deflect

Max's mother, protect her from the menacing figure poised — and Annie sensed a caged feral impatience — behind the bookcase?

"Annie, my dear, I am here to stay. I shall just take my place in some nook or cranny here in your delightful shop, and I shall be responsible for *everything*. You needn't worry again. You will be free to bend your every gallant effort to gain —"

"Laurel, you are *wonderful* to come. You are just in time." Annie's grip tightened, and tried to edge the willowy form toward the door.

Without any overt action, Laurel resisted and they were locked in a frozen tableau a scant two feet from the entrance.

Desperately, Annie reached far into her heart and said brightly, "You must go at once to see Mrs. Crabtree. We have reached the ultimate moment of decision — and you may have carte blanche."

"Carte blanche?" The dulcet voice rose in delight. "Oh, Annie, my love, you will never regret taking this great step forward for mankind." The swift cool touch of lips on her cheek, a rustle of silk, and Laurel was through the door and gone.

Annie closed the door and turned back to the cash desk. She reached casually for her mail, began to thumb through it, stopping at the one particular envelope and staring at it in simulated surprise. As she began to open it, footsteps sounded lightly on the parquet floor.

Annie turned.

She wouldn't have recognized her visitor if she hadn't expected her. It was, Annie thought in a remote corner of her mind, astounding the way women could alter their appearance through dress.

The murderer wouldn't have caused notice on her bike ride. After all, many women now avoid the sun as much as possible, now that skin cancer is an everpresent specter. She wore a pomegranate-red and violet-blue flowered shift. An enormous sun hat was tied beneath her chin with yellow straps, and huge silver-tinted sunglasses obscured her eyes. In that garb, she was as effectively hidden as a mud-brown cottonmouth on a creek bank.

But Annie knew who she was.

The shiny sunglasses turned toward the central aisle.

"Not too busy today, are you?" It was so quiet in the store that the tick of the grandfather clock sounded like hollow footsteps in an alley. Annie wondered suddenly if she were hearing her own heartbeat. Even though she knew Chief Saulter waited at the back of the shop, her sense of threat, of evil unleashed, was so strong that she had trouble answering.

But the words she managed, a faltering, "Customers come in bunches," fell away, because there was to be no pretence, no skirmishing, no chance of survival for Annie Laurance. She knew, when she looked down at the gun held so steadily in the gloved hand, that the decision had already been made. Annie Laurance was to die.

"Put up the CLOSED sign and lock the front door." Sheridan's voice was as cool and self-possessed as when she'd greeted guests at her party.

Stiffly, Annie moved toward the entrance.

"If you try to open the door, I'll shoot you." Not a flicker of concern in that well-modulated, confident voice.

Annie's chest ached. She mustn't trigger the attack, because she had to get the right words on tape, the words that would free Max — no matter what happened. She locked the door, turned the sign, and came back to the desk.

She reached out for the envelope with Carla's name on it. "You killed Carla!"

It hung in the balance. Would Sheridan shoot, or would she talk?

But she had a killer's egoism. Sheridan smiled. "Of course I did." Then the smooth face hardened. "She was such a fool." Sheridan moved between Annie and the door, keeping the gun aimed at Annie's heart. "Give that to me."

Clutching the envelope, Annie took a step backward down the center aisle.

Sheridan pressed forward. As Annie retreated, she repeated, "Give me the envelope, Annie."

"What's in it?" Annie demanded. "What did Carla know?" She shook her head in bewilderment. "But you had an alibi. Chief Saulter said it was good. What did you do, bribe Harley?"

"Of course not. My alibi is superb, unbreakable. I planned it that way."

Annie knew, but to hear it in Sheridan's voice sickened her. She continued to edge backward down the aisle. She was even with the caper-comedy shelving now. Another ten feet to go and Chief Saulter would have a clear aim at Sheridan.

"Then how did you kill Shane?"

Sheridan laughed. It was a soft, throaty, satisfied sound that sickened Annie. "Annie, you're so *stupid*. I didn't kill Shane.

Carla killed him — all for the love of me. Isn't that wonderful?"

"For the love of you?"

An eyebrow quirked above the mirrored sunglasses. "Dear, naive Annie. You have so much to learn. It's too bad you've run out of time."

"You had an affair with Carla? Persuaded her to murder Shane?"

They had reached the coffee area now, past the horror sci-fi shelves, and Sheridan stepped to one side. No one looking into the shop would be able to see her. Annie had no trouble foreseeing the future: one quick shot, the envelope retrieved, and a departure through the rear door into the alley.

As if in confirmation, Sheridan glanced toward the storeroom with the EXIT placard above the door, then she said contemptuously, "Dear Carla was so suggestible. And it worked beautifully. I've always been good at planning, you know. She shot him when she went downstairs for a few minutes. She hid the gun outside, behind the steps by the third entrance to the football stands. I came for it very late that night. I thought it might come in handy. And didn't it! Let your Max explain away that gun."

"You planned all of it? But you couldn't have! How could you be so certain Carla would cooperate?"

"Oh, I knew." Sheridan gave a little shiver beneath the voluminous folds of her dress. "The idea came to me when I heard about the play. It was perfect. I knew Shane could get the role. He didn't want to, of course. God, he was so lazy, bone lazy, but we'd planned his drowning by then, and I convinced him that there might be suspicions he'd disappeared rather than died since it was a double indemnity policy. I told him no one would think he'd run away if he were involved in a play. God, he didn't want to bother to learn his lines."

"You set us up after the murder, didn't you? You knew that Shane was lying at the party about my chasing after him."

The wide-brimmed sun hat quivered with her laughter. "I loved it. It was so nice of him to provide such a luscious motive for his own death."

"You had Carla kill him during rehearsal Tuesday night because he was to capsize his boat that night — and he had to die before then."

"Wasn't it wonderful? Shane dead, two million in insurance, and a widow who could never be suspected because she was in bed with another man at the time of the murder."

"But it devastated Carla when she found out about you and Harley."

The cherry-red lips thinned. "Carla was so *tiresome*. I told her that Harley didn't mean a thing to me. It was an *alibi*. But she was jealous. So stupid of her. I couldn't take a chance on her after that."

"You took the belt from Max's condo before you ever talked to her. You were going to kill her even before you knew she was upset."

Sheridan gave a little shrug. "It occurred to me. I like to keep things tidy."

Her thumb caressed the trigger.

The black mass hurtling through the air made a tiny whistle and Sheridan's mouth opened as the heavy weight slammed into her, knocking her backwards. Then the bowling ball thudded heavily on the wooden floor. A flash of navy blue, a neat tasteful woman's suit, sprang across the room, and a sensible black shoe with low heels stamped down on Sheridan's hand, kicking free the gun.

Chief Saulter yelled, "What the hell?" Then he was there, snapping handcuffs on a writhing, screaming Sheridan.

Absolutely stunned, Annie gasped at the chief, then turned to the newcomer.

Her gray hair neatly styled in a feather cut this morning (and Annie wondered how she managed all those different hairstyles), her dark eyes snapping, Henny Brawley smoothed down the rumpled blue skirt. Then she smiled cherubically at Annie. "You know, I've always loved mysteries."

Sister Mary Helen, of course, the delightful sleuth created by Sister Carol Anne O'Marie.

17

A standing ovation greeted the triumphant cast of *Arsenic and Old Lace* as the curtain lifted for the third time. Cheers rose and feet stamped.

Henny stepped forward for yet another curtsey.

The play — and the players — were a smash. In the wings, Annie saw Burt beaming with delight as he and Harley Jenkins shook hands. Summer theater on Broward's Rock was saved. And Sam hopped ecstatically in too-tight black dress shoes as Broadway producer Solomon Purdy clapped him on the shoulder.

As the curtain fell for the last time and cast members hugged and kissed each other, Henny threw both hands above her head, kicked into an exuberant rhumba, and cried, "Hurry, everyone. Let's go to Annie's party!"

Death on Demand was a mob scene, jammed with first-nighters. Annie tried to squeeze down the central aisle, hoping

Ingrid had arranged for enough food. Time had evaporated during that weekend. After Sheridan's capture, all of Saturday was absorbed with the attendant statements taken by a good-humored Chief Saulter and a suddenly sullen Circuit Solicitor Posey. Rehearsals picked up again at the crack of dawn on Sunday and continued through Monday. Annie had scarcely had time to eat and sleep, much less plan for the party, which she'd offered to host at a midwinter meeting of the players. Still, everything looked well. Obviously, the party was a smash. So what accounted for the uneasiness that plucked at her subconscious? No, it wasn't concern about the party. It was an almost unrealized sense of something missing. Something she should have —

Laurel.

Annie realized with a shock, and she stopped dead, that she hadn't heard from Laurel since Saturday morning.

Her unexpected halt caused Max to bump into her.

He bent and yelled in her ear (nothing less than a shout could be heard above the din), "What's wrong?"

"Your mother! Where's your mother? Have you seen Laurel?"

"Oh, I saw her somewhere." He waved his arm vaguely. "Let's ask Ingrid."

They wormed their way to a flushed Ingrid, who was rapidly pouring champagne into glasses. At their question, she nodded and yelled, "She's been here and gone. Took a load of books with her."

"But she doesn't read mysteries," Max objected.

Ingrid grinned. "She does now. She asked if we had any books about weddings. I told her sure. I gave her *So Long as You Both Shall Live*, *The Wedding March Murder*, *The Bride Regrets*, and *The Bride Wore Black*." She paused and downed a glass of champagne. "As she left, I heard her murmur something about red, not black."

Annie's eyes widened. *Where* was Laurel? What had she *wrought?*

Then a strong arm slid round her shoulder and Vince Ellis bent down to give her a wet kiss. "Annie, you were great tonight." He reached out his other arm to embrace a pink-cheeked Henny, dramatic in white satin party pajamas. "You and Henny both. But what I want to know is how you two tracked down Sheridan?" With the skill of a professional journalist hot on an inside story, he maneuvered them into the relative calm of the store-room, followed by Max, Chief Saulter, and an inquisitive Jed McClanahan, carrying two glasses of champagne, which he downed in quick succession.

"An inspired guess," Max suggested, but his eyes twinkled over his champagne glass.

Chief Saulter shook his head. "Gutsy and smart, that's what they are."

Henny's fox-sharp nose quivered with pleasure. "Actually, Ariadne Oliver has always been a great inspiration to me. She just *knows* who the criminal is." For an instant, her geniality faded. "But actually, it's character that makes the difference, you know. Sheridan had a bad character. Just like Jacko Argyle in *Ordeal by Innocence*. So, I didn't care how good her alibi was, I knew that woman was somehow responsible. I decided not to let her out of my sight — and I didn't, not for a moment. When she came sneaking out of her back door in that costume and got on her ten-speed, I knew she was up to no good. I followed her. And I had my favorite bowling ball in my front basket." There was a curious pause. "Like running with hand weights," she added casually.

Saulter was nodding with interest. "But

— uh — what was the getup? I mean, I've never seen you ride a bike in a navy-blue suit."

Henny beamed. "I like to get in the spirit of things."

Saulter's face creased in continued puzzlement, and Annie made a mental note to explain to him Henny's penchant for appearing as famous fictional sleuths — mostly geriatric and always female.

But for now, it was credit where credit was due. "So Henny saved me and Max both," Annie said admiringly.

A red-nosed McClanahan (Annie wondered perhaps a trifle uncharitably if he'd come to opening night because he'd heard there was a party afterward with free booze) tried to steer the conversation his way. "Of course, I would've ripped 'em to shreds in court."

Henny gave him a skeptical glance and generously shared the limelight. "Now, Annie honey, you tell us how you knew."

"When I talked to Carla Thursday evening, she was obviously brokenhearted — and it *had* to be connected to Shane's murder. After she was killed, I kept trying to figure out what she'd *seen*. I asked myself, Who would she protect? When I learned her lover must be another woman,

410

I thought first of Cindy or Janet. But neither seemed the kind of woman to set out to entrap and exploit Carla. Then I thought of Sheridan and I remembered what she looked like the night of her party, standing beside the Steuben oil derrick in that gold lamé dress, overpowering, arrogant, and totally self-absorbed. But Sheridan had an alibi. Oh, yes, of course she did. Of *course* she did. Everything was clear to me then. That was why the murder happened when it did. Carla and Sheridan had it all planned. Sheridan would have an unbreakable alibi. And, so far as anyone knew, Carla had no real motive to kill Shane. So it should work beautifully. And it did. The trouble was, Carla had no idea that Sheridan planned to be in bed at the time with Harley Jenkins. When she found out, she was wild with jealousy. That was the beginning of the end for her. The real turning point was when I realized the importance of Sheridan's alibi, then I understood and knew that Carla hadn't *seen* anything. Carla was the murderer — because of Sheridan."

The chief's faded brown eyes glinted with anger. "I told Annie, that woman is a bitch, pardon my language. She deliberately set out after Miss Fontaine. And she'd planned the murder for a long time. We traced those two guns, the one that killed Shane and the one she carried Saturday when she came after Annie. She'd used it to kill Freddy. She stole them from a house on the island in early April. Stole *both* of them. Looks to me like she was planning on getting rid of Carla even then."

"And Sheridan knew Posey was after Max, even before that session at the school, because she unloaded that story about me and Shane to Posey on Wednesday. That's why she took Max's belt when she hid the murder weapon in his condo," Annie explained. Her eyes darkened. "We should have known when Freddy was killed that someone malicious was behind the troubles. She engineered all the sabotage through Carla, of course. That was done to muddy the water, to focus attention on the players. But it showed real evil to kill that cat. She knew how Shane hopped in bed with everybody, and I think maybe it bothered her more than she'd ever admit. She didn't have to kill a cat to put something ugly in the window seat. It was aimed right at Janet and Cindy." Then she clapped a hand to her head. Cat! "Chief, my mind's crazy. I keep forgetting things. What about Shane's cat? That beautiful cat on the boat?"

Chief Saulter looked down at the floor in an embarrassed way and said gruffly, "Oh, he's okay."

"Are you sure?" she demanded.

The chief scuffed the floor with his boot. "After you and Shane's girlfriend made that statement on Friday, I got a search warrant. Posey couldn't ignore everything you'd said, though he claimed the two of you cooked it up. Anyway, when I went to talk to Sheridan, I took the big fellow with me. Turned out she hated cats, wouldn't let him in the house. He lived on the boat. So, I just took him along home with me. Seems to be a pretty nice fellow."

Max refrained from smiling too hugely. "Uh, is he taking up residence at your place?"

The chief shrugged. "Couldn't let him starve. Like I said, he's kind of a handsome fellow." He scratched at his chin. "Actually, he seems like a pretty high-toned cat. So I named him Lord Peter."

There was a round of applause, which left Jed McClanahan looking puzzled. And bored. There wasn't much scope in the Death on Demand storeroom for the best trial lawyer in the United States of America. He looked around (for more

413

champagne?), then moved toward the door. "Well, folks, all's well that ends well, I always say. Course, we would've done great in court. Now, if you folks ever need a good lawyer again, give me a call." He took a dog-eared card from his pocket. "My number's on there. It might be the most important number you ever had, so take care of it." He thrust it at Henny. "And you be careful, little lady."

He opened the door and stepped out into the frantic melee of the party (it sounded rather like someone had brought a pair of bongo drums).

Henny clapped her hands above her head. Castanets clicked. "Careful, hell!"

Saulter looked a little shocked.

Henny grabbed his arm. "Come on, everybody. We're *party animals.*"

Max's blue eyes shone with approbation. "Let's party all night," he yelled, sweeping Annie through the door.

As they plunged into the heart of the throng jammed in the coffee area, Vince hurried after them.

"Hey, Annie," he yelled. "One more thing." He pointed at the watercolors, dimly visible through the smoky haze. "Has anybody turned in the names of all five yet?"

Annie had been too busy to care. She shook her head.

Vince looked around to see if anyone was listening, then shouted in her ear "*Rebecca* by Daphne du Maurier, *The Yellow Room* by Mary Roberts Rinehart, *My Brother Michael* by Mary Stewart, *The Mistress of Mellyn* by Victoria Holt, and *Dream of Orchids* by Phyllis Whitney."

Annie stared at him in astonishment.

Vince flushed, then said doggedly, "Broke my leg at my cousin's house a couple of years ago, and all she had were those kind of books." Then he lifted his chin. "Darn good writers."

"You get a free book," Annie said hastily, not wanting to be mistaken for a sexist pig.

"A free book." Vince squinted in concentration. "How about the latest Nancy Pickard?"

"Right on," she cried.

Ah, sweet mystery of life — the impenetrable puzzle and incalculable catholicity of a whodunit fan.